What the critics are saying...

5 *Stars* "*Erin's Fancy* is a fabulously deliciously sensual story. As soon as I started reading this book I was immediately captivated. I did not put it down until I was finished...This is the second book in *Ms. Walters'* extremely popular "*Awakening Desires*" series. If you, like me, love sensually realistic characters weaved into an equally captivating plot, then this book is a MUST READ, there is no way you will be disappointed!" ~ *Dianne Nogueras, eCataRomance*

"I was beginning to despair over finding an erotic romance that would touch more than just my—ahem—well—something that would engage my emotions as well as my senses. I found one last month when I read *Katie's Art Of Seduction* by *Ms. Walters*, and I've found another in *Erin's Fancy*...The sex scenes are numerous, earthy and sexy. The pace is fast, and there is a unique twist near the end that was unexpected, but entirely pleasing." ~ *Terrie Figueroa, Romance Reviews Today*

5 *Angels* "This is an exceptional book. *Ms. Walters* not only tells a very erotic story but also a very emotional one...You do not want to miss this book—it is definitely a keeper." ~ *Tewanda Fallen Angel Reviews*

N.J. Walters

ERIN'S
AWAKENING DESIRES
Fancy

ELLORA'S CAVE
ROMANTICA PUBLISHING

An Ellora's Cave Romantica Publication

www.ellorascave.com

Erin's Fancy

ISBN # 1419952862
ALL RIGHTS RESERVED.
Erin's Fancy Copyright© 2005 N.J. Walters
Edited by: Pamela Cohen
Cover art by: Syneca

Electronic book Publication: May, 2005
Trade paperback Publication: November, 2005

Warning:

The following material contains graphic sexual content meant for mature readers. *Erin's Fancy* has been rated *E-rotic* by a minimum of three independent reviewers.

Ellora's Cave Publishing offers three levels of Romantica™ reading entertainment: S (S-ensuous), E (E-rotic), and X (X-treme).

S-*ensuous* love scenes are explicit and leave nothing to the imagination.

E-*rotic* love scenes are explicit, leave nothing to the imagination, and are high in volume per the overall word count. In addition, some E-rated titles might contain fantasy material that some readers find objectionable, such as bondage, submission, same sex encounters, forced seductions, etc. E-rated titles are the most graphic titles we carry; it is common, for instance, for an author to use words such as "fucking", "cock", "pussy", etc., within their work of literature.

X-*treme* titles differ from E-rated titles only in plot premise and storyline execution. Unlike E-rated titles, stories designated with the letter X tend to contain controversial subject matter not for the faint of heart.

Also by N.J. Walters:

Annabelle Lee
Harker's Journey
Katie's Art of Seduction

Erin's Fancy
Awakening Desires

Dedication

Thank you to my husband, Gerard, for his continued support, advice, love, and encouragement. Also, thanks to Pamela, as always for her hard work, guidance, and belief in me and my stories.

Chapter One

Erin Connors ran her index finger over the glossy magazine cover with the scantily clad cover model and underlined the article, "Seven Sex Positions That Will Drive You Both Wild!"

Taking a deep breath, she opened the cover and scanned the table of contents. She flipped through the pages, stopping at, appropriately enough, page sixty-nine, and spread the magazine wide on the scarred wood table in front of her. Bold pink letters flashed up at her from the page. *Legs on shoulders, Doggy-style, 69, Standing Backwards Position, Face-to-Face, Spooning and Scissors.* She could feel the heat creeping up her face as she perused the pictures of half-naked couples, with strategically placed clothing and blankets, demonstrating the techniques.

Glancing up, she peeked out the open back door and noted that the yard was empty. Her brother Jackson was busy in the barn and Nathan had already left for work. The coast was clear. Sighing, she rubbed the back of her suntanned neck. It was pathetic that a woman of twenty-five had to hide the fact that she was reading a woman's magazine. Especially a magazine that gave advice about sex. That's what came from still living at home at her age, and having two, very large, very protective older brothers, one of whom was a local deputy sheriff. They still treated her like some kind of nun who supposedly never even thought about sex, much less had sex.

That was entirely the problem. She hadn't had sex. Well, technically she had, but she didn't count graduation night in the back of Brad Hutchinson's pickup truck out at Peak's Pond. That had been a lot of fumbling, a little pain, and a whole lot of nothing! It had been such a disaster that Erin had never quite worked up the nerve to try it again. Not that she'd had much of an opportunity.

The fact of the matter was that men didn't notice her. Well, they noticed her, but not for the right reasons. Erin was what was known as "a big girl". Six feet tall in her stocking feet, her arms and legs muscular, and her shoulders wide from working side by side with her brothers, tended to be off-putting to a lot of men.

It wouldn't have been so bad, but the only part of her that wasn't large was her breasts. She'd gotten shortchanged in that department. Though nicely rounded, they tended to disappear in the overalls and loose shirts she wore for work.

Still, she wasn't ugly. Her hair was deep auburn, but it was a thick, curly mess that wouldn't hold a style, so she usually kept it confined in a single braid that fell to her waist. She had the Connors blue eyes, the pale blue of a sunny summer sky, just like her brothers Jackson and Nathan. Her nose tilted up just slightly and had a light dusting of freckles, and her lips were wide and full. It was a nice face, a comfortable face, and that was part of the problem.

Erin looked like the proverbial girl-next-door with her wholesome looks. Tagging behind her older brothers, doing the same work, had quickly labeled her a tomboy. By the time she'd become interested in what it meant to be a girl, everyone was used to her being just one of the guys. Except for Carly Ames, none of the girls in the neighborhood or at school had liked her because she was a friend to all the boys. Conversely, all the guys liked her because she didn't act like a girl.

The problem was that when all the boys grew into men and the girls grew into women, Erin was left out. The men started dating and she was still just one of the boys. Everybody's pal, that was her. And she hated it. Maybe not all of it. But damn it, she was a woman too, with women's needs, except no one ever seemed to notice. If she was ever to get the sweaty, grinding, orgasmic sex that she wanted, she needed help.

Turning her attention to the article, she began to read aloud. "Any man who's being truthful will tell you his favorite position is doggy-style. It's very primal and sexy to your man."

Okay, she'd grown up in a farming community, so she could understand the animalistic appeal to a guy.

"Just get down on all fours and stick your ass in the air. No, it's not the most dignified position in the world." Erin pictured it in her head and thought that this was an understatement. In fact, she figured it would look pretty ridiculous, but what did she know. These people were the experts or they never would have gotten published in this magazine.

As her eyes drifted closed, the image in her head changed slightly and came into sharper focus. She saw herself kneeling on the kitchen linoleum with her face pressed to the cool floor and her ass stuck up in the air. A man stood behind her, but she couldn't quite picture his features, but his deep voice washed over her, filling her with pleasure...

"Spread your legs wider and offer yourself to me."

Erin could feel her juices run down her legs as she slid her knees as far apart as they would go. She could feel the heat rolling off of him as he knelt behind her. Without warning, he gripped her hips with his large hands and thrust his cock deep inside her. Moaning, she ground her bottom against him. He laughed and slipped his hands up to cup her breasts. "You know you want me to fuck you, don't you?"

"Yes," she cried. "Fuck me. Hard." He began pumping into her from behind.

Erin's eyes popped open and she gasped for breath, desperately trying to focus on the magazine page in front of her.

Grabbing her tall glass of iced tea, she took a huge gulp and continued to read. "We guarantee he'll go crazy. As he enters you from behind, he'll go in very deep and will hit your G-spot. He can also stimulate your breasts and clitoris in this position." She paused to take a deep breath.

"He most certainly can," she panted. Her underwear was wet and she could feel her inner muscles contracting slightly. She wasn't even sure where her G-spot was, but she was certainly feeling hot. The glass was sweaty and cool, and she rubbed it against her cheeks and neck. It made her feel slightly better.

Plunking the glass back on the table, she continued reading the article. "The standing backwards position is simple. Standing about two feet from the wall, turn around and face it, bracing your hands against it. Stick out your behind and allow him to enter you. He can thrust harder because you can brace yourself, and he can still stimulate all parts of your body as well."

Erin could feel her nipples pushing against her sports bra and had an almost overwhelming urge to rub them. Uncomfortable with her thoughts, she squirmed slightly to get comfortable in her chair, but that only made things worse as she could feel the heat between her thighs. So far the only thing she'd learned was that men really seem to like to have sex from behind. That, and make herself incredibly uncomfortable and aroused.

Again a picture formed in her mind of her naked and facing a wood-paneled wall. His voice rumbled behind her.

"Bend over and lean against the wall." He stood behind her, towering over her making her feel small and feminine for the first time in her entire life.

His hairy thighs brushed against her smooth ones as he inserted himself between her legs. She could feel his hard cock pressed against the dark cleft of her ass and it made her shiver. He reached a hand between her legs and parted her slick folds before pushing himself deep inside her. The feeling of fullness was incredible and the urge to move was too powerful to ignore.

Erin plastered her thighs together and squirmed on her chair. God, she'd never been this close to coming before. The buzz of the dryer shocked her and her eyes popped open. She glanced frantically around the kitchen. For a moment, she'd forgotten where she was, the feeling were so real, so intense. Wrapping her arms around her waist, she took a few deep breaths to calm herself before venturing back to her magazine.

More determined than ever to learn all she needed in order to seduce a man, she smoothed the pages of the magazine wide open. If she didn't learn, then she'd never have sex. And at this very moment, she wanted it more than anything she'd ever wanted in her entire life. Boldly, she returned to the article. "Face-to-face," she read. Finally, she sighed to herself, something a little different.

Clearing her voice, she continued. "Sit on his lap, facing him, and wrap your legs over his hips and lock your feet behind his back. Once, he's inside you, keep it slow and steady, and just rock. He can use his hands for support on the bed. Take advantage of this position for some heavy necking…" Her voice faded as she finally got a face to go with her fantasy man. No longer was he a nameless, faceless body. This was not just any man. This was *the* man. With his intelligent pale green eyes, high cheekbones, square jaw and full, kissable lips, it was a face no woman in her right mind would ever forget—Abel Garrett.

He had grown up on the farm next to theirs and was friends with both her brothers. For as far back as she could remember, she'd wanted him to notice her. As he'd grown from tall, lanky boy to an incredibly handsome man, her infatuation with him had intensified. But she'd never been more to him than Jackson's younger sister, treating her with the same careless affection and kindness as one would a cute little puppy, ruffling her hair whenever he came over to spend time with her brothers. He'd leased his family's land to her family and left home right after high school. And except for a short yearly visit, he'd stayed away for the last fourteen years.

If she was left with nothing but a fantasy, then this man more than fit the bill. Licking her lips, she went back to the article. "Legs on shoulders," she whispered. This one looked promising. "Lie on the bed and have your man kneel between your legs. Place your ankles on his shoulders as he enters you. He has access to your breasts and clitoris and can hold your behind if he wants to thrust hard. A great position for both of you."

Erin closed her eyes on a groan. The images flashed through her mind like a motion picture.

Her reddish hair was spread across the stark white pillows as she held her arms out to the man in front of her. Tall, muscular and totally aroused, he wedged his body between her spread thighs, his pale green eyes never leaving hers. His full lips smiled as he picked up her ankles one at a time, and kissed each tenderly before placing one on either of his broad shoulders.

She could feel his cock pressed against her wet slit and moaned in anticipation. Teasing her, he rubbed his hardness against her wet folds, lubricating himself with her juices. Her heels dug into his shoulders as she rotated her hips, trying desperately to get him inside her.

Laughing, he reached out and traced his fingers around her breasts, coming close, but never touching her nipples. They were hard nubs that were begging for his touch. "Abel, please," she panted. Her whole body was on fire now, straining for release. Grabbing his wrists, she moved his palms until they covered her breasts. Then she began to move his hands on her even as she pushed her hips hard against his heavy cock.

A harsh growl came from deep inside him as he slid his cock deep inside her. Her inner muscles pulsed around his arousal driving her even closer to the edge. Ignoring her hold on his wrists, he began to lightly flick her nipples with his fingers. Pleasure washed over her and she felt her breasts swell under his attention. Bending forward, he pushed his way even deeper inside her as his tongue lapped at her breast. "More," she urged him.

Abel began thrusting inside her, slowly at first and then quicker as they both grew more frantic. His mouth continued to devour her breasts, licking and sucking until she thought she'd go mad. Her skin was damp and she could feel herself coming. He sat back suddenly, anchored his hands around her waist and began to thrust quick and hard. Her orgasm hit her fast and furious, her inner muscles clamping down hard on him as he continued his frantic pace. He was so close now. She reached out to stroke his glistening chest. "Abel," she moaned.

"How'd you know Abel was home?" The screen door closed with a bang.

Like a bucket of ice water, her brother's voice washed over her. In an automatic gesture of self-preservation, she flipped open an old copy of the *Apple Farmer Journal* and hid her own magazine from view. Her face was flushed, her pulse pounding, as her inner muscles continued to rhythmically contract and relax, soaking her already wet panties. She'd just had her very first orgasm, and once again one of her brothers was thwarting her sex life.

Scowling at him, she was ready to blast him when his words penetrated her sexual haze. "What do you mean?" she croaked.

Jackson had his back to her and was filling a glass with iced tea from the refrigerator. His head tipped back and he emptied the glass once before refilling it and returning the jug to the cooler. Turning around, he kicked the door closed and tromped over to the table, pulled out a chair and plunked himself down next to her. "You were saying his name when I came in. I thought you must have heard."

"Heard what?" Honestly, she was going to smack him if he didn't answer her soon.

"Abel's home." Jackson took another swig from his glass and reached out to grab her magazine. Erin managed to snag it just before he did and scooped up both of them at once, raising herself slightly and plopped them under her behind. He scowled at her, but thank heavens didn't try to retrieve them.

"When did he get here? How long is he staying?" Her heart was pounding hard just at the thought of seeing him. Paper crinkled under her as she pressed her bottom hard against the chair, squirming slightly to try and find a comfortable spot. Aftershocks of her orgasm pulsed through her body and it took every ounce of control she possessed not to drop her head to the table and moan. She didn't know if she could even face Abel after his starring role in her daydream, but she sure as heck wanted to try.

"Don't know for sure, but Jed's wife, Alma, who works at the Stop and Shop said he filled a grocery cart to the brim first thing this morning."

It was hard, but Erin tried to focus on what her brother was saying. "Jed was already here?" Jed Saunders delivered the mail every day, but usually didn't make it their way until lunchtime and it was just after nine in the morning.

"Yeah," Jackson laughed. "He had a lot of mail for Abel and I'm sure Alma sent him to dig up more gossip. That woman has a heart of gold, but she does love to talk." Jackson pushed away from the table and motioned to the small stack of mail on the kitchen counter that she hadn't even noticed. "Nothing to worry about today. No bills, just some flyers and catalogues."

One of Erin's jobs was to deal with the mail and make sure all the normal household bills were paid in a timely fashion. Any bills incurred in the running of the apple orchard, she piled on Jackson's desk in the study for him to handle. They all worked the family farm, but it really belonged to Jackson. Erin also managed a small blueberry operation of her own.

"I think I'll take him one of the apple pies I just took out of the oven." It was almost impossible to keep her voice calm and normal. "Just to welcome him home."

"You don't fool me." Jackson shook his finger at her, and for one moment her heart stopped, as she feared he'd somehow guessed her carnal intentions towards his friend. Her heart started once again as he kept right on talking. "You want to get the latest gossip before anyone else."

"Guilty," she admitted. Anything to get her brother out of the house so she could grab a long, cold shower and deliver one of those pies.

Stopping long enough to rinse out his glass and pop it in the drain tray next to the sink, Jackson headed back out the door. "Why don't you ask him for supper?"

"Okay," she agreed, but she was talking to herself as Jackson was already striding across the yard. "I just might do that," she said as her mind began to work.

Energized, she popped out of her chair, grabbed up her magazine, ignoring the farming periodical as it fell to the floor. Holding it close to her chest, she hurried out of the kitchen. Taking the stairs two at a time, she ran down the hall to her bedroom. Quickly, she lifted her mattress and stuffed the magazine under it, now more determined than ever to finish studying it.

For now, she had more important things to do. First, she needed a shower, most definitely a cool one. Second, she needed to wrap up one of her deep-dish apple pies. And thirdly, she needed to go and try and entice her next-door neighbor into a summer affair.

Chapter Two

It was shortly after ten in the morning when she drove the short distance to Abel's house. It was only a couple of miles, but the closer she got, the more nervous she became. Butterflies crowded into her stomach and her palms were slippery on the steering wheel. Though anticipation and fear warred within her, her yearning was greater. Gripping the wheel tight, she made the turn and drove down the private road, pulling to a stop behind his house. Gratefully, she noted that no one could see her truck from the road.

Turning off the vehicle, she sat there for a moment and waited. The yard was empty and she could detect no movement inside. Opening her door, she climbed out and gently pushed it closed. The air was sultry and sweet as she walked towards the back door. The sun was climbing over the hills in the distance as she put her key in the lock, turned the knob and let herself inside.

Erin knew her way around the house, having visited here many times as a child. Mrs. Garrett had always been kind to her and any cooking and household skills that Erin now possessed had come from her patient instruction and tutelage. Erin had desperately wanted a mother, and Mrs. Garrett had wanted a girl to mother. It had worked out well for both of them and Erin had been heartbroken when she'd been killed. It had been like losing her own mother all over again.

She saw bags, several suitcases and boxes piled just inside the door, so she knew that Abel was around somewhere. Quietly she laid the pie on the kitchen counter and peeked inside all the rooms on the bottom floor, but each of them was empty.

Butterflies fluttered in her stomach as she climbed the stair of the farmhouse. Assuming that Abel had taken up residence in his old room, Erin made her way to the bedroom at the front of the house. The door was partially closed, so she gently pushed it open, relieved when it didn't squeak.

It was now or never. She could still walk away and nobody would ever know she'd been here. For a moment, as all her doubts and insecurities rose up to taunt her, she almost turned and ran. As she hesitated, her conscience piped up and whispered that there could be dire repercussions, for both her and Abel, if either of her brothers ever discovered what she was doing.

Poised at the threshold, with one foot edging forward into the bedroom, and the other still planted firmly out in the hallway, she chewed her lip in indecision. When she realized what she was doing, she made herself stop and rubbed her abused lips with her finger. It was a nervous habit that she'd never been able to break no matter how hard she tried.

Erin could feel a bead of sweat roll down her back. As much as she wanted this, she didn't know if she had the nerve to do it. It was one thing to think about doing something she saw in a magazine, but it was quite another to actually do it.

A movement from inside the room caught her eye. The covers on the bed moved as Abel rolled over in bed to face the door. She held her breath as she waited for him to speak, but he said nothing. In fact, he made a soft snoring noise and settled back to sleep. Erin breathed a sigh of relief before her gaze was drawn to him.

God, he was gorgeous. He was so large, he filled the double bed completely and his feet stuck out over the end. His chest was bare, and the sheet was bunched around his waist. The muscles of his arms and torso stood out even when he was at rest. He had a perfect six-pack stomach and a light sprinkling of dark hair that angled down from between his flat brown nipples, traced a line straight down his belly, and disappeared under the covers. It was impossible for a man this size to look vulnerable, but his face appeared relaxed as he slept.

She couldn't abandon her plan now. Seeing him here like this, there was no way that she could stop herself from climbing into bed with him. He was everything she had ever wanted in a man. He was loyal, kind, hardworking, and smart. The fact that he was gorgeous was icing on the cake. Restless, Abel sighed and turned once again until he was lying flat on his back.

Chewing on her bottom lip for a moment, she came to a decision. It might be easier for her if he just found her naked in bed next to him. That way she wouldn't have to say anything but let nature take its course. After all, no hot-blooded male would ignore a naked willing woman in his bed.

Creeping to the end of the bed, her eyes never left his sleeping form as she toed off her sneakers before shimmying out of her jeans overalls and panties. Bending forward, she tugged her shirt over her head and dropped it on top of her jeans. Her fingers unhooked her bra and a second later it joined the pile of clothing on the floor. Acting on instinct, she took the rubber band from the end of her braid and shook out her hair. Fully naked, she stood there, trying to decide the best way to handle this. There was hardly any room on the bed at all.

She froze as he shifted in bed again and a moment later grinned at his new position. As if he'd guessed her predicament, he had rolled until he was lying on his side and there was a space in front of him that looked to be just big enough for her to crawl into. Erin tiptoed around the side of the bed, picked up the sheet and eased down on the bed. Her whole body was tense as she lowered herself next to him, and when she was finally in position with her head on the pillow next to his, her breathing was shallow and quick and her heart was racing.

Erin's breathing eventually slowed and deepened to match Abel's as she lay there next to him. She waited for him to move, to wake, to speak, or to do anything. Finally, she came to the conclusion that she'd been too stealthy while sneaking into his bed. Abel was sound asleep and showed no signs of waking up anytime soon. She rolled her eyes and huffed out a breath, slightly miffed that he didn't sense her presence. This was like something out of a romantic comedy, she thought with amusement—aroused woman gets nerve enough to climb in bed with hero who sleeps through the whole thing!

Well, she was here now and she wasn't leaving. He had to wake up eventually and when he did, she sure hoped he liked his surprise. Grinning to herself, she rolled onto her side, facing away from him and snuggled into his pillow. She caught a whiff of his soap as her breathing got slower and deeper. The hypnotic sound of his breath and the heat of the day relaxed her. While she waited, her mind drifted to her upcoming blueberry harvest, and all the work she had to get done before then. Without her even being aware, she drifted off to sleep.

Abel Benjamin Garrett drifted in a hazy state somewhere between wakefulness and sleep, enjoying the remnants of a pleasant dream, as his thoughts wandered. Nightmares had plagued him for months now and sleep had become a luxury. He'd gotten used to always being tired, but by the time he'd finally made it home this morning he had long passed being tired and was now completely exhausted.

He'd driven all night and rolled into the small town of Meadows just after eight this morning. The grocery store was already open, so he'd forced himself to stop and load up a cart full of food. He couldn't even remember what he bought, but he recalled a brief conversation with the lady who checked him out, as well as piling the grocery bags into the back of his truck.

The drive to his childhood home was nothing but a blur. It had been crazy and dangerous to keep driving, but Abel was filled with a burning desire to go home and shut the world out. Gathering the last of his energy, he'd dragged in his luggage and the groceries and dropped them in the kitchen. He'd shoved the perishable food into the refrigerator and left the rest piled on the floor.

Stumbling up the stairs, he'd stripped off his clothes and fallen into bed, immediately falling into a deep sleep. The usual images of violence and anger that were such a regular part of his dreams were missing for once. Instead, a comfortable feeling of well-being filled him, as he'd wrapped his arms around one of the pillows.

Totally relaxed as he lay there in bed, Abel let go of all thought and began to sink back towards sleep and the woman who still waited for him in his dream. He could still smell her. An elusive perfume permeated his senses, but he couldn't quite place it. It was familiar to him somehow, and he knew that at some point in his travels he'd met this woman. The mattress shifted, indicating that she'd stretched out next to him. Giving himself totally to his dream, he lay there and waited to see what she would do.

A lock of hair tickled his nose, but instead of moving away, Abel leaned closer and breathed in the scent of fresh air, sunshine, and woman. He immediately became aware of soft feminine flesh snuggled close to him. Not wanting to wake from this delicious fantasy, he wrapped one arm around his prize and pulled her close until her behind was snuggled up tight against his throbbing erection. She squirmed a bit, trying to get comfortable, and he could feel his cock growing even larger.

Sighing, she mumbled something before drifting off to sleep again. Abel decided that it was time for him to explore. Even though he knew he had to be dreaming, he kept his eyes closed tight and inhaled the essence he was quickly becoming addicted to.

Because of her height, his dream lady matched his body better than any other woman he'd ever been with. Her ass cuddled his erection with ease, while his knees fit right behind hers. The sleek contours of her back fit nicely against his wider chest, and her head tucked right beneath his chin.

Indulging himself, he rested his hand on her flat stomach and spread his fingers wide, easily touching both her hipbones with his fingers. The heat from her belly warmed his palm, and it occurred to him how nice it would feel in the dead of winter to warm himself with her body.

Slowly, he used his index finger to trace a path up to her belly button, circling it before moving higher. Unerringly, his hand found her breast and cupped it. His large palm covered it completely, and a feeling of raw possession filled him. *Mine.* A wave of emotion filled him and he gripped her tighter, pulling her even closer until her back was plastered against his chest.

When she began to struggle lightly, he reluctantly eased his grip, and she quieted once again. Her nipple was stabbing the center of his palm and he felt a growing urge to taste it. He growled at the thought of savoring every square inch of her succulent flesh. His body was hot and his cock was swollen to its limits, but he didn't take her. Not yet. In case he never got another opportunity, he wanted to enjoy every moment of this dream.

Her skin felt soft against his roughened finger as he traced the velvety skin around her nipple. She moaned sensually, pushing her ass back against him once again, while her hips made a little circular motion that almost drove him out of his mind. Clenching his teeth, he continued to explore her breast, testing the shape and texture of her nipple with his fingers.

Shifting his upper body slightly away from her, he kissed a path from the top of her head to the nape of her neck. Nibbling her neck, he continued to tease her breast and grind his erection against her behind. She sighed and raised her arm until it was wrapped around his head, holding her to him.

His muscles tensed slightly as he felt her fingers lightly skim his hair, and he found himself wishing that his hair were longer so that she could run her fingers through it. He kept his black hair cut fairly short for convenience sake, but the sensation of her hand caressing his scalp was a pleasant one. Sighing, he angled his head so it was easier for her to touch him.

It was hard not to protest when her hand slid from his hair. But instead of losing contact, she rolled over onto her other side so that she was now facing him, allowing her fingertips to trail along the side of his neck and over his shoulder, until her palm was flat on his chest. As she traced the muscles there, he could feel his body start to tense. His cock flexed, demanding attention. It had been a long time since he'd wanted a woman this badly.

Her fingers lightly rasped one of his flat male nipples. A moan of pleasure slipped from his mouth, and for a moment he was afraid she would stop. Instead, he felt her breath on his lips just before her soft mouth covered his in a sweet kiss that tasted of cinnamon. His heart was racing now as he waited to see what she would do next. She didn't disappoint him.

Delving into his mouth, her soft, wet tongue explored every inch of him. Unable to hold himself still any longer, he gripped her head in his hands and turned it slightly so that he could have better access to her sweet lips. Taking his time, he sucked on her tongue before foraging his way into her mouth. There, he tasted and savored her sweetness.

His cock continued to throb, but it was almost a pleasant kind of torture. For a man who liked sex and women as much as he did, he'd all but lost interest in both in the last few months as his work had consumed him. The fact that he was actually thinking about sex again reassured him that he'd done the right thing by coming home. All he needed was a rest. A place to recharge his batteries and rethink his life.

Moving his hands slow as to not frighten his mystery lady, he allowed his hands to follow the line of her spine, gently urging her closer to him. She murmured something in response, but he couldn't quite understand the words, and at this point he didn't care. Cupping one of her firm tits in his hand, he used his thumb to rub the hardened nipple.

"Make love to me," she whispered.

Abel froze as the sounds of the birds outside the windows penetrated his foggy mind. His hand covering her breast stilled and she made a small sound of disappointment as she gripped it in her own hand and began to move it once again. Prying open his eyes, his dream became a reality. The fragile slope of her neck was moist from his kisses and one creamy shoulder was exposed. The sheet had slipped low and his eyes followed the contours of her side and the indention of her waist, barely catching a glimpse of the side of her breast that was covered by his hand.

"You're real." His voice sounded surprised even to him.

"Did you think I was a dream?"

"Yes."

She was a beauty. Her hair, pushed back from her face, was the color of a cinnamon stick. Pale blue eyes seemed to be cataloguing all his features as she reached out and traced his lips with her finger. Fine skin with a smattering of freckles across her slightly tilted nose, and full, lush lips completed the picture.

All in one motion, Abel grabbed her shoulders and flipped her until she was flat on her back. Rolling on top of her, he covered her body with his, trapping her under him. Capturing her hands, he raised them over her head and held them there with one of his hands. Her back arched and the hard nubs of her breasts stabbed his chest. He almost moaned as he felt her soft curves conform to the hard planes of his body. His arousal was poking her in the stomach, but there was nothing he could do about that. She was totally at his mercy.

Abel was the kind of man that other men walked softly around. Built on a massive scale, he was eight inches over six feet and more than two hundred and fifty pounds, all of it solid muscle.

But it was more than just that. It was the look in his eyes that said he had seen it all and done it all, and nothing scared him any more. Abel hated the thought of frightening a woman, but it couldn't be helped. He needed answers. The one thing he did remember was that he'd locked the door behind him. If nothing else, this woman was guilty of breaking and entering.

He leaned over her, ready to reassure her that he wouldn't hurt her if she answered his questions. Bracing himself to ignore the fear in her eyes until he got his answers, he opened his mouth to speak and then clamped it shut. She was smiling at him. A soft, sensual smile that had him swallowing hard.

"I'm glad you're home, Abel." Her voice was soft and sultry and made his toes curl. He wanted to hear that voice crying out in pleasure in the dark of the night. All the nerve endings in his body were humming in anticipation of that happening. He would have her, of that there was no doubt, but first he had to find out who the hell she was.

"Who are you and how did you get in here?" Her smile disappeared and he was filled with the ridiculous notion that his words had hurt her somehow. His first instinct was to do whatever it took to have her smile at him again.

"I guess you don't recognize me." She closed her pretty blue eyes and took a deep breath as if gathering her strength. "It's me, Erin."

For a moment the name didn't register, but the moment it did, he wanted to throw back his head and howl at the injustice of it all. Erin Connors. His best friend's little sister. He remembered her as a little girl following his every move with her enormous blue eyes. She'd still been a kid when he left home, and over the years, he'd only caught glimpses of her here and there. Jackson might be the closest thing he had to a brother, but what he was feeling towards Erin right now was certainly anything but brotherly. She sure as hell wasn't a child any longer. Now, she was a woman grown, and what a woman! Tall and curvy, she fit him perfectly.

Dropping his forehead to hers, he pushed his hips towards her unable to help himself. "God, I wish you weren't." His cock throbbed, and it took every ounce of willpower he possessed to keep from coming on her stomach.

To his surprise, she pushed back, grinding her hips against him. "What's that supposed to mean?"

In spite of his aching arousal, he felt himself smiling as he looked into her disgruntled features. It was amazing. In a short few minutes with this woman, he had experienced more emotions than he had for a long, long time. Arousal, amusement, and curiosity filled him all at once.

"It means that you're Jackson's sister and therefore off-limits." Because he could no longer resist them, he kissed the smattering of freckles on her nose. "Which is too damn bad, because I want to fuck you. Bad."

She gasped for a moment and he prepared himself to be blasted by her for his blunt words, but she surprised him. "I want that too." Leaning forward, she licked his lips. "Fuck me, Abel."

Abel hadn't expected her to take him quite so literally, but all the reasons why he shouldn't make love to her were suddenly unimportant as she shifted, cradling his cock against her wet pussy. She was naked in his bed and more than willing.

An awful thought crossed his mind. "Neither of them will come looking for you, will they?" She knew who he meant and was already shaking her head.

"No. I told Jackson I'd be home in time for lunch."

Abel smiled and glanced at the clock. "That doesn't give us much time, but we can work around it."

He felt her surprise as her body jerked slightly. "But it's just past ten."

"I know. I'd better get to work." Releasing her hands, he rolled off her, turning her until her back was to him once more before licking a line down her spine all the way to the dimples just above her luscious ass. He kicked the covers off the bed as he moved until they were both naked. She made a slight sound of distress. "I plan to see and taste every inch of your luscious body, honey, and keep you naked as long as possible."

"Okay." Her voice was small and tentative, but the fact that she agreed so readily sent a wave of lust through him that was followed by a rush of tenderness.

Molding his hands over her ass, he squeezed both cheeks. "I love the way you pushed your ass against my cock until it was settled right here between the folds." He moved his thumbs to the dark cleft and traced a path down towards her feminine heat.

Erin moaned and tried to hide her head under the pillow, but he wouldn't allow it. Reaching up, he tugged the pillow off her head and smacked it against her bottom before tossing it next to him on the bed. "None of that." Leaning over, he lightly bit her on the cheek before licking both her dimples. "You've got a gorgeous ass and I plan to enjoy every inch of it."

Erin could hardly believe she was lying naked in Abel's bed with the bright morning sunshine coming through the window. She felt exposed, yet she also felt decadent and sexy as her sensitive skin brushed the cotton sheets. It was a bit disconcerting to have her behind exposed to him, but the moment she felt his tongue on her flesh she forgot all about being embarrassed.

Her fingers clenched the sheets as his hands continued to shape and mold her bottom. It had never occurred to her that a man would find that part of her anatomy sexy or that she would enjoy his touch so much. She moaned as his clever fingers traced a line down the cleft between her cheeks. Almost against her will, her bottom rose to meet him. He laughed and it was a low, husky sound that sent shivers down her spine.

His lips were soft and firm as he kissed his way up her back. She could feel his large erection pushing against her bottom. Although she'd read that most men had a hard-on when they awoke in the mornings, she still felt special, as if it was all because of her. One of his large hands gripped her waist, and he pulled her back until his cock was once again sandwiched between the cheeks of her ass.

Once he was satisfied with her position, his hand slid to her stomach before he spread his fingers and combed them through her pubic hair. Slowly, he repeated the motion again and again until she was desperately trying to open her legs. Carefully, he lifted her top leg and placed it over his. It widened her legs enough for him to slip his fingers through her hair and down to the damp folds of her throbbing sex.

Erin whimpered and arched her head back against him. She needed more, but didn't know how to ask him for what she wanted. He shifted for a moment and she felt his other arm slipping under her shoulders. When his hand cupped her breast she didn't know whether to cry in frustration or to moan with ecstasy she was so aroused. The sound that came out of her throat was somewhere in between.

"You like that, do you?" His breath tickled her ear and sent tingles of sensations through her body.

"Yes." She wanted to say more, but that was all she could manage. Her body was taut with arousal and she was perched on the edge of orgasm. It was exhilarating and slightly painful as she lay there waiting, anticipating his next move.

His fingertip brushed the tip of her distended nipple at the same time he pressed another finger against her clitoris. He didn't move the hand between her legs, but just applied a steady pressure as he continued to lightly brush her nipple. She could feel his cock pulsing in the cleft of her behind. That combined with all the hours of anticipation was too much for her and she felt her body convulsing.

Crying out, she clamped her hand over his fingers between her legs to keep him there. Her body shook as the powerful release washed over her. Finally, when it was over, all her muscles relaxed and she lay quietly next to him. Neither one of them had moved position. His hands were still caressing her, but his touch was more soothing now than arousing.

Turning her head slightly she smiled up at him. She'd never felt this good in her entire life. "Thank you." Her gratitude was heartfelt and real.

"You're very welcome, but we're not through yet." His eyes were dark with arousal and need, and his hands tightened briefly on her body as if he was afraid she might try and leave him. She could have told him that she had no intention of getting out of this bed until he'd finally made love to her, but decided to show him instead.

Clenching the muscles of her ass, she gripped his cock tight. He hissed an oath between his teeth and his entire body went rigid. His eyes were dark slits as his mouth covered hers in a heated kiss. All signs of play were gone. This was a seriously aroused man and he meant business.

Erin could barely breathe as his mouth plundered hers. Their tongues tasted and tested one another and she knew that she'd never get enough of him. His hands were once again in motion. Two of his large fingers slid inside her slick opening and the sound in her throat was almost a purr in response to his action. Once his long fingers were seated to the hilt, he spread them wide, opening her further. The edge of his palm pressed against her clit. He swallowed her cries as his mouth continued to devour hers.

His other hand continued to shape and mold her breast, and she felt it swell even more with arousal. With his thumb and forefinger, he lightly pinched her nipple. Her body was alive and every inch of her was sensitized. She was overwhelmed by the urge to push.

With his arms wrapped around her like a vise it was hard for her to move, but she managed to swivel her hips slightly and push her breast even closer to his hand. Abel tore his mouth from hers and placed hot kisses across her cheek. When he reached her ear, he swirled his tongue around the outer rim before flicking the inside.

"Abel," she moaned.

"Tell me what you want," he ordered as he continued to stimulate her entire body.

"I want you." Reaching behind her she grabbed his ass and tried to bring him even closer to her.

"You want me to what?"

Erin's breasts ached and the emptiness between her legs was almost unbearable. "I want your cock inside me."

His wicked tongue thrust into her ear as his fingers toyed with her nipple. "You want me to fuck you?"

Erin was panting hard now, her entire body vibrating with desire. "Yes," she wailed. "Fuck me. Now."

"Hell yes," he groaned.

She cried out as he pulled away from her, but before she could protest, he drove his cock deep inside her. Her inner muscles clasped him hard as he pulsed within her. Erin closed her eyes. The connection she felt with this man was so intense. It was more than sexual. It was intimate, like having him inside her body, mind, and soul all at once.

He shifted, gripping her waist and pulling her downward until he was seated inside her to the hilt. "Damn, you feel good." His voice was a low whisper in her ear and she nodded unable to speak.

With one hand on her waist, and the other on her breast, he began to thrust slowly and deeply. Erin could hear his harsh breathing and realized that her own was just as ragged. He pulled out as far as he could go before surging back inside her. She helped him as much as she could but he had all the leverage. The most she could do was lie there and enjoy the ride.

The hand on her waist slid downward until he was touching her clit with one finger. That single touch was enough to send her spiraling out of control and she cried out as she came once again. Abel thrust even harder a few more times before she felt him stiffen. He came deep within her. The hot liquid discharge intensified her own release and she cried out once again.

When they were both spent, they lay boneless against the pillows. Erin felt mellow, yet happy. She stretched her leg that was still draped over his and he gave a half laugh. "You're going to kill me if you keep that up." She groaned as he lifted her leg off of his. Her leg had gotten stiff in that position. Then she groaned with pleasure as his fingers dug into the sore muscles and he rubbed the stiffness from them.

"That feels so good."

"So do you." He breathed deep as he spoke. "You smell like sex and woman. I can smell myself on you. I like that."

His primitive words sent a shaft of pleasure through her as they continued to lie there side by side. Neither one of them was in a particular hurry to move. A pang of disappointment went through her and she sighed when he finally pulled out of her. She felt empty without him and turned to face him. As if he understood and shared her feelings, he wrapped his arms tight around her.

Abel rolled onto his back, pulling her with him. Settling herself into the crook of his arm, she toyed with the hair on his chest. Pushing a lock of hair out of her face, he kissed her on the nose. "That was amazing."

"It's called spooning." The words were out of her mouth before she could stop herself.

"What is?" He continued to sift his fingers through her long hair.

"What we just did." She made little circles around his nipples as she spoke. "I read about it in a magazine."

"Did you now?" He sounded interested. "What else did you read?"

Keeping her eyes glued on his chest, she concentrated on the motions of her fingers. "There was an article that listed what they said was the best seven sexual positions, and the one we just did was called spooning."

"What were some of the other ones?"

The fact that he sounded so nonchalant about the whole thing gave her the courage to continue. "They all have different names like scissors and doggy-style, and a whole bunch more." He stiffened the moment she mentioned the first one, and she suddenly lost her courage to continue.

She felt his chest begin to rumble. It took her a second to realize he was laughing. He rolled suddenly until she was lying flat on her back once again with him looming over her. There was a grin on his face as he cupped her face in his hands and gave her a quick kiss. "The scissors thing sounds painful, but I think I'd like the doggy one. In fact, I know I would."

Erin could feel the heat rise in her cheeks and knew she was blushing. She tried to avert her gaze, but he captured her face in his hands, making her look at him. He was the epitome of the well-sated and indulgent male as he kissed the tip of her nose.

"We can try anything you want to." One of his legs covered hers as he leaned over her. His eyes were dark green and serious as he spoke. "The only rule is that you tell me if I do something you don't like. You can always say no. Understand?"

She nodded and gave him a tentative smile that seemed to satisfy him because he settled back next to her and cuddled her tight. "We'll work our way through any of the positions you want to try." His voice was low and sleepy. "And some more you probably never even thought of."

Promise or threat, Erin didn't care. Her entire body tingled as her mind conjured pictures of the two of them in various sexual positions. Allowing her hands to drift over the hard planes of his chest, she snuggled closer to Abel.

The heat and exertion made them both drowsy and their conversation trailed off as they both drifted off to sleep wrapped around each other.

Chapter Three

It was the heat that finally woke her. The rays of the sun were pouring through the bedroom window, making it hot and uncomfortable. She sprawled on top of the sheets, too lethargic to even move. Stretching slightly, her leg brushed against something hard and firm. Abel. Smiling, she opened her eyes and just stared at him. They were lying close together, but not touching, both of their bodies damp with perspiration.

His hair was plastered to his skull, his chin was shadowed with morning stubble, and his lips were pressed together in a firm line. Even though they were closed now, Erin loved the way his green eyes subtly changed shade, lightening and darkening, depending on his moods. His face was as tanned as the rest of him, evidence that he spent quite a bit of time outdoors. Even resting, his body was a study in rippling muscles and toned flesh. There wasn't an extra ounce of fat anywhere on the man. Simply put, he was gorgeous.

She sighed, knowing she could easily pass a day just looking at him. But strangely, that was not what really attracted her to him. Even when she was only a kid, Erin had sensed an innate kindness in Abel, as well as a sense of fair play and justice. He always stuck up for the underdog and didn't tolerate bullies. She'd found that out when he'd stopped several older boys from teasing her about her height and her red hair. Although she'd only been eight, after that incident she'd followed the fifteen-year-old Abel around, openly adoring him. Not once had he ever scolded her for it or made her feel bad in any way.

The senseless death of his parents had changed him so much. He'd gone from open, smiling young man to one who was grim and silent. The man who'd shot his mother and father in a convenience store holdup had been arrested and charged with their deaths, and Abel had gone to the trial proceedings every day, absorbing every detail. His first book had come out of that incident. It had simply been entitled, *A Son's Search for Justice* by A. B. Garrett.

Almost a dozen more books had followed, each one chronicling the tragic events of some crime. Erin had read only one. The story had been gripping and so real it had given her nightmares for weeks. She owned them all, but had never read more than the opening and final chapters of any of them.

No matter where he had lived or traveled for his work, Abel had always made a pilgrimage home once a year. Sometimes he was here for as long as a week, other times he'd be gone after two or three days. No one ever knew when he was coming or when he was leaving, but he always wrote to them. Well, really he occasionally wrote to Jackson who shared the letters with her and Nathan. They were always filled with details of where he was and what he was working on. Erin had traveled all the way around the country through those letters.

Erin didn't know how he could keep his sanity investigating gruesome crimes such as serial murders and rapes, and then writing about them. She sensed from his letters that it had taken a toll on him. Over the years, his letters had gotten further apart and sparser on details, but permeating them all was a sense of aloneness. It broke her heart to think of him buried in his work, hardly coming up for breath between projects. It was if he was driven to write each one, as if that would somehow make dealing with the death of his own parents easier to handle.

Reaching out, she placed her hand on his arm, simply wanting contact with him. She admired him as a person, but she adored him as a man. This morning, he'd made her feel sexy and womanly for the first time in her life and for that alone, he had earned a special place in her heart forever.

Flawed he might be, but she didn't think she'd ever met a finer man. Their time together might be short, but she planned to take full advantage of every second. He didn't move a muscle, but suddenly she knew he was awake. She peeked up at him and sure enough, his green eyes watched her with such a look of sexual intent that it almost took her breath away.

"Hi," she said.

"Hi back." Taking her hand from his arm, he kissed her palm before laying her hand on the bed between them. "I'm sweating like a pig in this heat, honey. You don't want those gorgeous hands on me until I get a shower.

She placed her hand on his chest. "I don't mind. I'm sweaty too." Leaning forward, she dropped a kiss on his lips. "Besides, I'm a farm girl. I don't mind a little honest sweat."

Laughing, he grabbed her in a bear hug and tugged her on top of him. "Then I'm a very lucky man."

She nodded emphatically. "You certainly are." Pushing her hips against his already half-aroused penis, she added, "And maybe you might get even luckier."

"Think so?" he teased.

"I know so." She loved bantering with him. Never had she felt this comfortable in any man's presence, including her brothers. Her glance happened to stray to the bedside table where the clock radio sat. She blinked, not believing her eyes. It couldn't be that late. But when she looked again, the clock still said that it was just after eleven.

"Omigod." Screaming, she rolled out of bed, ignoring Abel's surprised yelp as her knee came too close to his groin for comfort, and began to frantically search for her clothing. Bending over, she grabbed her underwear, but before she could tug them on, she was captured from behind in a bear hug and tossed back on top of the bed.

With her panties still clutched in her hand, she glared up at him. Smiling, a very pleased, satisfied male smile, he surveyed her naked body from head to toe. Her flushed skin felt even hotter and her nipples tightened, but one more glance at the clock had her sighing. "I've got to go."

Abel leaned over her, planting a hand on either side of her head. Bending down, he lowered his mouth to hers. His lips skimmed her own and she parted hers in response. Quickly taking advantage, his tongue swept inside, engaging hers in a sexual duel. Her arms crept up around his neck, pulling him closer to her. Taking his time, he kissed her with a thoroughness that left her breathless when he finally did pull away.

"Good morning, again." Taking her hand in his, he placed it over his obvious erection. "I know you have to go, but we could take a shower together before you do. It's the environmentally responsible thing to do, you know, to conserve water."

His grin was wicked and she couldn't resist teasing him. "Well," she drawled. "I suppose if it's for the environment, I can sacrifice myself."

Standing, he tugged her up from the bed and pulled her along behind him as he left the bedroom and padded down the hallway. "Abel," she cried. "We're naked." She was desperately trying to cover part of herself with her free hand.

He stopped in his tracks and threw back his head and laughed. Erin, not amused by his humor, tried to free her hand from his hold. Although he wasn't holding her tight, his grip was unbreakable. Finally, she stopped trying and settled for just standing there and glaring at him. Really, the man lacked all sense of modesty.

Getting himself back under control, he scooped her up in his arms, threw her over his shoulder, and proceeded to carry her down the hallway. Erin yelped when he picked her up. She was no lightweight, but he carried her with ease. At first she struggled against his hold, but he smacked her on the ass. "Settle down, honey. There's no one here but us, and besides, we'll be in the shower in just a second. It doesn't make any sense to get dressed."

"I know," she muttered, squirming slightly as his hand soothed the slight sting on her bottom. The heat on her bottom aroused her, which surprised her greatly.

Her reaction to their nudity made her feel like a prudish old maid. "I'm just not used to it." She felt the need to justify herself.

"That's okay. I'll make sure you get plenty of practice." He deposited her on the countertop in the bathroom and then leaned over to turn on the taps in the oversized shower stall. The smooth countertop was cool against her behind and she could barely resist the urge to spread her legs and push her hot pussy against it.

Swinging her feet back and forth, she watched him as he went about readying everything for their shower. Anything to distract herself from the throbbing ache between her legs. All his movements were fluid and sure for such a large man. Opening a cabinet door, he rummaged around and pulled out a couple of towels, setting them on the hamper next to the shower. Checking the water, he adjusted it to his satisfaction.

Sauntering back to the counter, he spread her legs wide with his hands and stepped between them. Startled, Erin splayed her hand on the countertop for support. Abel leaned down and drew one of her engorged nipples into his mouth and sucked hard.

Erin moaned, dropping her head back and widening her legs even further. Abel's fingers lightly pinched the other hard nub as his teeth lightly bit the other. Lightning ran from her breasts to her pussy. "Fuck me, Abel." She was panting hard now and so close to coming again.

Abel lifted his head from her breasts and moved his fingers down to her wet pussy. "Not yet." Thrusting two of his fingers deep inside her, he widened them before pulling them out again with maddening slowness. "I like my pussy hot and begging." His fingers pinched her throbbing clit. "You're not there yet, but you will be." Scooping her up once again, he carried her to the shower and set her underneath the spray.

Erin sputtered as water covered her face, but the cool liquid felt so good against her heated, sensitive skin. She didn't know whether to smack him, yell at him or beg him to fuck her. Before she could decide, large hands began to comb through her hair, wetting the curly locks.

Surprised, she started to turn to see what he was doing, but he placed his hands on her waist, keeping her faced away from him, and whispered in her ear. "Let me?" His voice sent shivers running down her spine, and she slowly nodded.

Curious now, she stood in the shower with the water cascading over both of their bodies and waited to see what he would do. She could hear the sound of him opening a bottle and the sound of something being squeezed out. Then his hands were back on her head as he rubbed the shampoo into her hair. Taking his time, he massaged her scalp and worked the lather all the way down to the tips of her hair before rinsing it off.

Erin had never felt anything like it in her life. His hands were strong and rough, yet when he washed her hair, they were gentle and soothing, yet strangely arousing. Never, had she felt as pampered in her life, and the wonder of it was that he wasn't finished yet.

With her hair rinsed free of soap, he leaned back over and picked up another bottle. A moment later, his hands cupped her breasts and began to lather her skin. His fingers slid easily over her wet, soapy skin, taking special care to make sure that both mounds were completely soaped. With his thumb and forefinger, he pinched them rhythmically until Erin was sure she'd come any second. Moaning, she leaned back against his chest for support as her knees went weak.

Abel shifted his hands from her breasts and continued to soap her upper body, her arms and her stomach. Erin sucked in her breath as his fingers slid through her pubic hair, parted her and slipped right inside her. Spreading her legs to allow him easier access, she enjoyed the feel of his fingers inside her. With one hand on her breast and the other between her legs, he easily aroused her to a fevered pitch.

"I need you." She could feel his cock hot and heavy behind her and knew that he was more than ready for her as well.

"Is your pussy hot?" His breath was hot on the back of her neck as he teased her. His fingers continued to slip in and out of her hot, slippery slit.

"Yes," she cried. If she was any hotter, she'd self-combust. If he didn't fuck her soon, she was going to trip him and throw herself on top of him.

Instead of answering her, he turned her until she was facing the tiled wall of the shower stall. "Put your hands on the wall."

She immediately followed his instructions and placed her hands against the slick tile. His hand caressed the back of one of her legs before coming to rest behind her knee. Bending her leg, he lifted it to a little ledge in the wall. "Keep your foot propped up here."

Erin nodded and her whole body clenched in anticipation. She could feel him behind her as he fitted his body to hers and drove his wet cock deep inside her. Because of the soap and water, he entered her easily even though it was a tight fit. His cock seemed to lengthen even more as he held himself within her. The feeling was not uncomfortable, but she felt full. Filled to her very core by him. She tried to move, but her balance was precarious.

"Let me do all the work," he whispered as he started to move. With his feet braced apart and one arm wrapped around her and the other against the wall, he began to move. Pulling back slightly, he'd almost withdraw from her before plunging back into her pulsing vagina.

Erin forgot all about the time, work, and getting home on schedule to fix lunch. Nothing mattered but making love to Abel and for both of them to reach sexual fulfillment. Her insides churned as he continued to ease out of her before plunging back inside her waiting heat. His strokes got harder and harder, and the slap of their wet skin aroused her even further.

Her nipples were throbbing, so she leaned her face and upper body against the tiles and pushed her breasts against the wall to help ease the ache. "Harder," she commanded. She sensed his momentary surprise, but then he gripped her tighter and began to pound in and out of her body.

That was all it took for her to explode. Screaming her release, she came long and hard as Abel continued to plunder her body. A moment later, she felt him swell and then he erupted inside her. Erin felt herself sliding down the wall and was grateful when Abel's arm tightened around her. His head rested on her shoulder and he was panting as hard as she was.

The water was freezing cold now, but neither of them cared. Erin's body still felt warm and flushed even as the icy water bathed her skin. When Abel eased himself out of her, her body clenched in protest.

Abel groaned before giving a slight rumble of laughter. "They say that a lot of household accidents happen in the shower." He kissed her shoulder, his teeth grazing the sensitive flesh at the base of her neck. "As much as I'd like to stay here, we'd better get you out of the shower and home before Jackson comes looking for you."

That reminder was enough to get Erin functioning again. They both rinsed off quickly before Abel turned off the water, stepped out of the shower, and shook out a big fluffy towel. Motioning her out, he waited while she stepped out of the shower stall. The moment she was out, he wrapped her in the towel, bent down and planted a kiss on her lips. It wasn't a passionate kiss, but it was a slow, intimate one that left her feeling languid and satisfied.

Stepping back, he picked up the other towel and began to wipe the moisture from his body. Erin watched him, entranced by the beads of water sliding over his large, muscled torso and down his strong, sturdy legs. He glanced at her and his lips curved up in a knowing smile. Erin gave herself a mental shake and began to briskly dry herself.

"I don't know that we actually conserved any water." She gave him a saucy grin as she wrapped the towel around her body and tucked the tails in at the top over her breasts.

"No, but we sure had fun." Abel pulled a dry towel from the cabinet and handed it to her. "For your hair."

Erin squeezed most of the water from her hair before wrapping the towel around it like a turban. "Can I borrow your hairdryer?"

"Sure. I think there's an old one in here." He rummaged around the drawer, pulled out a dryer and plugged it in over the counter. The mirror wasn't steamed up too badly where they'd left the door open and the water had been mostly cold. Abel leaned against the counter with his towel wrapped around his waist and watched her as she dried her hair. It was slightly disconcerting as, in many ways, Erin found this even more intimate than sleeping with Abel.

As quickly as she could, she dried her hair and finger-combed it before she put it back into her familiar braid and realized she didn't have anything to hold it with. Abel held out his hand and she gladly took it, holding the tail of her braid in the other. Erin felt light and happy as they padded back to the bedroom, and reluctantly let his hand go so she could dig a rubber band out of the pocket of her jeans to secure the ends of her hair.

"We've never talked about birth control." Abel's voice brought her back to reality in a rush. He raked his fingers through his hair. "I should have taken care of it, and I'm sorry for that. It was up to me to protect you."

"I'm on the pill," she confessed. "The doctor put me on it several years ago to help regulate my period." Erin was embarrassed to be discussing this even though she knew it was necessary.

"I promise that I'm healthy. I've never forgotten to use a condom before in my life." He sounded aggravated with himself, and in a perverse way, she was pleased that she could make a man as self-contained as him lose all control. She knew she'd feel very different if she hadn't been on the pill, but since birth control wasn't an issue, she decided to enjoy herself.

Erin tugged on her clothes and watched Abel as he hauled on his jeans. When they were both dressed, she walked up to him, went up on her toes, and kissed his cheek. "Don't worry about it, everything is fine."

"You're sure?"

"Positive," she answered. A glance at the clock told her that she was out of time. If she hurried, she'd get home the same time as Jackson. He was getting soup and sandwiches for lunch if he wanted to eat at all.

Chapter Four

Abel kept his hand on the small of her back as they walked down the stairs. "How did you get in the house and how did you know I was here?"

Erin's smile was genuine and her eyes were alight with mischief. "Now you know that the entire town knows you're back. After all, you did stop for groceries this morning."

Abel chuckled and was surprised by the sound. He had all but forgotten how to laugh, but had done so several times since discovering Erin in his bed this morning. "I'd forgotten how fast the local grapevine works."

"Anyway, Jackson told me you were back. He got it from Jed, the mailman, who got it from his wife, Alma, at the Stop and Shop."

"I get the picture," Abel interrupted her. "But did you come here just to seduce me? Not that I minded," he added, letting his hand fall lower so he could squeeze her luscious ass.

His body was primed and ready to go again, but his conscience was reasserting itself. It didn't matter that Erin had climbed in bed with him. He was the older and more experienced of the two of them, and he'd taken advantage of her. Yes, she was an adult, but she'd lived a sheltered life and was one of his best friends' baby sister.

"Why, I brought you a welcome-home present." She batted her eyelashes coyly. "I know you like apple pie."

That explained the cinnamon smell from his dream. "But how did you get in?"

"We've got a key. Who do you think takes care of this place while you're gone?"

Erin's words struck him. He'd never thought about that in all the years he'd been gone. Whenever he'd stopped back for a visit the house was always clean and smelled fresh, something he'd always taken it for granted. The thought that she'd kept his home ready and waiting for him moved him deeply. "I'm sorry." The phrase was totally inadequate to express how he was feeling. "Thank you."

"It was my pleasure." Quickly she brushed aside his praise. "I liked your mother, and couldn't bear to see her home fall into disarray. It's her pie recipe I used." Erin bit her lip and bounced on her toes, looking for all the world like a child who needed approval.

Abel stopped at the bottom of the stairs, and drew her into his arms. Leaning down, he traced the soft contours of her lips with his tongue. He knew he couldn't let this go any further, but damn it, it had been way too long since he'd taken such pleasure from having a woman's body next to his.

The soft mounds of her breasts were flattened against his chest as Erin kissed him with abandon. The woman didn't seem to have any protective instincts, giving herself to him totally. She made little sounds of pleasure as he stroked her tongue with his. Her hands clutched at him, her nails digging hard into his shoulders.

Moving slightly, he grabbed her behind with one hand and tugged her close to him. One of Erin's hands slid from his shoulders and cupped his rigid cock through the stiff denim of his jeans. Abel tore his mouth away from hers and he buried his face in her neck, inhaling her intoxicating scent. The smell of her arousal was driving him mad. She was ready and willing, ripe for the taking. And his.

So lost was he in his own desires, that he almost came in his pants when she wrapped her arms around his neck and hoisted both her legs around him, locking her ankles behind him. She pushed her mound against his cock, moaning as she pleasured herself. The sight of Erin, totally abandoning herself to the passion that sizzled between them snapped his tenuous control.

Blind with need, he shoved her against the wall and tugged at the top of her overalls, pulling the straps down over her arms. She struggled to help him, releasing her hold on him long enough for him to push up her soft cotton shirt and sports bra to expose her breasts. Small, but perfectly proportioned, the pert nipples were like ripe strawberries just waiting to be plucked. He'd always been partial to strawberries.

Plumping her breasts with his hands, he bent his head, nibbling and tasting her lush flesh. Her skin was salty and sweet, and her soft moans of pleasure filled the air as she continued to grind her pussy against his cock. Even between their layers of clothing he was unbelievably aroused.

Abel could feel the sweat rolling down between his shoulder blades as he struggled to regain a thread of control. It took an effort, but he kept reminding himself to be careful with her, but she wasn't making it easy. Erin tugged eagerly at his clothing, and he pulled back long enough to tear his own shirt over his head and toss it on the floor.

Slowly, he covered her torso with his chest as he lowered his mouth to hers. The rasp of her nipples against his chest and his cock against her hot pussy was incredible. Needing even more, he devoured her mouth, plundering the dark, moist cavern. Their bodies touched everywhere, but it still wasn't enough.

The hand on her bottom squeezed tight for a moment before sliding along the cleft of her jeans. He could tell that she was wet and ready for him as even the fabric was damp. "You're ready for me again, aren't you, baby?"

"Yes," she groaned and ground her hips hard against his cock.

"Come for me," he coaxed her. He needed to pleasure her. Wanted her pleasure. "You can do it," he encouraged. His fingers rubbed hard against the crotch of her jeans even as he nibbled his way down her jawline and bit lightly on her neck.

"Abel..." she cried just as her body convulsed. He could feel her pulsing against his crotch and he ground his teeth and prayed he wouldn't come in his pants. With her head tilted back in the throes of her pleasure, she was the most beautiful sight he'd ever seen. She held nothing back from him.

Holding her tight, he cradled her in his arms until she finally stopped shivering. Sighing, she went boneless in his embrace and her legs slid down his sides until her feet were touching the ground again. Levering himself away from her, he gazed at her, pleased by the smile that played across her lips. "I'm not going to apologize for that."

"I'd be angry with you if you did." Snuggling closer to him, her hand grazed the front of his jeans and he grabbed her hand in an iron grip before moving it away.

"That's not a good idea." He was riding the razor's edge at the moment and the last thing he wanted to do was disgrace himself. Erin had him hotter than a teenage boy with his first girl.

"I think it's a wonderful idea." Squirming against him, she rubbed her bare breasts across his chest.

Abel pulled away from her and stood there totally bewitched by the erotic picture before him. With her back against the wall, her legs spread, her breasts bare, and her lips rosy, she was every man's wet dream. He wanted nothing more than to heft her over his shoulder, carry her back upstairs to his bed and keep her there for at least three days. He raked his hands through his hair and over his face, trying to regain his composure.

Erin continued to stand there and smile at him. Finally in an act of self-preservation he reached out and tugged her bra and shirt down to cover her tempting breasts. "Enough, Erin."

Shooting him a look of irritation, she pulled her overall straps back over her shoulders and tucked her shirt back in. Abel waited until she was finished pulling herself back together. God, she looked good enough to eat. He shook his head at his wayward thoughts and allowed his nose to lead him towards the kitchen. "Come on," he growled as unfulfilled lust roared through him. "I've got to taste that pie." He really wanted to eat her pussy, but pie would have to do.

Erin followed Abel to the kitchen. It was either that or be left behind. What she really wanted to do was drag him back to the comfortable bed upstairs and demand he make love to her again. But that was impossible. One didn't drag a man of his size anywhere.

She couldn't take her eyes off him as he strode towards the kitchen. That man looked great coming and going. Right now, she was enjoying watching the way his tight butt filled out his jeans. It looked good enough to take a bite out of. Look what that magazine had done to her. She'd had more lustful thoughts today than she had in the last seven years combined. Maybe she was just long overdue for some fun.

Abel looked even better than she remembered, and her memory was excellent. The faded denim of his jeans were molded to the muscles in his thighs and cupped the large bulge in the front, displaying it to perfection. His waist was thick due to his size, but there wasn't an inch of flab on him. Erin was just glad that he hadn't felt the need to put his shirt back on. The muscles of his back and arms looked like they were sculpted out of bronze.

Sighing, she wished he'd turn around again just so she could ogle his washboard stomach again. She knew she was being disgraceful. After all, she had two strong, muscular brothers not much smaller than Abel. A great male body shouldn't have her panting after him like this. But there was just something about Abel that called to her as a woman and made her glad to be one.

He stood beside the counter for a moment and just closed his eyes and inhaled the scent of the pie. The sheer look of pleasure on his face made every moment of making it and baking it well worth it. Hurrying past him, she opened a cupboard and took down a plate. Tugging open the drawer next to him, she pulled out a fork and knife. Abel hadn't moved a muscle. He was still standing there with his head tilted back and his eyes closed, breathing deeply.

It occurred to her then that Abel was tired. Not a regular tired, but a deep down to your soul exhausted. She didn't know how she knew, only that she did. This was a man at the end of his rope, mentally and physically. What he needed was some old-fashioned TLC, and she was just the woman to provide it. Biting her lip, she reminded herself that this thing with him had to be a summer fling. He wouldn't be around much longer than that, and if she let her heart get involved she was asking for a world of hurt.

Reaching in front of him, she snagged the pie plate and dragged it in front of her. Wielding her knife with skill, she cut a huge slab of pie. Actually, it was more like a quarter of the pie. She slid the fork underneath it and scooped it onto the plate. He still hadn't moved.

"Abel." She laid her hand on his forearm and could feel the muscle jump under her palm. "Come sit down and eat."

It seemed to take an effort on his part, but he opened his eyes, rolled his shoulders, and allowed himself to be led to the table. When he was seated, she popped the plate of pie in front of him and handed him a fork. "Eat."

He gave her a glance from under his heavy eyelids that warned her that he wouldn't always obey her orders. But she didn't care as long as he ate. "Do you want something to drink?" She knew she was hovering, but she couldn't help herself.

"I think there's some milk in the fridge." He forked up a piece of pie. She watched as his mouth opened and the pie disappeared inside. His teeth scraped against the fork as he pulled it back out and his tongue licked his lips.

Liquid flowed from her crotch and she ached with emptiness. Her imagination conjured up all kinds of things he could do with that talented tongue. Right now, Erin wanted to do nothing more than sit on his lap facing him, haul off her shirt, and offer him her breasts to feast on. She could feel her nipples poking against the front of her bra and thanked the lord that she was wearing overalls. It wouldn't do for him to know that she could get all hot and bothered just by watching him eat.

"Erin?" His voice brought her back to her senses. "Are you all right?"

"Fine. I'm fine. Everything is just…fine." Turning on her heel, she hurried to the refrigerator and opened the door. The cold air felt good as it washed over, allowing her to regain at least part of her composure. She rummaged around until she found the carton of milk and plunked it, and two glasses from the cupboard, onto the table.

Taking her time, she filled the two glasses with the cold milk. She wanted to make sure she approached this in the right manner. Abel seemed oblivious to her turmoil as he continued to shovel down the pie. Scraping his plate clean, he sat back with a contented sigh and took a mouthful of milk to wash it down. It was now or never.

"I want to have a summer fling with you."

Milk spewed everywhere as Abel began to choke and sputter. "Woman," he roared. "Are you trying to kill me?" He started to cough, so she leaned over and thumped him on the back a few times.

Pushing her away, he stood up from the table and crossed his arms over his chest. He looked very intimidating, and for a moment, she hesitated. But only for a moment. She'd known him all her life and she trusted him.

Sitting back in her chair, she saluted him with her glass of milk before taking a sip. "No. I'm offering you a no-strings summer affair." She carefully set the glass back on the table.

Leaning forward, he gripped her upper arms and plucked her out of her chair as if she was a child. "What happened between us shouldn't have happened, and I take full blame for that. But it wouldn't have happened if you hadn't caught me so unaware." He said each word slowly as if she was dimwitted and he was trying to make her understand him. "You are Jackson's baby sister."

"What's that got to do with anything?"

"What's that got to do with anything?" he repeated, his tone incredulous. "That's got everything to do with it."

"Why?" Taking advantage of her proximity to him, she placed her palms on his chest and kneaded the tense muscles there. "We're both adults. I want you, and I know that you want me." Slipping one hand down the front of his stomach and over the front of his jeans, she cupped his bulging cock.

"Damn it, Erin." He pulled away from her, backing up as he continued talking. "Just stop. I know it's like closing the barn door after the horse is out, but it can't happen again. I apologize for taking advantage of you earlier, but this is not going to go any further. It can't."

The counter was right behind him, so she stood in front of him and wrapped her arms around his neck. His arms went behind his head to remove her hands, but before he could, she stepped up on the tip of her toes and kissed him.

He froze immediately with his hands wrapped around her wrists. Emboldened, she feathered soft little kisses across his lips while pushing as close to him as she could. His stiff cock pressed against her stomach and once again she felt the answering ache pulsing between her legs.

For a moment he did nothing and just allowed her to kiss him. When he didn't respond, she began to lose her courage. She could feel the heat crawling up her cheeks, and she closed her eyes as shame washed over her. Because of what he'd done in the bedroom, she'd felt bold and womanly. She'd forgotten for a moment that she was just plain old Erin. A man like this didn't need her when he could get any woman he wanted, and he'd probably only had sex with her because he was horny and she'd made herself readily available. Closing her eyes against the pity she was sure would be there in his eyes, she tugged her arms from his neck.

He pounced the moment she moved. As if she had awakened the sleeping giant, she found herself hauled into his arms, and clasped so tight, she could barely breathe. One large hand cupped the back of her head and angled it for his comfort as his lips took hers in a searing kiss.

Heat sizzled through her veins and she knew that she was in danger of becoming a puddle at his feet. This man could kiss. There was no part of her lips, mouth and tongue that he didn't taste, explore and savor. As if he had all the time in the world, he consumed her slowly, one kiss at a time. Giving herself over to his skillful embrace, it wasn't long until she was returning the favor. She'd always been a quick learner.

The other hand moved down her back until he was cupping her behind. Pulling her tight to his arousal, he used his grip to urge her to move her hips in a circular motion. His hand dropped from the back of her head and suddenly both of them were gripping her ass. That was her last thought as her feet left the floor. Wrapping her arms tight around his neck and her legs around his waist, she was ready to do whatever he wanted her to.

Moaning, she peppered his face with kisses. Both of them were breathing hard now, and she could feel his hot breath on her neck as he placed stinging little love bites there. "Fuck me, Abel."

The minute she uttered the words, she knew she had made a huge mistake. Her voice seemed to shake him out of his sensual haze. His large body froze, every muscle drawn tight. Slowly, he released his grip on her, and she felt her legs slide down his until her feet touched the floor.

She stumbled slightly and his hand shot out to steady her before pulling away. Feeling unsteady, Erin groped behind her and gripped the back of a chair. Carefully, she lowered herself until she was sitting.

Abel looked like a man in pain. It was etched across his face and evident in every straining muscle in his massive body. "Erin," he began. Rubbing his hand over his face, he took a deep breath and tried again. "It's not you."

Erin couldn't bear to hear the "it's not you, it's me" line. This was the beginning of the pity speech that every plain girl got when being turned down by a gorgeous guy. Next thing he'd be telling her what a great personality she had. Every woman knew that that was the code word for at best, plain, at worst, ugly.

"You're a great girl."

She held up her hand to stop him. If he kept going she'd probably disgrace herself by crying, and that just wouldn't do.

"You don't have to say anything more. I'm sorry for throwing myself at you." She gave a little laugh, trying desperately to lighten the mood and not let him know that her stomach was cramping, and her heart was crushed. "I forgot who I was for a moment."

"What's that supposed to mean?" His frustration was evident now.

It was time for her to end this and leave while she could still manage it with some dignity. "I'm plain old Erin, everybody's buddy." Standing, she inched towards the back door. "Jackson and Nathan's baby sister."

Abel stalked towards her, looking more displeased than she'd ever seen him. "What the hell are you talking about?"

She had to get out of here. Now. "Gotta go. You're invited to supper." Her hand was on the back door. Safety was a few steps away.

Turning, she pushed open the door and heaved a sigh of relief. Just when she thought she'd made it, a large hand clamped over her shoulder and spun her around. "You're not going anywhere until you explain that last statement."

Anger bubbled up inside her. What did he want? Her heart on a platter. She was sick and tired of people acting like she really didn't have any feelings at all. Tired of being seen as an extension of her two older brothers. She was a person in her own right, and although people didn't seem to realize it, she was a woman. She had wants and needs too.

"What don't you understand?" Taking the offensive, she poked him in the chest as she spoke. She'd learned early to never give ground when dealing with a man. If they sensed fear or weakness, they pounced in a moment. It was something she always kept in mind when dealing with her brothers, but for a moment with Abel she'd let down her guard. "I made an offer. You declined. Simple."

"It doesn't seem that simple," he muttered.

"You've made it obvious that I don't appeal to you and that's fine. You don't need to use your friendship with Jackson as an excuse. I understand that a man like you is probably used to having beautiful women fall all over him." She was horrified as a thought crossed her mind. "You don't have a girlfriend, do you? Or a wife?" Her gaze shot to his left hand. It had never crossed her mind to look for a wedding ring. What had she done?

"No. No girlfriend. No wife."

Relief filled her, but he wasn't finished.

"What the hell kind of man do you think I am?"

Before she could reply, he held up his hand to stop her. "I don't think I want to know."

She bit her lip hard to keep the tears at bay. This was getting worse and worse. First she threw herself at him, and when he tried to let her down nicely, she insulted him. Erin wanted to die on the spot. She'd felt silly and foolish lots of times in her life, but she couldn't remember a time when she'd felt quite this bad before.

Before she ran home and crawled under a rock, she owed Abel an apology. His expression was still thunderous and she couldn't blame him. She'd all but accused him of being a two-timing snake, and it would have been all her fault if it had happened.

"I'm sorry." She couldn't think of what else to say. "I'm really sorry." The look he was giving her told her that he wasn't finished talking to her yet, but she was done. "You're invited to supper. Jackson is looking forward to seeing you. Bye."

Turning, she ran as fast as her long legs would carry her. In five seconds flat, she was in her truck, had it started, and was tearing down the road towards home. The dirt was flying behind her, but she didn't even glance in the rearview mirror. She couldn't bear to see him and her dreams disappearing in the distance.

Chapter Five

Abel stood in the back doorway and watched until the truck faded from view. Even after she'd disappeared from sight, he stood and surveyed the land behind his home, contemplating what had just happened. Finally he let out a long sigh and took himself back into the kitchen. Snagging the remainder of the pie off the counter, he sat at the table and dug into the rest of it.

Rolling the tasty apple around in his mouth for a moment before chewing it, he replayed everything over in his mind. There was more to Erin's reaction than him just turning down her offer of an affair. It went deeper than that. For a moment, when her defenses had dropped, she'd seemed shattered. The last thing he'd wanted to do was hurt her.

He stared down at the pie, wondering about the woman who would take the time to bring him a freshly baked apple pie. And not only that, but she'd used his mother's recipe.

Then there was the house. Yes, he leased most of his land to her family, but there had never been any kind of agreement over the house. They had a key because they were the closest neighbors, and you never knew when there would be an emergency of some kind. Especially when he was gone most of the time.

The place should have been dusty, musty, and run-down. Instead, it smelled fresh, like someone had opened a window recently. The table and furniture were polished to a sheen and the kitchen sparkled. It was obvious that someone had been taking good care of the place. And without even having to ask, he knew it was Erin.

What was worse was that he still wanted her. Badly. His body was screaming for release and his dick was still rock-hard and waiting, jammed against the zipper of his jeans. They'd damn near set the place on fire, they'd generated so much heat. How in the heck could she ever come to the conclusion that he didn't want her? It was just past noon and he'd already fucked her twice. Almost three times, if you count the close call on the stairs.

As he continued to eat, it came to him. Only an inexperienced woman, one not sure of herself, could ever think he didn't want her. She'd put herself down in a way that seemed natural. Too natural. As if she'd been doing it for so many years, she actually believed the crap she was spouting.

The more he thought about it, the angrier he got. What was wrong with all the men around here that a woman as gorgeous as Erin didn't know just how desirable she was? For that matter, why weren't the men beating a path to her door? The fact that she turned to him, a virtual stranger, was telling.

Scraping back the chair from the table, he placed the empty pie plate in the sink, giving himself a mental reminder to wash it and take it with him when he went to the Connors' home for supper. After this morning's performance, there was no way he would miss it. Glancing at his watch, he noted that it was just after half-past twelve. Plenty of time to put away the rest of the groceries, unpack, and take a shower before he had to leave.

Jackson's sister or not, he decided he might have to rethink his strategy. An affair might be out of the question, but there was no reason he couldn't flirt with her a little. Build her confidence. The more he thought about it the more he liked the idea.

He snorted at himself. Yeah, great guy that he was he was doing this for her own good. The truth was he wanted her more than he'd wanted any other woman. Just to touch her, kiss her, and maybe pet her a little would be an exceptional treat. The hardest part would be trying to retain some kind of control over his horny body.

With that in mind, he decided that another cold shower was the first thing on the agenda. His cock was still at full salute and he knew that if he stood a chance at having any control, he'd have to take care of that little problem. He'd just imagine it was her soft little hand wrapped around him. His cock twitched. For once, they were in agreement.

* * * * *

He could hear the loud voices as he approached the back door of the house. So caught up in their argument, they didn't even noticed that he'd arrived. Propping himself against the open back door, he crossed his arms over his chest and waited for them to notice him.

The mouthwatering smells drifting from the kitchen told him he was in for quite a treat for supper. If he wasn't mistaken, that was baked chicken with stuffing he was sniffing. He'd also bet his last dollar that it was his mother's special recipe for stuffing that he was smelling. His stomach growled in anticipation.

Erin was bent over, peering into the oven at whatever she was baking, giving him a perfect view of her behind. Her faded jeans perfectly cupped her luscious ass, making his fingers itch to do the same. She'd fit his hands perfectly this morning. The soft cotton shirt she was wearing hugged her pert little breasts to perfection. He was so caught up in his lustful thoughts that it took a moment for the argument to register in his brain.

"You knew I needed your help with this."

"I'm sorry, Jackson." Slamming the oven door, she then proceeded to lift the lid off one of the pots on the top of the stove. "I had other things to do. I'll help you in the barn after supper."

Jackson was sitting in a chair at the head of the table with his long legs spread in front of him and a bottle of beer in his hand. Taking a slug of beer, he rubbed the cool bottle against his forehead before dropping it back on the table. "I really wanted to get that done this morning, Erin."

"Well, too bad. I was busy this morning." Lifting one of the pots from the stove, she drained it into a colander in the sink.

Clunking the empty pot down on the counter, she shook out the remaining water and dumped the contents into a clean bowl. Abel watched with glee as Erin added milk, salt and pepper and began to whip the potatoes. He licked his lips in anticipation.

"Yeah, delivering pie." Jackson's reply was curt as he took another pull from the bottle. "Your time and muscle would have been put to better use moving hay bales. Old man Adams is coming to pick up a load tomorrow. You know we need the extra money that pulls in."

Erin set the potatoes aside before she turned and let him have it. "The darn hay will get moved tonight before I go to bed."

"Yeah, but not getting it done means I have to work tonight, and I had plans for some pool and maybe a little dancing and romancing later." The smile on his face left no doubt that he had more on his mind than just dancing.

Erin snorted. "Sorry to upset your love life, but I've been up since the crack of dawn this morning. I cooked breakfast, did four loads of laundry, most of which belonged to you and Nathan, cleaned the house, made a grocery list, and baked three pies. After I delivered a pie to Abel, I made your lunch and then I spent the rest of the afternoon in my berry fields. The blueberries will be ready to harvest in about another two weeks." On a roll now, she barely paused for a breath. "Then, I left work early so I could hurry home and cook for you and the guest that *you* invited to supper. But, I can promise you that your damn hay will be moved tonight."

Jackson held up his hand. "All right, already. You win. You're as busy as I am."

Abel's brow creased in a frown. That was the understatement of the century. While his buddy sat on his butt, Erin worked nonstop. Even while she'd been putting Jackson in his place, she'd been busy dishing up carrots, peas, and ears of corn. Just when it seemed as if Erin was gearing up for another round, the sound of someone thumping down the stairs stopped her.

"Is supper ready yet?" Nathan Connors appeared in the kitchen, his hair still slightly damp from his shower. He'd traded in his police uniform for a comfortable pair of old blue jeans and a soft blue shirt.

Before Abel could announce his presence, Nathan spotted him. "Hey, Abel. Come on in."

Erin spun around from the counter, her eyes wide. He could tell she was wondering just how long he'd been standing there. The moment they made eye contact, she turned away and pretended to be busy. Abel couldn't help but notice that her face was flushed, and he had a feeling it was more than the steam from supper causing it.

Abel sauntered into the kitchen and laid the empty pie plate on the table, his eyes never leaving Erin. Before the moment could get awkward, his attention was drawn away from her as he was enveloped in a bear hug from Jackson. Slapping each other on the back, in a way that would have felled lesser men, Abel felt as if he had finally come home.

Jackson released him before stepping back and sizing him up. "Well, if it isn't Mr. Big-Time Author come to supper."

Abel just grinned at him, knowing full well that Jackson had read every book that he'd written. "You know me. I'll never turn down a free meal. Especially not one that smells as good as this."

"Cooked it myself," Jackson joked.

Abel motioned to the beer bottle on the table. "Yeah, I can tell how hard you were working."

Nathan pushed past his brother and slapped Abel on the back on his way to the refrigerator. Pulling out two more bottles, he opened them and took a mouthful of beer before handing Abel the other bottle. "If we had to depend on our cooking to survive we'd starve to death. It's a good thing that Erin takes pity on us and feeds us occasionally."

His eyes went back to Erin, but she ignored them all as she continued to prepare supper. Both her brothers seemed more than content to sit back and let their sister do all the work. Plunking his bottle of beer on the table, he walked over to the counter, and laid the empty pie plate that he'd brought with him on the counter. "What can I do to help?"

Erin's mouth dropped and her face was filled with astonishment. You could hear a pin drop in the kitchen. Jackson and Nathan were staring at him like he was some alien life form that had wandered into their midst. Shaking his head in disgust, he picked up the bowl filled with the whipped potatoes and another filled with carrots and carried them to the table.

"But you're a guest..." Erin sputtered.

"Yeah," Jackson seconded. "Erin can do that."

For the first time in his life, Abel wanted to take his friend out back and beat him senseless. Instead, he settled for putting both hands on his hips and glaring at him. "I know she can do it. She just shouldn't have to do it all by herself."

His gaze was locked with Jackson's and he sure as hell wasn't backing down. For a moment, anger gleamed in his friend's blue eyes, but then it seemed as if his sense of humor got the better of him, and he began to chuckle. The tension that had filled the room moments before dissipated as Jackson moseyed up to the counter and picked up the large platter that held the steaming chicken.

Carefully placing it on the table, he picked up a carving knife and fork and began to slice the bird. "What?" he said as everyone continued to watch him. "This is men's work. I can do this."

Abel just shook his head. His friend was somewhat of a male chauvinist. It surprised him that he'd never noticed that before. He supposed that's what came of staying away for so long. You didn't really know people anymore. Oh, he knew the important things. He'd still trust Jackson with his life, but he no longer trusted him to be fair to his sister.

Erin was peeking at him out of the corner of her eye as she carried the last of the steaming bowls over to the table. She glanced at everything one last time, as if to assure herself that all was right with the meal, and then she finally pulled out her own chair to sit down. Abel moved quickly and managed to get there in time to hold her chair for her. That garnered him a look of surprise and a shy look of pleasure.

"Showing off your big-city manners," Nathan teased.

"No," he replied. "Just helping to seat a pretty lady." Winking at her, he grabbed the closest bowl and began to heap food on the plate in front of him. "This all looks fantastic, Erin."

"Thank you." Her voice was low and soft, and the smile she gave him was filled with pride.

"That's a good man. Butter her up and you'll get more free food while you're here." Jackson's voice broke the tentative link between him and Erin. But before he could berate his friend, he was already onto another topic. "Speaking of which. How long are you home for this time?"

Erin had sucked in her breath the moment Jackson asked the question, telling him that she was interested in his answer. Acting as nonchalant as possible, he tasted some of the potatoes and savored their flavor before he answered. "Indefinitely. But for the rest of the summer for sure. Possibly longer. It's time I went through the boxes of stuff belonging to Mom and Dad. I've put it off for far too long." He smiled to himself when she released her pent-up breath on a deep sigh.

He had seated himself right next to Erin when he'd sat down for supper, and after he'd enjoyed his first few mouthfuls of food, he decided it was time to have some fun. The conversation flowed around the table as Nathan related something funny that had happened when he'd been out on patrol today. Erin had finally relaxed and was smiling while she listened to her brother. Abel casually allowed his left hand to slide under the table next to him.

Her whole body stiffened in shock when his large hand cupped her knee. Taking his time, he trailed his fingers up the inside of her thigh, stopping just before he reached the top.

Color slowly seeped up Erin's face until her cheeks were a nice rosy hue. Abel continued to eat his supper as he trailed his fingers up and down her legs in a slow and easy fashion.

"You okay, Erin?" Jackson was looking at his sister with a quizzical look. "I didn't notice earlier, but you seem really red. Did you get too much sun today?"

Erin had to clear her throat twice before she could speak. "No, I'm fine. Just a little flushed from working over a hot stove."

Jackson nodded, satisfied with her explanation. "Erin's made herself a nice little business selling berries with your family's land."

"Really?" Abel turned slightly to face her, noting that her breathing was a little more rapid. Giving her a break, he moved his hand lower and settled it just above her knee. "Tell me about it?"

Erin took a deep breath and let it out slowly before responding. "I worked with the wild blueberry bushes that were already there and planted some more. It's a totally organic operation." She shrugged as if it were no big deal. "I pick so much and sell it to local stores and restaurants, and I also have a u-pick operation when the berries are in season. I put in a new road where our property line meets and built a small shed for equipment and such." She ate a mouthful of potatoes and chased it down with some milk before continuing. "I'm really busy from the end of July until mid-September, but it works out well for me."

Nathan snorted. "It works out better than well. Erin employs about a dozen kids from the high school during harvest time, either part-time or full-time."

Jackson nodded. "Yeah, she does. We use the rest of the fields to plant some hay and alfalfa. It works out well for us."

"It works out better for me," Abel added. "I want to thank you for taking care of the house. It certainly wasn't part of the agreement. To tell you the truth it just never crossed my mind."

Both men were looking at him with blank looks in their eyes, strengthening his belief that it was all Erin's doing.

"I told you it was no big deal." She glanced at her brothers and back at her plate. "I'm over that way all the time and it only takes a few minutes to open a window or run a dustcloth over things."

Abel responded by sliding his hand up the inside of her thigh again, and this time he didn't stop until he reached the top. He could feel her feminine heat seeping from her crotch even through the layer of denim, and he felt his dick begin to stir in response. He licked his lips, imagining just how good she would taste. The urge to haul down her jeans, spread her legs wide, and lick every inch of her sweet pussy was almost overwhelming. It didn't matter that her brothers were sitting right next to him and would probably kill him if they could read his mind.

Erin jumped when his palm cupped her intimately, choking on a piece of chicken. Abel was forced to remove his hand long enough to thump her on her back.

"Are you sure you're all right?" Jackson watched as Abel continued to pat her on the back.

"I'm sure," she sputtered. Jumping up from the table, she went straight to the sink and poured a glass of water for herself. Taking her time, she sipped slowly all the while keeping her back turned to them. When she finally regained her composure, she went to the oven, grabbed a potholder, and pulled out a casserole dish that had been left warming there.

Abel watched her as she dished up a steaming chocolate pudding mixture and topped each serving with fresh cream. He could sit and watch her all day long. There was something about the way she moved that was restful. Even when she was busy, her movements were unhurried and precise. Some of her hair had escaped from the confines of her braid, and little locks curled slightly in the heat. Her skin was flushed and her full lips were parted in concentration as she worked.

Abel would much rather have her for dessert than chocolate. Or even better was Erin covered in chocolate. He shifted in his seat, trying to get comfortable. His erection was pushing hard against the front of his jeans, and kept him from offering to help. There was no way he could leave his seat right now without both her and her brothers noticing that his cock was straining against the zipper of his jeans, demanding to be let out.

Jackson pulled his attention away from her with his next question. "Are you working on a new book?"

Abel stiffened, not wanting to talk about his work. He never did. But this was different. He knew it wasn't morbid curiosity that prompted his friend, but a genuine interest in Abel himself. "No. I just finished one that should be out by Christmas."

"What's it about?" As a deputy sheriff, Nathan was always interested in Abel's opinions on the various court cases he researched and wrote about.

"The Trenton Slayer." Everyone was silent for a moment, and then Nathan let out a long, slow whistle.

"That was a hell of a case. Mark Smithson spent over ten years murdering young girls before they caught him." Nathan shook his head. "I read some of the reports on that one, and they were pretty gruesome."

Erin placed the dishes of dessert on the table in front of all of them. Everyone ignored them as they listened to Abel recount some of the story.

"Yeah, it was the worse case I've ever investigated." That was saying something, as they all knew that it was his parents' brutal murder in a convenience store holdup that had led him to his career as an investigative journalist and later a crime writer.

"I talked to the cops and all the families." He toyed with the dessert spoon for a moment before looking up at them, and his eyes were bleak. "But the worst of it was talking to Smithson. He's one sick son of a bitch. It was all just a game to him, and he didn't regret one thing he did. In fact, he promised to do worse if he ever gets out."

Now it was her turn as Erin slipped her hand over to his lap and squeezed his thigh. There was comfort in her touch and he could feel her concern for him. It gave him the strength to pull himself away from the story. If he wasn't careful, it dragged him down like it had for the last year of his life, eating at him and sucking him dry.

"Anyway, I'm finished with it. The book is done and I don't want to think about it any longer." Abel tried his best to inject some humor into his voice. "I'm looking forward to a long vacation filled with sleeping, eating, fishing, and the occasional ice-cold beer."

Jackson teased him in an attempt to lighten the mood. "A man of leisure. If you get bored, come on over here and I'll put you to work doing a real job. We'll have those puny muscles of yours built up in no time."

They all laughed as Jackson had intended. Abel was more muscular than Jackson was and that was saying something, as there wasn't an ounce of fat on Jackson after years of hard farm work. "If I ever feel the need to get into shape, you can be my personal trainer." Abel's smile was genuine now.

Reaching down, he grabbed Erin's hand before she could pull it away. Slowly, he slid it up over the top of his thigh and over his throbbing cock. He knew she could feel him pulsing through his jeans, and her hand automatically covered him and squeezed gently. It was all too easy to imagine her on her knees in front of him opening the front of his jeans. His cock would spring loose and she would take him deep into her mouth and suck him. Hard.

Abel broke out into a cold sweat as he struggled for control. Maybe it hadn't been such a good idea to start a game like this. Erin's touch affected him deeply and his reactions were quick and extreme. Right now, he wanted to sweep the dishes off the table, throw her on the top, and fuck her until they were both senseless with pleasure. It didn't even matter that her brothers were sitting right there in front of them. He was in way over his head.

Thankfully, Nathan broke the erotic spell that she was weaving around him when he pushed back from the table. His chair made a scraping noise on the floor as he stood and stretched. "Come on, Jackson. I'll give you a hand in the barn and Erin and Abel can do the dishes."

"Are you sure?" Erin glanced from one brother to the other. "I can help him after I finish the dishes."

Nathan winked at her before heading for the back door. "I'm sure. You've already had a long day." Abel realized then that he wasn't the only one who'd heard the heated exchange between brother and sister earlier. "Besides, I'm bigger and stronger than you," he teased her.

"And uglier," Jackson added as he rose from the supper table.

"I never claimed otherwise." The screen door slammed behind him and they could all hear him whistle as he walked towards the barn.

Jackson nodded at Abel. "Come on out if you want."

"Thanks," Abel responded, surprised he could talk with Erin's hand slowly moving up and down over his cock. "But I'm still beat. I drove straight through last night and only slept for a couple hours today. After I help with the dishes, I'm gonna go on home and make an early night of it."

"I'll see you tomorrow then." Jackson headed for the door, but turned at the last second and glanced back over his shoulder at his sister. "Thanks for supper." His voice was gruff and he was gone before Erin could respond.

She was stunned for a moment before she laughed with delight. "Well, that was a first. You're obviously a good influence on him."

Abel trapped her hand against him and squeezed hard. He wanted her so bad his teeth ached. She was fast becoming an addiction. One taste wasn't enough, but left you wanting more.

He knew he wanted her. Had to have her. But not until she understood where he stood in his life right now. All he had the energy for at the moment was sweaty, grinding, hot sex. And lots of it. The last year had left him feeling raw.

It took more strength than he thought he possessed to remove her hand from the front of his jeans and place it back on the table. Standing, he towered over her for a moment, soaking in her beauty. "We have to talk." His voice was gruff as he struggled with the desire pulsing through his veins.

Stiffening in her chair, she slowly looked up at him. "So talk."

Chapter Six

Erin didn't wait for him to speak, but stood up and began clearing the dishes off the table. Quickly and efficiently, she scraped and piled plates on top of each other. Carrying a stack to the counter, she deposited them there and returned to the table for another load. Her body was rigid as she moved. Abel could tell he had ticked her off with his actions.

Sighing, he picked up several of the now empty serving bowls and took them over to the counter, dumping them next to the other dirty dishes. When he turned, he realized that Erin was standing there watching him, practically devouring him with her gaze. The hungry look in her eyes startled him, and then he felt an answering hunger rise up within him.

She was a tall woman with wide hips and long legs. Swallowing, he leaned back against the counter and closed his eyes to shut her out. It didn't help. Her image was burned on his brain, and his imagination was filled with erotic pictures of her. He didn't have to hold back his sexual appetites for fear of hurting her with his sheer size. They fit together perfectly. Those long, luscious legs wrapped around his waist easily, while his hands locked on her ample hips so he could thrust into her. Hard.

This wasn't good. He was so primed at the moment, it wouldn't take much for him to come. For a man who prided himself on his self-control, he was rapidly finding that he didn't have much, if any, when it came to this woman standing in front of him. He rolled his head from side to side, hoping to loosen the tension there.

Erin continued to move around the kitchen, opening and closing cupboard doors. Abel felt her standing next to him, but before he could open his eyes, she picked up one of his clenched hands, pried it open, and dropped something in it.

"I'm sorry. I didn't mean to give you a headache." He could tell by her tone that she was trying to joke with him. "This might help."

Opening his eyes, he stared at his open hand, and the over-the-counter pain reliever that she'd put there. She waited patiently next to him with a glass of water in her hand. Again, he felt a tenderness for her well up within him. It had been a long time since anyone had bothered to worry about him.

"Thank you," he replied solemnly before popping the pills into his mouth and chasing them down with the glass of water.

"We can talk tomorrow if you want." Erin went back to work and he noticed that while he'd had his eyes closed, she'd finished clearing the table and wiping it down.

"No. I'd rather get it over with. Besides, I told you I'd help with the dishes."

Erin shrugged and started running water into the sink. "Suit yourself."

"I usually do," he replied laconically.

She squirted some liquid detergent into the sink before pointing to a drawer next to him. "Dishtowels are in there." Turning away from him, she plunged her hands into the water and began to wash glasses and cutlery with a vengeance.

Abel pulled out a clean towel, picked up a glass and started to dry it. He decided it was prudent to give them both a little space. They worked in silence, but it was a companionable one, and Abel was pleased that Erin was not one of those women who felt the need to fill every quiet moment with mindless chatter.

Ten minutes later they were almost finished the dishes and Abel was no longer feeling quite so pleased with the quiet. It was almost as if she'd forgotten he was even there. It took him a second to realize that his male vanity had been pricked by her lack of attention and interest. He chuckled to himself. Obviously, he'd never have to worry about getting a swollen ego with her around. Other parts of his anatomy might swell, he thought as he glanced down at the bulge of his jeans, but never his ego.

Deciding it was time for some action, he dropped the cloth on the counter and moved until he was standing directly behind her. Placing his legs on either side of hers, he crowded her until her stomach was pressed tight against the sink. Bracing his hands on the counter, he had effectively caged her in his embrace. She went motionless.

"What are you doing?" Her voice was low and her breathing was getting faster.

Pushing his hips forward, he allowed his rigid cock to push against her ass. She could not mistake his arousal. Leaning down, he whispered in her ear. "Oh, I'm just making sure you remember that I'm here."

She shivered before pressing her bottom hard against his erection. "I never forgot for a single second."

Now it was his turn to shudder as his dick hardened even more. He was gripping the countertop so hard, he was surprised that a piece didn't crack off in his hands. Every cell in his body was screaming at him to fuck her. Immediately.

When she rotated her bottom, grinding against it, he was lost. All logical thoughts of talking disappeared from his head. They were both adults and she was as turned on as he was.

Dropping his head, he licked the curve of her shoulder and was rewarded when she gasped and tilted her head to one side, giving him better access. He nipped at the fragile skin at the nape of her neck even as his hands reached around her and cupped both her breasts.

Erin felt as if she'd died and gone to heaven. It had been pure hell sitting at the table during supper trying to pretend that this morning hadn't happened. Her body remembered all too well what it felt like to have sex with him, and responded to his presence. Dinner had felt more like foreplay. Her skin tingled at his nearness, her breasts felt heavy and tight, and she could feel the creamy heat between her thighs.

His voice was a low rumble that she felt deep inside her feminine core even when he was just chatting with her brothers. He'd showered and changed since she'd seen him earlier, and he smelled of fresh soap and hot male. It was a seductive combination. His long legs were encased in a faded pair of jeans and his broad shoulders were covered in a crisp white linen shirt. The top two buttons were left open on the shirt, teasing her with a glimpse of his tanned chest, and he'd rolled back the sleeves to reveal thick wrists and strong forearms.

She loved the way his green eyes grew darker when he was aroused. His lips were sensual and his smile knowing. This was an experienced man who enjoyed his own sexuality, and his whole demeanor promised that any woman in his bed would not be disappointed. Now that she'd had a taste of his passion, Erin desperately wanted to be the woman in his bed. Abel represented her best chance to experience her sexuality fully and completely. She'd been crushed when she'd left his house this morning, but tonight had offered her another unexpected opportunity.

Rather than being aloof with her as she'd half expected, or worse, treating her like his friend's kid sister, he'd been attentive. Helping with supper, pulling out her chair, and including her in the dinner conversation were all signs he was interested in her. Or at least she hoped they were.

She darn well knew he was sexually attracted to her if his performance under the kitchen table was any indication. When his hand had covered her thigh and then moved higher to finger her crotch, she thought she might melt into a puddle and slide to the floor. It was shocking to realize that her brothers hadn't noticed a thing. Erin felt as if she'd been wearing a huge sign on her forehead with big bold letters proclaiming, "Fully Aroused Woman".

The fact that he'd stayed to help her with the dishes had made her both excited and terrified. Excited that he might be interested in her and terrified that she was about to get the "you're a great girl, but" speech all over again. When he'd closed his eyes and leaned back against the counter, her heart had dropped. She'd given the man a headache. Wasn't that the oldest cliché in the book?

Burying her disappointment, she'd given him something for the pain and started washing the dishes. The faster they were done, the quicker he would leave. They'd worked well together, and it had been nice to have him next to her as they cleaned the dishes. It was such a small thing, but she almost always cleaned up after meals by herself. Her brothers always had something else to do, and besides which, having Abel dry dishes was a lot more thrilling than having Jackson or Nathan do them.

He'd surprised her when he'd moved behind her, encircling her with his body. The heat pouring off his large frame was enormous, but she'd wanted to get closer. After this morning, however, she'd waited to see what he would do first. When he pressed up close to her, she could feel his erection pushing against her bottom. It had been pure instinct to push backwards and then move her hips to circle his hardness.

His response was electric. When he'd whispered in her ear, desire had shot clear to her toes, and he'd barely touched her. His tongue, slightly rough and warm, had traced a moist path from her shoulder to the nape of her neck. Wanting more, she'd tilted her head to encourage him, but he was already moving. His teeth had nipped at the nape of her neck, and she'd felt both vulnerable and aroused at the same time. The gesture was one of pure male dominance, especially when his hands had come up to possessively cup her breasts. She was totally surrounded by him, and she loved it.

Her body felt languid and heavy as she leaned back against his chest for support. One hand left her breast and she whimpered in protest. Her disappointment was forgotten in a second when he angled her head to one side and tipped her face towards him. His eyes were blazing as he lowered his mouth to hers and covered it in a searing kiss.

Her eyelids grew heavy and slipped closed as she lost herself in the passionate kiss. His lips were soft, yet firm, as they enveloped hers. This was no tentative seeking, but a declaration of possession. Abel's tongue swept into her mouth, claiming it for his own. He sought out and tasted every crevice until he had mapped the entire territory. His fingers tangled in her hair, anchoring her to him, while his other hand caressed both her breasts until her nipples were hard buds stabbing at the center of his palms.

Abel pulled away from her and dropped his forehead to hers. "I want you." His voice was harsh and his breathing labored.

"Yes," she whispered. She wanted to scream out her answer, but was having a hard time just breathing. Raising her hand, she caressed his face, leaving a trail of hot soapy dishwater on his cheek. She'd forgotten she'd still had her hands in the water.

Abel leapt back and swore as he wiped soapsuds from his cheek and the corner of his mouth. Erin slapped a hand to her mouth in horror and ended up sputtering herself as soapy water covered her lips. They both looked at each other, frozen in place. One corner of Abel's mouth quirked up, then the other. Erin felt an answering grin cross her own face. Then they were both laughing.

Abel grabbed the dishtowel from the counter and swiped at her face before doing the same to himself. All that sexual tension had been converted to humor and neither of them could stop laughing. Abel managed to lean against the counter and support himself, but Erin just slid to the floor in front of the sink, holding her stomach as she laughed so hard that tears gathered in her eyes.

Finally, she buried her face in her hands, not looking at him, until she gained control over herself. Wiping her eyes with the back of her hand, she peeked at him from under her lashes. He was still smiling down at her, but he too had gotten a hold of himself.

"You're good for me." His simple comment gave her stomach butterflies, and she flushed with pleasure. The ever-present desire for him flared to life once again.

"You're not so bad yourself." Her voice was soft and flirty and didn't sound like her at all. Yet it was, just another part of herself she'd never explored before.

Abel's eyes darkened as he reached down and pulled her to her feet. Wrapping his hands around her waist, he hoisted her onto the counter and stepped between her open legs. The humor and laughter of a moment before had disappeared, replaced by raw sexual need.

"If you want me to stop it has to be now." Abel's rough voice raised goose bumps on her skin as his hands reached for the button of her jeans.

Erin said nothing, but unzipped her jeans and raised her butt off the counter and helped him tug her sneakers, jeans and panties off. The kitchen counter felt cool and hard against her bottom. She felt exposed and vulnerable half-naked with Abel fully dressed.

Abel picked up her feet one at a time and placed them on the counter, opening her wide to his view. "I wanted to eat your pussy for dessert instead of chocolate." His fingers traced the moist folds of her sex as he spoke. "But now I think I want both."

Reaching across the counter, he scooped a glob of chocolate out of the casserole dish, and rubbed it over her sex and across her clit. The smell of sex and chocolate wafted on the air, and Erin flexed her hips towards him, wanting his mouth on her pussy.

Leaning down, Abel nuzzled her pubic hair with his nose. "You smell sexy." His tongue lapped at a glob of chocolate that slipped down her inner thigh. "And good enough to eat."

"Yes," she moaned, tugging his head closer.

Slowly, his tongue went up one side of her sex and down the other, lapping and licking the chocolate from her flesh. He sucked her clit, taking care to run his tongue over every inch of the swollen bud. Erin moaned and spread her legs wider.

"Pull up your top and show me your pretty breasts." Abel's rough hands stroked her thighs as he continued to lap at her swollen clit.

Erin hesitated and Abel slipped one of his long fingers inside. "Do you want me to stop?"

She'd die if he stopped now. Barely giving herself time to think about the fact that her brothers were just outside, she hauled her top and bra up, exposing her breasts and their tight rosy nipples to him.

"Beautiful." Abel stood and cupped both breasts in his hands, tracing the hard nubs with his fingers.

"Now, Abel." Erin reached down and squeezed his cock through the layers of his jeans. He was hard and thick and she wanted him buried inside her.

Abel swore softly, but stepped back long enough to open his jeans. His cock sprang free, full and ready. Moving between her legs, he angled her hips and thrust inside her. Her pussy clenched tight around him, tugging him further into its depths.

Scooping his fingers into the casserole dish once again, Abel rubbed his chocolate-covered fingers over her lips. Using her tongue, she lapped the pudding from his fingers before taking two of them into her mouth and sucking them. Abel groaned, but slipped his fingers in and out of her mouth as he began to slowly shift his hips back and forth. Erin loved the feeling of being filled by him, her pussy filled with his cock and her mouth filled with his fingers.

Abel pulled his fingers away, and she moaned with disappointment. But before she could protest, he'd slammed his mouth down on top of hers, devouring it. His tongue plunged past her lips, stroking in and out before capturing her tongue and sucking on it. Erin clutched at his head, neck, and shoulder, frantically stroking whatever parts of him she could reach.

Pulling away, he kissed and nipped his way down her face and neck, sucking and biting her breasts until she thought she would scream with frustration. She could feel his cock swelling and pulsing inside her, but she needed more.

"Abel." He answered her plea immediately. Gripping her waist in his hands, he pulled his cock almost all the way out before plunging back in. Erin tipped backwards, grabbing at the counter for support. Her back hit the windowsill and she heard the toaster crash to the floor as her hands sought something to hold on to.

Blindly, Erin reached out until she was holding the faucet with one hand and the edge of the counter with the other. Abel continued to pound into her, driving her closer and closer to fulfillment. Close. She was so close.

Abel banded one of his arms around her and continued thrusting while he slipped his other hand between them and stroked her clit. That was all it took. Her entire body clenched and then spasms of pleasure shook her. She could feel her pussy clenching his cock and then Abel gave a yell, jerking and heaving as he came.

She was still shaking with the last strains of her orgasm when she heard the voices. Frozen into place, she watched the back door in horror. She had completely forgotten about her brothers. Abel had stilled, but made no effort to pull himself away from her.

"I think it's in the house." Erin could hear Jackson's voice getting closer and closer.

"Get it after," Nathan's voice rang out. "I want to finish this now."

"Fine." She didn't hear what else was said, as Jackson's voice faded away.

Abel's shoulders started to shake. The motion shot straight between her legs and she felt her pussy clench down hard on his semi-erect cock. Abel's chuckles of laughter turned into a groan as he slipped his cock out of her wet slit.

"That's not funny." She smacked at his shoulder, almost toppling over when her hand slipped off the counter. Struggling for balance, she flattened her hand on the counter. But instead of hitting the countertop, her hand ended up buried in what little was left of the chocolate pudding in the bottom of the casserole dish.

Bringing her hand up, she swiped at his face. Quick as a cat, he grabbed her hand and licked her chocolate-covered palm, a wicked gleam in his eye. "Dessert was excellent."

Erin's sense of humor got the better of her and she gave a laugh. "Glad you liked it." Letting her legs dangle over the side of the counter, she sat up and pulled down her top with her clean hand.

Abel stepped back and tugged his jeans back over his hips. Taking his time, he tucked in his shirt and zipped up his jeans. He looked exactly as he did when he'd arrived this evening.

She, on the other hand, was a mess. Her entire body felt sticky and she was in desperate need of a bath. Turning on the tap, she rinsed the remainder of the sticky pudding from her hand, before gingerly hopping off the counter. Abel's large hand steadied her as she shook out her clothing and tugged on first her panties and then her jeans. As she was pulling on her sneakers, she noticed the toaster lying on the floor.

She looked at the counter and noted with some amazement that the curtains were half off the rod, a canister of flour was tipped over, and there were chocolate smears all over the counter and even some on the wall behind her. Erin said a small prayer of thanks that the canister of flour hadn't opened.

Abel's arms came around her from behind, hugging her tight. Erin allowed herself a moment to luxuriate in his embrace. She felt his lips on the top of her head, and then he heaved a huge sigh and released her. The wonderful feelings of a moment before had all but disappeared, and she was now filled with trepidation. The sound of a chair being pulled out told her that he'd settled himself back at the kitchen table. Briskly, she picked up the toaster, righted the canister, and fixed the curtains. Wringing out a cloth, she began to scrub the counter.

"Erin," he began. "You know I'm sexually attracted to you." He gave a wry laugh. "That's an understatement."

Tossing the cloth in the sink, she turned and faced him. He held up his hand before she could say anything. "Hear me out."

Nodding, she propped herself against the counter, crossed her arms across her chest, and waited. He leaned forward, resting his elbows on his knees, and clasped his hands in front of him, thinking for a moment before continuing. "The last year has been..." he trailed off. "Well, it's been hellish and draining. I don't have anything to give to a relationship."

Burying his face in his hands, he sighed and rubbed his palms against his cheeks before raising his head. Erin wanted to wrap her arms around him and ease his pain, but she knew that now was not the time. Now what he needed most was for her to listen.

"You're a beautiful, desirable woman, but you just happen to be my best friend's sister. You deserve more than I can offer you." He looked at her and his eyes pierced her heart with the sorrow that was there. "But I want to fuck you anyway."

Unable to keep still any longer, she pushed away from the counter and walked towards him. Wrapping her arms around his head, she pulled him close.

He buried his face in her stomach, breathed deep, and kissed her belly through the fabric of her t-shirt, before tugging her down to sit on his lap. "It's okay," she reassured him.

"I don't know where my life is going from here, but I do know that I want you naked and willing in my bed for as long as I'm here." He rested one hand on her thigh while the other one wrapped around her back. "We're both adults and this is your decision to make. I only hope that when it's over, I don't lose your friendship, or Jackson and Nathan's, for that matter."

"That won't happen," she promised.

"You say that now, but sex always muddies the water." He dropped a kiss on the top of her head. "I just don't care anymore."

Abel shifted his hold on her and lifted her in his arms as he stood, which was no easy feat given that she wasn't a small woman. Shocked, she flung her arms around his neck for support.

"Don't decide now." His eyes were serious as he stared down at her. "Think about it overnight. Think hard. If you decide that hot mind-blowing sex is enough to satisfy you, then come to me tomorrow night and we'll take it from there."

He released her legs until she was standing with her arms still slung around his neck. Bending down, he planted a hard, quick kiss on her lips before gently prying away her arms and heading to the door.

"Don't forget to bring that magazine if you decide to come," he shot back over his shoulder.

Erin had completely forgotten about the magazine, but readily agreed. "I think we covered two of the positions this morning. The shower was a variation of the standing backwards position." She knew that she sounded slightly bewildered as she continued to talk. "It never occurred to me to try it in the shower."

His grin was wicked as he winked at her. "You give me the list and I promise I'll improve upon it."

Erin laughed. If nothing else, he had a healthy ego, but so far he had more than backed up any claims he'd made. Another thought crossed her mind. "The article was right."

"About what?" She strolled towards him and Abel held the door for her as they both stepped outside.

Shading her eyes with her hand against the glare of the setting sun, Erin glanced up at him. "Men do seem to like having sex from behind. Do you think it's an animal instinct?"

"I don't know about animal." Reaching behind her he gripped her behind with both hands. "Personally, I think it's because you have such a great ass."

She glanced nervously towards the barn, but relaxed when she saw no sign of either of her brothers. "That's what all the men say." Erin couldn't believe she was flirting so outrageously with Abel. Something about him allowed her to be more herself. She felt freer and more womanly around him.

"As long as all they do is talk," he growled.

Erin was surprised by the possession behind his remark, but decided that it was because he wanted to make sure she wasn't seeing anyone else as long as he was here. It must be a guy thing, she mused. "Don't worry. You're more than I can handle." He seemed pleased by her remark, so she decided that she had been right in her assessment. It was simple male possessiveness, kind of like marking his territory, no need to read anything more into it.

Abel opened the door to his truck and climbed inside. He closed the door and leaned against the open window while he started the vehicle. "I'll be cooking supper tomorrow night if you decide to come over."

She chewed on her lower lip as she considered the possibilities. It was going to be harder than she anticipated if they were going to keep their relationship a secret. Her mind pondered the logistical problems involved. "I can tell the guys I'm going to my friend Carly's house. She'll cover for me."

Abel frowned. "I don't like skulking around like we're doing something wrong. We're both adults. I'll talk to your brothers."

"No!" The scowl on his face deepened at her reply. "I don't want them to know. I have to live with them when you're gone."

Abel's expression grew even darker at her words. "Trying to get rid of me already?"

"Of course not, but we both know you won't stay here forever." Erin searched for the right words to make him understand. "I just don't want to cause any trouble between you and my brothers."

He nodded slowly, and she could tell, with great reluctance. "If it becomes a problem for you, I will speak to them." His voice was firm, brooking no argument.

"That's fine, but for now just let things be." If Erin had her way her overbearing brothers would never know about her and Abel.

"It's settled then. I'll see you tomorrow night about six." Abel gave her a look of understanding as he put the truck in gear. "If you don't show up, there'll be no hard feelings. And thanks again for the meal. It was the best I've had in years." Passion flared in his eyes once again. "Especially dessert."

With that, he was gone. She stood there watching until his truck had faded from sight. The night seemed empty and lifeless without him. Deep down, she knew that he didn't expect her to take him up on his offer. He'd made no effort to pretty up what he was offering her. Erin knew that he wanted her in his bed, but he also liked her. That was enough for her.

When it was over, it was over. She was woman enough not to pout or complain about that. Her brothers would have to be kept in the dark as they'd never approve or understand. There was no way she'd let Abel lose their friendship. Not when he was giving her what she desired most.

Hearing her brothers' voices again in the distance, Erin hurried back into the house, rushed to the sink, and pulled the plug. Giving the kitchen one last look to make sure everything was in order, she headed for the stairs. The dishes that weren't dry could stay in the drain rack overnight. Erin had more important things to do.

Chapter Seven

Erin relaxed and enjoyed a long, hot bath. It had taken her quite a while to calm down after the sexually charged episode in the kitchen. She still couldn't believe that she'd had sex on the kitchen counter with her brothers only steps away in the barn. But it had been incredible. Just the thought that they might be caught had added to the excitement and set her blood to pumping. Maybe, she was a little more daring than she'd given herself credit for. Abel was the quintessential healthy male animal and gave off a sexual heat that was incredibly exciting and arousing. Her skin tingled as she thought about what might happen tomorrow night.

For the first time in her life, she'd had fun performing all those feminine rituals that she usually found a chore. Shaving her legs was a sensual experience, as she'd wanted them to be silky and supple when they rubbed against Abel's rougher, hairier legs.

Once she'd toweled off, she'd taken her time, and smoothed them with a cocoa butter lotion that she'd bought when she'd gotten dry skin last winter. She wished she had something that smelled seductive, but it would have to do. Just the action of sliding her hands up and down her legs caused her breathing to accelerate as she imagined Abel's hands doing it instead. The difference was, he wouldn't stop at the tops of her thighs, but keep going higher until he reached her moist, feminine core. His fingertips would be rough and exciting as he parted her folds and probed at her opening.

Her breathing deepened and she could feel the muscles of her pussy tightening and relaxing. Her whole body felt languid and her breasts felt heavy. They had sex three times already, but she couldn't wait to have his hard cock inside her again. It had only been one day, but her body was beginning to crave the satisfaction he had introduced her to so thoroughly.

Groaning, she pressed her thighs together to ease the throbbing ache between them. It didn't help. Licking her lips, she thought about touching herself to ease the ache. She'd read an article about that in her magazine as well. They said it was quite normal for a woman to bring herself to orgasm, and not only that, but some men liked to watch their partners do so.

It made her head spin to think about touching herself while Abel watched. If there was even the slightest chance that he might ask her to do so, then she should practice when she was alone.

Gathering her courage, she spread her legs slightly and trailed her fingers up from her knees. Taking a deep breath, she inched them higher. Her hips arched in anticipation and she could feel her nipples pucker. Her body was generating a heat from within, and her skin was warm and moist from her bath.

"You done in there?" Jackson's voice was like an ice-cold bucket of water, immediately dousing her arousal.

Giving a little shriek, she grabbed her towel, and held it in front of her body. She knew that her brother couldn't see her, but just the thought of standing there naked and aroused while she talked to him was more than she could stand. "Almost!" she shouted. Hurrying now, she awkwardly tugged on her robe, dropped the towel, and belted it tight around her waist.

"Get a move on. I want to shower before I go out." He banged on the door twice more for effect.

Scowling, Erin tossed her dirty clothing and towel down the laundry chute and took one last look around to make sure she had everything she needed. Swiping some of the steam off the mirror, she noted her cheeks were flushed, but that couldn't be helped. Jackson would probably just assume it was from her bath. Her hair was bundled up in a towel and she still had to dry the mess before she went to bed, but she'd do that in the privacy of her own room.

He thumped two more times on the door and was going for a third when she tugged it open. "What is your problem tonight?" Blocking the doorway, she glared at her brother.

Reaching down, he flicked her playfully on the nose. "You were in there so long, I thought you might have drowned. Usually you're in and out in five minutes." He sniffed the air. "What's that I'm smelling? Perfume?"

Erin felt the heat climb up her cheeks. This was one of those times she wished she'd been an only child. The only thing to do was brazen it out. "It's cocoa butter, you idiot. The sun has dried out my skin."

"Ah, I was only teasing you." He put his hands on his hips and grinned at her. "Where would you wear perfume?" Laughing as if he'd made a joke, Jackson grabbed her hand and tugged her aside and out of his way. Stepping around her, he walked into the bathroom, and closed the door in her stunned face.

"Where indeed?" she muttered as she scuffed down the hall. Barely resisting the childish urge to slam her door shut, she closed it carefully and crossed over to stand in front of her mirror.

The same image she saw every morning and night was reflected back at her. Tall, big-boned, curvy, and sturdy were all terms that had been applied to her at various times in her life.

Dropping the plain white, terrycloth robe to the floor, she appraised her body with a critical eye. Yes, she was tall and her hips were well-rounded, but her legs, arms, and shoulders were strong and toned. Farm work had kept her in good shape and her waist dipped inward and her stomach was flat. Unfortunately, her chest wasn't as large as the rest of her. She might be a B-cup, but her breasts were round and firm.

For whatever reason, Abel was attracted to her body and she planned to take full advantage of that fact. Looking in the mirror, she smiled. For the first time in her life, she felt desirable and womanly. Her nipples tightened as she examined herself, sending shivers down her spine. It was almost a surprise to her that they were so sensitive. During her one previous attempt at sex, her partner's clumsy attempts to caress her breasts had left her cold and unsatisfied.

Opening a dresser drawer, she pulled out one of her old cotton sleep shirts and dragged it on over her head. Releasing the towel, she allowed her long hair to fall around her face. She wished she could whip it into some fantastic style that would make her look soft and sultry, but that just wasn't going to happen. Picking up her comb, she patiently worked it through the tangles in her thick locks. When that was done, she picked up the hairdryer, set it on low, and gently blew her hair dry.

It was still early by the time she was finished, but there was no way she was going downstairs anymore tonight. Lying back against her pillows, she tried to imagine what tomorrow morning would bring. Smiling, she snuggled down in her bed and tugged a sheet over her body. Images from her magazine flitted across her mind, but instead of the nameless models, she and Abel were featured in all the pictures.

Drifting into a partial dream state, she tried to imagine what it would be like to pleasure herself in front of him. Would he want her to cup her own breasts or rub her thumbs across her nipples? Slowly, her hands inched up her belly until they were covering her aching breasts, and her nightshirt was bunched around her neck and shoulders. For a moment, she simply held both of them, feeling their weight and texture. Shifting her grip slightly, she allowed her thumbs to skim the peaks of her nipples.

She hissed out a breath as desire engulfed her. Her breasts swelled and she could feel her nipples tighten even more. Giving herself over to her own pleasure, she continued to touch herself, feeling an answering throbbing between her legs as they moved restlessly across the sheets.

Taking a deep breath, she pinched her nipples between her thumbs and forefingers, rhythmically squeezing them. She could feel the juices from her pussy sliding down the cleft of her behind. Nipping them a little harder now, she moaned as her pussy clenched tight. She felt empty and needy, her legs moving restlessly on the bed.

Braver now that she was so aroused, she allowed her thighs to fall wide open. Giving her breasts one final squeeze, she slid both hands between her thighs. Remembering the instructions in her magazine, she used one hand to hold open the folds of her sex, and used the other to gently trace her slightly swollen vulva and clitoris. She gasped as she touched just the right spot. Her toes curled, and her legs automatically clamped tight around her hands to hold them in that spot.

Forcing herself, she opened her legs and began to lightly flick her clitoris with her thumb. Pleasure raced through her entire body even as the ache at her core got even worse. Panting hard, she slipped one of her fingers inside herself. It was immediately coated in her arousal, and it was easy to slide it in and out as her thumb continued to move. She shoved a second finger in to join the first one.

A thin cry escaped her as she widened her fingers as she stroked. It wasn't the same as having Abel's cock fucking her, but it still felt good. Looking down at herself, she watched as she drove her fingers deep inside her pussy, wishing it was Abel's long, thick fingers instead. Her nipples were hard, red nubs that were demanding attention. Leaving one hand buried between her thighs, she slipped the other one back to her breasts. Cupping one of them in her hand, she pinched the nipple. Lightly at first, and then harder.

The pleasurable ache grew inside her as she watched her fingers slide in and out of her pussy. Erin was unable to take her eyes away from her own body. She shifted to the other nipple and pinched it as well. Back and forth, she moved her hand, stroking her breasts and tugging at both of the swollen buds.

She was so close. The sound of her breathy gasps filled the room as she reached for completion. Arching her hips up, she drove her fingers as deep as she could as she pressed her thumb hard against her clit.

Once. Twice, she stroked. On the third stroke, she self-combusted. Her entire body tensed and then a powerful orgasm ripped through her body. The slick inner muscles gripping her fingers tight as she held them inside her. Her legs clamped shut around her hand and she rolled to her side and rode out the incredible sensations.

"Oh, my lord. Oh, my lord," she chanted over and over. Every muscle in her body relaxed as she sank deeper into her mattress and sighed. Lying there, completely spent, she enjoyed the pleasant little aftershocks.

Jackson's boots thumped down the hallway. The reality of it quickly intruded, and Erin realized she still had her hands tucked between her legs. Quickly she pulled them both away and tugged her cotton shirt back down around her body. The material rasped against her nipples making her clench her teeth as tiny spasms of arousal shot through her.

She could hear the sounds of her brothers' voices and then the slamming of the truck doors. The engine roared to life, and the sound of the truck faded off into the distance as they drove away.

Rolling over in bed, Erin covered her head with the pillow and took long, deep breaths trying to ease the ache that throbbed between her legs. She was still very aroused, but she now knew that the only thing that would satisfy her would be Abel. The thought of having his hard, hot length inside her created an answering pulse within her.

She thought about just sneaking out of the house and going over to Abel's, but she wasn't ready to take that chance just yet. Jackson might look in on her when he came home, and she wasn't ready to deal with the problems that would arise if he didn't find her in her own bed. But tomorrow night. Well, that was a different story altogether.

"Enough," she muttered as she turned over again, punched her pillow with her fist, and thumped her head back down on it. There was nothing she could do until tomorrow.

Erin didn't know how long she lay awake before her body finally calmed down enough for her to drift off to sleep. She refused to look at the clock, knowing that would only make it worse. Still, she knew it had taken several hours, as she'd heard Jackson and Nathan come home after their evening out playing pool at the local bar. But since they'd come home together, she knew that neither of them had gotten lucky last night. Erin took a perverse pleasure in that thought as she squirmed restlessly in bed.

Sleep had come to her at some point after that and it was almost a shock when the alarm went off the next morning. Her hand had shot out so fast to turn it off, she'd almost knocked the darn clock on the floor. Scowling, she settled the clock back on the nightstand and listened for a minute. When she heard neither of her brothers, she'd relaxed.

Jumping out of bed, she fixed up the covers and hauled on her clothes. She didn't waste time wishing she had sexier clothes to wear. The fact was that she had to go to work this morning and get through lunch without raising any suspicions with Jackson. Erin was just thankful that Nathan ate at the café in town for lunch. He claimed he liked the lunch specials, but Erin personally thought that he liked her friend, Carly. It would kill her to wait, but it was too early to call Carly now. She'd have to catch her at work during the lunch hour.

Hurrying downstairs, she started a pot of coffee while she popped a couple of slices of bread in the toaster. The quicker she got to work, the quicker the day would pass.

* * * * *

"So will you cover for me?" Holding the receiver with her left hand, Erin absently chewed the fingernails on her right hand, as she waited for a reply. Carly had been too busy to talk at lunchtime, so she'd been forced to wait until late in the afternoon to call her back. The two of them had been friends their entire lives, but not once in all that time had she ever asked her friend to lie for her.

"Sure I will."

Erin sighed in relief at her easy agreement. "Thanks." Twisting the cord in her hand, Erin really didn't know what else to say. "This really means a lot to me."

"I know and I expect payment. You'll have to tell me all the juicy details." Carly called out to someone in the distance before she continued. "He must be quite a guy if you're willing to risk your brothers' wrath to date him. I hope he's worth it."

"Yes," she whispered softly. "He's worth it."

"That's good enough for me, but honey, please promise me you'll be careful."

"I will," Erin promised.

"Tell him that if he hurts you, I'll beat the crap out of him up."

Erin laughed, as her friend knew she would. Carly Ames was only five-foot-three and looked like an angel, but behind her angelic exterior was a strong woman with a wicked sense of humor and a penchant for mischief. It made her perfect for overseeing the operation of the family diner, Jenny's, which was named after her mom who'd run it for over thirty years. Now that her parents had retired, Carly managed the whole operation and spent many long hours working as a waitress, as well as handling all the business aspects of running a successful diner.

"Have you seen Nathan lately?" Erin teased. Her friend had had a huge crush on Nathan since she was a teenager, but she'd never approached him to ask him out. Nathan, on the other hand, spent many hours perched on a stool in the diner watching Carly work, staring at her as if he wished she was on the menu. Neither one was willing to make the first move, although it was obvious to everyone who knew them that they were crazy about each other. It was funny, ridiculous, and slightly sad.

"He was here for lunch." She sighed and Erin could picture her friend with that goofy half-smile she got on her face whenever she talked about Nathan. "I know you're worried about Jackson finding out that you're an actual grown woman who has a sex life, but I think Nathan could handle it."

Erin laughed. "You think Nathan could walk on water."

"No, I don't," she protested. "I'm well aware that the man has faults. He just has so many good qualities that the faults don't matter."

Erin sobered at the note of longing in her friend's voice. "Ask him out. You've both wasted years circling and sniffing each other." It hurt Erin to see two people who were obviously so right for each other, hiding their attraction behind polite façades.

"Maybe I will." There was a determination in her voice that Erin had never heard before. "If you can do it, so can I." Erin heard someone calling to Carly. "I've got to go. We're getting busy again. But don't worry, I've got you covered for tonight. I plan on curling up in bed with a good book and a chocolate bar tonight."

"I'll call you tomorrow," Erin promised her.

"You better. See ya."

The phone went dead in Erin's ear. Slowly she placed the receiver back in the cradle, thankful for having such a great friend. Carly had agreed to help her no questions asked. You couldn't ask for more than that.

Now that she'd taken care of her alibi, she started to get excited about this evening. She'd already stashed the magazine in a bag under the seat of her truck so she wouldn't forget it. Butterflies were beating against her stomach, which was ridiculous. They'd already had sex together, for heaven's sake! It wasn't like Abel hadn't seen her naked. No matter how many times she told herself to be logical about the coming evening, she could barely contain her excitement and her nerves. He was cooking her supper. It was almost like having a real date.

The back door slammed and Erin turned. It was time to begin her performance. Jackson was tromping through the kitchen, heading towards the upstairs bathroom where he always took a shower before supper. He was rubbing the back of his neck as he went and rolling his shoulders to work out the kinks.

"There's fried chicken in the oven and potato salad in the refrigerator." Casually, Erin walked to the sink and filled the coffeepot with water. "I'm going over to Carly's for the night."

"This is a busy time for you right now." Leave it to Jackson to state the obvious.

"Yes, but I've got at least another week before we can start picking blueberries. If I don't go now, I may not get a chance for at least a month." Erin kept her back to her brother, filled the coffeemaker and turned on the machine. "I'm going to take a change of clothes and go straight to work in the morning from Carly's. I'll be home in time to make lunch."

"Oh, for god's sake, Jackson, lighten up." Without either of them hearing him, Nathan had come home and now stood leaning against the back door watching them both. "Erin works harder than either of us and deserves to have a night out."

Jackson scowled at them both. "I'm not an ogre, you know." His voice was gruff, but the look in his eyes softened. "Go and have a good time."

"Thanks." Erin knew that Jackson worried about her and often treated her more like a daughter than a sister. Since their mother's death when Erin was little more than a toddler, he'd been more of a parent to her than her own father, who had been, at best, aloof. Whenever she'd hurt herself as a child, it had been Jackson she'd run to for comfort. It was Jackson who'd bandaged her hurts and kissed her boo-boos. Her father couldn't be bothered with her minor problems.

Plus, Jackson had been responsible for the farm since he was a teenager. It was very telling that none of them missed their father since he'd remarried and moved to Florida. They hadn't heard from him in over a year since they'd made the last payment to him to buy the farm. It belonged to the three of them now. Their years of hard work had paid off, but Erin worried about the toll it had taken on her oldest brother. Jackson needed more fun in his life. He'd never really had a chance to be young and carefree as he'd always had the responsibility for his younger siblings and the farm.

Jackson was almost out of the kitchen before he stopped. "I really do appreciate all that you do, Erin." His back was turned and his shoulders were tense.

"I love you too, Jackson," she said softly. He nodded once and continued up the stairs.

Nathan sighed and slung his arm around her shoulder. "I worry about that boy."

"Me too." Erin squeezed his arm before sliding out from under it. "I have to get going, but the chicken is warming in the oven and there's some fresh biscuits in there too."

Nathan patted her on the behind. "Get going. I'll make sure Jackson gets fed."

Giving him a grateful smile, she grabbed her knapsack with her change of clothes and hurried out the back door. All of a sudden she was very hungry, and it wasn't just for food.

Chapter Eight

Abel glanced at his watch for the fifth time in the last five minutes. It was almost six and he expected Erin any minute. It was the first time in years that he found himself looking forward to something so much, and although the feeling was strange, he liked it.

Being home, and especially being around Erin, reminded him of the young man he'd once been. The years of investigating and writing about the most gruesome parts of human nature had changed him. He'd lost faith in the goodness in humanity and seen only the pain and the horror. Erin was changing all of that.

She was exactly what she seemed to be—a hardworking, loyal, kind, compassionate, sexy woman. Just being around her was better than any medicine could be for curing the pain in his heart and the sorrow in his soul. In the couple of days he'd been home, he felt better than he had any time in the last year.

It was only when that thought went through his mind that he realized what he'd thought. Home. No matter where else in the country he'd roamed, he always considered the farm to be home. He was already reconsidering his career, so perhaps it was time to think about where he wanted to live. And more especially, who he wanted to be with.

Pacing back and forth on the deck did him no good, so he threw himself onto the oversized deck chair, spread his legs in front of him, and rested his hands on his stomach. There was nothing left to do but wait. The tossed salad was chilling in the fridge and the potatoes were baking on a low heat in the oven. He had two steaks marinating on the counter just waiting to be thrown onto the barbecue.

Glancing over to the side, he checked the pile of charcoal that he'd piled in the center of the barbecue. He'd light it as soon as Erin arrived and while they were waiting for the coals to turn white, he'd offer her a glass of the nice crisp white wine he'd bought especially for tonight. If he decided to move back home, he'd have to invest in a gas barbecue, but for now the old charcoal one would serve the purpose.

He tapped one of his fingers on his stomach before sighing and closing his eyes. The heat of the summer sun felt good on his skin, and he finally felt some of the tension leach from his body. The longer he sat there, the more the sounds of a late summer afternoon seeped into his consciousness. Birds sang in the distance, a slight breeze rustled the leaves in the trees, and the scent of freshly cut hay wafted on air.

Patience was a virtue he usually had in spades, but tonight, it had all but deserted him. He told himself that it was only because he hadn't cooked a meal for a woman in over eight months, but deep down he knew it was because he couldn't wait to see Erin.

Abel patted his jeans pocket to make sure the little present he'd bought for her was still there. He'd driven several hours today to find a store that carried what he'd wanted, but it had been well worth the effort. Especially if she liked what he'd purchased. His cock shifted and began to swell at the mere thought.

The sound of a vehicle approaching had him out of his chair in a moment, striding across the deck, and down over the porch stairs. He shaded his eyes, smiling when he recognized Erin's truck. By the time she pulled to a complete stop, he was already standing by her door and opening it.

"Hi." She smiled shyly at him as she slid her long, jeans-clad legs out of her truck.

He didn't give her a chance to move away from him, but hauled her up against his chest and enfolded her in his arms. She responded immediately by scooting as close to him as she could, twining her strong, supple arms around his neck. He lowered his head slowly until their mouths touched. Her lips were firm and soft against his. He felt her hands wrap around his skull, tugging him closer.

Giving into her unspoken request, he deepened the kiss. His tongue teased the seam of her lips until they parted, and then he slowly forged his way inside. Her mouth was warm and her tongue met his, stroking it sensually. Cupping her chin with his hand, he angled her head as he deepened the kiss. She melted against him, silently offering herself to him. Reluctantly, he dragged himself from her sweet lips.

"I've been wanting to do that all day." His voice was husky with need as he caressed the side of her neck for a moment before allowing his hand to drop back to his side.

A slight tinge of a blush covered her face as he continued to stare at her. "Me too," she responded almost shyly before reaching behind her and pulling out a battered, canvas knapsack. Abel took it from her and waited while she rummaged under the front seat and pulled out a plastic bag. He started to take that from her too, but she clasped it to her chest.

Wondering what she would be hiding from him, he stared at the outline of the item in the bag. It was about the size of a magazine. That's when it hit him. Of course, this was the famous magazine that she'd spoke of yesterday morning. He couldn't stop the wicked grin that spread across his face. "You're going to have to show it to me at some point if I'm going to know what you want me to do."

"Later," she mumbled, not quite meeting his gaze.

Abel stopped teasing her immediately. Cupping her chin with his hand, he tilted her head until her large blue eyes were fixed on him. "Whenever you're ready, and whatever you want. Those are the only rules." He kissed her lightly on the lips before moving her away from the truck, and closing the door. "But supper first."

She nodded and allowed him to tuck her under his shoulder and lead her up onto the back porch. "I'll put your stuff inside," he told her. "Do you want a glass of wine while I'm in there?"

"Sure." She sent him a grateful smile and laid the bag with the magazine on top of the patio table.

Standing in front of him, with her hands clasped in front of her and a wisp of hair in her eyes, she looked so young and innocent. She was wearing faded blue jeans, a soft t-shirt of pale green, and a pair of white sneakers. Ordinary clothing, but somehow on her, they were more seductive than the most skimpy lingerie. The jeans hugged every curve of her ass and her strong thighs, while the soft shirt cupped her breasts and outlined their shape to perfection. Abel felt his mouth begin to water and his cock begin to lengthen and thicken.

"I'll be right back." He turned and went into the house before she noticed the large bulge pushing against the zipper of his jeans. The last thing he wanted to do was rush her straight into bed. He'd promised her supper so he'd feed her first. Even if it killed him. And it just might.

Erin gulped in a huge lungful of air the second that Abel was out of sight. Her head was still spinning from his greeting. She fanned her hand in front of her face, hoping to ease the flush she could feel on her cheeks. The man was lethal. His kiss alone was enough to drive all her senses into overdrive. Easing herself down into one of the chairs scattered around the patio table, she tried to calm her racing heart.

She was embarrassed by the fact that her nipples were hard nubs against the cups of her bra and were visible through the fabric of her shirt. Then there was the wetness in her panties. Erin squirmed in her seat trying to get more comfortable, but only succeeded in making it worse. The friction of her clitoris against the crotch of her panties and jeans almost made her moan. She felt like flinging her head back and screaming, she wanted him so badly. It was all she'd thought about since he'd left her kitchen last night.

More than anything, she would have loved it if he'd scooped her up in his arms and carted her straight to bed. She would have been much happier eating later, after they'd satisfied their other appetites. Dropping her forehead to rest on the top of the table, she counted to twenty.

She could hear Abel rummaging around in the kitchen, so she knew she didn't have much time to get herself under control. He'd gone to the trouble of preparing her supper. No man, other than her brothers, had ever cooked for her, and they had only done it the few times she was too sick to do it herself. This was special and she was determined to enjoy every moment of it and not ruin the evening he had planned.

Raising her head, she sat back in her chair, and crossed her legs. She hoped she appeared cool and relaxed. It was the look she was going for. The screened door opened behind her and Abel placed one glass on the table and handed her the other.

"I didn't know if you drank, but I figured I couldn't go wrong with white wine." He sauntered towards the barbecue on the corner of the back deck.

Erin watched his butt as he walked. The jeans he was wearing fit him like a second skin, leaving little to the imagination. And since she'd already seen all of him, her mind filled in all the details. The black tank top he was wearing stretched tight across his chest, outlining all the muscles in his torso and back. His wide shoulders and thick arms were bare, and the muscles rippled as he started the barbecue.

Catching herself before she sighed out loud, she glanced around the deck to distract herself from Abel's scrumptious body. The covered back porch actually ran the entire length of the house and Abel's parents had added a twelve-by-twelve foot patio area off one end. The patio table, where she was seated, was tucked closer to the house, so that it was partially shaded by the porch roof. The barbecue was located in the far corner of the patio, and a large metal deck chair that was covered with a soft cushion was situated right next to it. Erin picked up her wineglass and moseyed over, leaving the partial shade of the house behind her.

Abel glanced her way, but said nothing as she settled herself into the chair. There was plenty of room for two. It crossed her mind that maybe she could entice him to share it with her while they waited for the coals to burn down. She sipped her wine to ease her parched mouth. The crisp fruity flavor was soothing on her dry lips. Licking them, she peeked over at Abel, unable to help herself.

His eyes were a blaze of green fire as he watched her. Erin could feel the heat rising inside her. Feeling wanton and powerful, she slid her tongue across her lower lip again, slowly and deliberately. Abel's face tightened and his entire body seemed to clench. She could see the outline of his cock, straining against the zipper of his jeans.

"You're playing with fire," he warned her. He never moved a muscle, but his gaze still devoured her.

"Maybe I want to," she taunted, taking another sip of the wine before placing the glass on the deck next to the chair.

He moved suddenly, all fluid motion, as he plucked her out of the chair and into his arms. She could barely breathe as his mouth slammed down on top of hers. It seemed as if he wanted to eat her alive. For a moment, she wondered if she'd bitten off more than she could handle, but her own arousal continued to grow, and suddenly what was almost too much a moment ago was no longer enough. She needed more. Wanted more.

A picture flashed in her mind. It wasn't one of the positions in the article, but it was something else she'd read about that she was dying to try. It was hard to think as Abel had left her mouth and was licking a heated path down her throat. She tilted her head to the side, wanting to give him whatever he wanted. However, the erotic picture continued to fill her mind, and she knew she wanted to do it. Here. Now. Tonight. She had no guarantee how long their affair would last and she didn't want to lose her chance.

N.J. Walters

"Abel." Her voice was low and hoarse at first. Abel's lips were feasting on her neck making it hard for her to think, let alone speak. Desperately, she tried again. "Abel." This time it was more forceful and got his attention. He raised his head slowly and shuddered.

Gripping her upper arms tight, he steadied them both. "Sorry. That got out of hand."

She couldn't bear to have him apologize for something so wonderful. "I didn't mind."

"Then why did you stop me?" His voice wasn't sharp at all, but merely questioning.

"I want to do something."

A slow smile spread across his face as he stepped back and spread his arms wide. "I'm all yours, baby."

Now that it was time to state what she wanted from him, it was a little more difficult than she'd anticipated. She cleared her throat. "I want to try something I read about."

"In the magazine?" He looked intrigued and his eyes were still hot as they continued to skim her body. She could tell he was imagining all kinds of things, and just the thought of what he might want to do to her made her shiver.

"Yes, but a different article." Grabbing hold of her courage, she nodded at the chair. "You have to sit down for this to work."

He dropped into the chair and waited.

"Umm. You have to take off your shirt." Before she could blink, he'd crossed his arms over his back, grabbed the fabric of the black tank shirt, and pulled it over his head. Tossing it onto the deck beside him, he waited.

He looked absolutely gorgeous sitting there. His body was tanned and hard as stone. He resembled a pagan god come to life. Even the tufts of hair under his armpits looked sexy. Abel reached out a hand to her, but she backed away.

"Don't be afraid," he coaxed. "We'll do whatever you want."

"Just sit there and let me do everything. Okay?" Abel lowered his hand and nodded.

She could feel herself relax the moment he agreed to let her do what she wanted. Erin trusted him not to break his word to her. This was her show and she was going to run it exactly the way she wanted. She only hoped she could come up with enough nerve to strip in front of him. Tugging her shirt from the waistband of her jeans, she jerked it over her head and let it drop beside her. Abel's breathing caught and his fists clenched at his sides. That was all the encouragement she needed. She reached for the opening of her bra, skimming her hands over her breasts as she did so.

Abel couldn't believe what he was seeing. Erin had stripped off her top and her hands were now covering her breasts. His cock throbbed and his hands clenched at the thought of tearing the rest of her clothes from her body. He wanted to stroke her breasts and suck on her nipples until they became as red as ripe berries.

Her fingers moved to the front clasp between her breasts and hesitated for a moment. Mentally, he ordered her to open it. For one second she looked uncertain and he almost howled in frustration.

He never took his eyes off her hands, willing her to move them, and a moment later, she popped open the clasp. The cotton cups pulled away from her breasts, leaving them bare. She shimmied her shoulders slightly, making the straps slip down her arms. The bra fell behind her. Her breathing was rapid, causing her breasts to jiggle slightly. Closing his eyes against the potent sight of her standing naked from the waist up, he searched for control, knowing he'd need it to get through whatever she had planned.

The sound of a zipper had his eyes wide open before she finished pulling it down. Licking his lips in anticipation, he waited as she toed off her sneakers and then peeled the tight jeans down over her hips and thighs, letting them drop to her ankles. She bent over and stepped out of her jeans, pulling off her socks as she did so. Her breasts swayed seductively as she leaned forward, and before he could stop himself, his hand reached out to fondle one of them.

She jerked back, almost stumbling before a slow, seductive smile crossed her face. It was a soft smile, full of promise. He could see the reddish curls of her pubic hair through the light fabric of her cotton white bikini panties. His fingers itched to slide through them, through her slick folds, and straight into her waiting warmth. As he watched, her nipples tightened and she quivered slightly before hooking her fingers into the waistband of her panties and skimming them quickly down her legs.

As she kicked them away, she spread her legs slightly and stood there, bathed in the hot evening sun, allowing him to look his fill. The sunlight made the red strands of her hair glitter, and the blue of her eyes looked even lighter against her tanned face. Her full lips were parted as her tongue darted out to moisten them.

He was in total agony, but he knew that this moment was etched indelibly on his mind forever. There would never be another second of time more perfect than this one. Swallowing hard against the unexpected emotion welling up inside him, he held his hand out to her once more and waited.

Erin walked slowly towards him, but avoided his hand and dropped gracefully to her knees in front of him. He almost swallowed his tongue when she reached for the zipper of his jeans and slowly eased it down over his engorged cock. It sprang free immediately, as he wasn't wearing any underwear.

"Oh, commando. I've heard about this." She was staring at his cock as if it was the greatest thing she'd ever beheld in her life. Abel was supremely glad that he'd only hauled on his jeans after he showered.

Using one of her fingers, she traced his length from the base to the tip, swirling it around the head and laughing delightedly when a drop of pearly liquid appeared at the top. He desperately wanted her to grip him tight and pump hard, but even more than that, he wanted her to indulge herself. It was just about the hardest thing he'd ever done, but he sat there and waited for her to make the next move.

Tentatively, she wrapped a hand around his cock near the base and slowly began to slide her hand up and down. Her grip was light and her movements slow. Abel pushed himself against her hand. "Harder," he encouraged her.

Erin's fingers tightened around him, and she began to pump her hand once again. This time her rhythm was slightly faster and harder. She glanced up at him, and he realized that she was looking for some kind of response or direction from him.

"That's feels real good, honey," he praised her. "But let me take off my jeans. It'll be better that way." He lifted his hips as he spoke and Erin tugged the jeans down over his thighs. Yanking off his sneakers and socks, she flung them aside, and then hauled his jeans down his calves and over his feet. Now both of them were naked.

Reaching down, Abel dug into his jeans pocket and pulled out a little bundle of tissue paper. "I bought this for you today." He handed it to her and watched with anticipation as she unwrapped it.

Peeling back the white paper, she stared at the contents and looked back at him. He mentally sighed as she bit her lip, her eyes hesitant. "They look really pretty, but what are they?"

Abel reached out and plucked on of the items off the tissue. "It's a nipple clip." His finger tapped the little beads at the end, making them swing slightly. "It slips on over your nipple and we can tighten it until it's comfortable for you." Reaching out, he stroked one of her tight nipples. "These beauties stay nice and hard giving you pleasure."

She glanced from the clip in his hand to the one in her hand. "Does it hurt?"

"No, honey. If it hurts, then it's too tight and we adjust it." Cupping her chin in his hand, he turned it until she was facing him. "It's all about pleasure."

"You'd enjoy it, wouldn't you?" Her innocent question made his cock throb even harder.

"Oh, yeah." He said nothing else, not wanting to pressure her, but damn he wanted to see those cute little clips hanging from her nipples.

Tentatively, she held her hand out to him. He swallowed his disappointment and took it from her, ready to wrap them up and put them away.

"Will you put them on for me?" Her soft plea shot through him like a bullet.

Would he? Hell, yes. Instead of grabbing her like he wanted, he took his time and drew her closer to him. Digging into his jeans pocket again, he drew out a small tube, opened it and squeezed some onto his fingers. Using his fingertips, he lightly coated her nipples with the lubrication. Erin said nothing, but leaned closer.

"That will help them slide on so they don't hurt." Picking up the first one, he carefully pinched the first nipple. It was already swollen, but he took his time, pleasuring her with his fingers before sliding the nipple clip over it. The clip captured the hard nub securely, and then Abel slowly adjusted the fit.

"How does that feel?"

Erin watched the beads dangle from her breast as she took a deep breath. She moved experimentally and moaned as the beads swung from side to side. "That feels amazing." Her breathy reply had him reaching for the second clip.

When the second clip was in place, he sat back and looked at Erin. Kneeling in front of him with her legs slightly spread and the nipple clips dangling from her breasts, she took his breath away. "Put your hands behind your neck." Erin complied and her breasts were thrust forward.

Using his foot, he edged her legs wider. Erin spread them wide, panting for breath as she watched his every move. "Now you look like the perfect slave girl ready to pleasure her master."

His fingers traced the tight nubs before flicking the beads. He watched, enthralled as they swung back and forth. Leaning down, he placed a soft, light kiss on her lips. "Thank you for wearing them."

Her tongue came out to lick at his lips. "You're welcome."

Abel sat back in the chair, spread his knees slightly, and relaxed. Erin scooted between his thighs and gave him a wicked smile up at him. "And do you want your slave girl to pleasure you now?" A bead of pearly white liquid seeped from the slit at the top of his cock at her sultry question.

Abel nodded and Erin took his balls in one hand while the other wrapped around his engorged cock once more. Her concentration was absolute as she squeezed and caressed his swollen testicles. Her hand wrapped around his cock, squeezing it tight before stroking up and down.

Abel couldn't take his eyes off her. She seemed to have forgotten she was totally nude, but he certainly hadn't. Her face, arms, shoulders, and legs were tanned a golden brown, while the rest of her body was pale. The contrast accentuated her milky white breasts and hips. Wisps had escaped from her braid, and framed her compelling face. Her eyes darkened as her arousal grew, and her inner thighs were damp. She looked perfectly natural, more like a wild rose than a cultivated one. Not showy, but filled with a beauty all her own that would never fade.

The only thing she wore was the nipple ornaments he'd bought for her. A feeling of possession shot through him as he cupped her cheek in the palm of his hand, tracing his thumb across her lips. Her hands stilled. "You are so beautiful."

Erin shook her head and laughed nervously. "You don't have to say things like that."

"I know I don't." He kept his voice soft and even. "You have no idea how I see you. Right here, right now, you're the most beautiful woman I've ever seen."

Her eyes shone as she bent her head towards him, but he stopped her before her mouth reached him. "You don't have to do that." Even as he spoke, he swore at himself for being so damned stupid. Her mouth was so close to his dick he could feel her warm breath. His balls were tight with anticipation. He'd never wanted a woman to suck his cock this badly before, but it had to be her choice.

"I want to," she murmured as her tongue swirled around the tip of his arousal. Her tongue snaked around the bulbous head with great enthusiasm.

"God, yes," Abel groaned. His hand gripped the back of her head, holding her to him. She'd said yes, so now he wanted it all.

Erin lapped and licked his cock with abandon, and Abel used his hand to gently encourage her to take him deeper into her mouth. She gripped the bottom of his shaft with one hand even as her mouth descended upon him.

Abel's whole body tensed as her moist lips slipped over the head of his cock, taking his hard length into the waiting warmth of her mouth. She took him as deep as she could before slowly pulling back all the way to the tip. Twirling her tongue around the top, she then lowered her mouth on him again. The hand at the base of his cock moved in tandem with her sweet mouth.

Although, he'd had many women over the course of his adult life, Abel couldn't remember a woman ever pleasuring him quite so thoroughly. There wasn't any part of his cock that Erin didn't lick or suck. The sun glinted off her red hair and the tiny nipple beads, making her glow as she knelt before him, servicing him.

Abel flexed his hips and murmured encouragement to her. His testicles tightened and he knew if he didn't stop her, he'd come in her mouth. That was something he desperately wanted to do, but not this time. This time, he wanted his cock deep inside her hot pussy when he came.

He pulled back the next time her lips reached the tip and his cock popped out of her mouth. She looked surprised, but he didn't have time to explain. The need to have his cock buried to the hilt, being squeezed by her wet pussy was too great.

Gripping her waist, he urged her to her feet and then tugged her onto his lap. Shoving her knees apart so she was wide open to him, he dipped his fingers deep inside her. They were immediately coated with the slick evidence of her arousal. Muttering a prayer of thanks, he gripped her hips, and rammed his cock into her, seating himself right to the hilt. Erin moaned and gripped the back of the patio chair for support before dropping her head to rest on his chest.

Resting her forehead against his chest, Erin could feel his heart pounding, and it matched the frantic beat of her own. She breathed deep, inhaling his masculine scent—a mixture of soap, sunshine and something that was uniquely, Abel. Rubbing her nose against the sprinkling of hair on his chest, she wallowed in his addictive scent.

His erotic flavor was still on her lips and in her mouth. She hadn't been sure she would enjoy oral sex, but the article had said that it usually aroused both partners, and although some people didn't enjoy the act, most did. Enjoy was too tame a word. It was incredible.

Erin loved the taste of him and was thrilled by the fact that he seemed genuinely aroused at having her mouth on his cock. It was definitely something she wanted to try again. She loved the way that his dick was soft and hard at the same time, and how his unique scent had filled her nostrils. His enjoyment was obvious and had fed her own arousal. She felt her own juices on her thighs, the folds of her sex were hot and wet, her breasts ached, and her inner muscles contracted sporadically.

A sense of wonder and accomplishment filled her. She'd been uncertain that she'd even be any good at it, but according to Abel's reaction she was very good. He'd shocked her by pulling away from her so suddenly, causing her to wonder if she'd done something wrong. But before that thought had a chance to be completed, he'd dispelled it by pulling her into his lap and driving himself into her.

His present had both surprised and pleased her. She'd heard of nipple clips, but had never seen a pair before. In her wildest dreams, she'd never imagined wearing them. She could feel them snug around her nipples, and every time the beads moved, the pleasure got even better. Just wearing them made her feel different — sexy, wild, adventurous.

Now, he filled her so deeply, it bordered on discomfort. It didn't hurt exactly, but she squirmed around, trying to get more comfortable, pushing her knees deeper into the soft chair cushion. Abel slid forward in the chair, driving his cock even further inside her. Her bare bottom rested on his thighs and her knees gripped his sides for support.

Erin raised her head and met his heated stare. He was totally aroused, primed and ready, but he waited for her to take the lead. Her heart swelled with emotion as she leaned forward and kissed him. Their lips met, and their tongues dueled as she swept her hands over his back, testing and feeling the sheer strength of him.

His hands urged her closer to him as they drifted down over the line of her spine before coming to rest on her behind. He cupped each cheek with a hand and squeezed. "I love your ass," he muttered as he trailed hot kisses across her cheek and down her neck.

She felt him nip at the base of her neck where it sloped into her shoulder before he soothed the small sting with his tongue. He continued his way down the curve of her shoulder, peppering it with stinging little love bites. Erin moaned as she felt his cock throbbing deep inside her body. Pressing her breasts against his chest, she rubbed her tight nipples over the hard planes of his chest.

"Lean back," he ordered. Erin positioned her hands behind her and rested them on his thighs before easing back slightly. Carefully, Abel removed both nipple clips, ignoring her wordless protest. "I don't want them to get sore."

He dropped them onto the deck and immediately began to nuzzle her breasts. The stubble on his chin rasped their sensitive undersides, and the sensation was delicious. Taking his time, he licked his way around one breast before doing the same to the other. His tongue was slightly rough and wet, making her shiver with desire. Her nipples were drawn tight and ached to be touched by him. She arched her back, encouraging him, but still he took his time. There wasn't an inch of flesh that he didn't taste before he finally lapped at her nipples. First one, then the other received his attention. A loud moaning filled her ears and it shocked her to realize that the sounds were coming from her. She was filled with such need. Such longing.

"Please," she gasped, needing more than he was giving her.

He responded by drawing one tight nub into his mouth and rolling it carefully between his teeth while flicking the hard tip with his tongue. A low keening sound escaped her throat, and she felt her inner muscles clenching around his cock as she came and came, the ripples of her orgasm washing through her entire body.

She heard him swear and his hands gripped her ass even tighter, his fingers digging into her flesh. Every muscle in his body was rigid when she finally collapsed against him.

He sat back in the chair, his breathing ragged as his hands swept up around her shoulders, soothing her. "That was incredible." His voice was the sexiest thing she'd ever heard.

With great effort, she finally managed to raise her head. "That's my line," she admonished him.

He shook his head and grinned at her. "It was my pleasure."

Snuggling closer to him, she could feel him still very hard and heavy inside her. A bead of sweat rolled down her neck as she languidly began to circle her hips. The heat and their lovemaking had drained her energy, but amazingly enough, she could feel herself becoming aroused once again. This man had the most amazing effect on her!

"Lord," he groaned. "You feel so damn good." He rested his hands on her waist, supporting her as she rolled her hips.

"You feel hot and hard." Her voice was sultry as she enticed him. "And ready."

"I want you to turn your back to me and mount me." His fingers slid between her legs and began to lightly stroke her swollen clit. Her hips began to gyrate in rhythm to his fingers. "You'd still be in control, but I'd fill you even fuller and deeper."

Both his words and his actions were driving her past being able to think. Every nerve ending in her body was alive and begging her to do whatever he wanted. "Show me." Her words galvanized him into action.

She caught her breath and hissed slowly as he eased her off his cock. Her body made a sucking sound as he withdrew, as if reluctant to let him go. The smell of sex wafted on the hot evening breeze, and the separation was almost more than she could bear.

He lifted her off of his lap, and helped her stand. The deck was hot on the soles of her feet, and she shifted unsteadily. Guiding her with his hands, Abel positioned her until she was kneeling on the chair cushion once again, only this time she was facing away from him.

Once he had her arranged to his liking, he slowly squeezed his cock back inside her body. It was harder this time, because the sensitive flesh of her vagina was swollen from her orgasm. It was a tight fit, but it felt so good.

"More," she demanded. "I want more of you." She pushed her bottom down hard against him, driving his engorged cock deep inside her. She could feel him growing even larger within her.

His hands reached around her torso and grasped both of her breasts, rolling her nipples with his fingers. Erin responded by reaching between her own legs until she was touching his testicles. She massaged them gently, stroking around them and between them.

"Move, Erin." His voice was hoarse with need, so she removed her hand, and gripped his thighs. Using them for leverage, she began to move up and down, carefully at first until she found the right stroke.

The pleasure was unbelievable as his thrusting penis seemed to stimulate her even more from this angle. As if that wasn't enough, he dropped one of his hands from her breasts and began once again to stroke her engorged clitoris.

Erin tried to hang on. Wanted desperately to prolong the enjoyment, but it was beyond her control. Her body convulsed on a downward stroke, and her inner muscles contracted, grasping him tight.

He drove heavily into her for three more strokes. His cry of release echoed her own as he pulled her down hard on his cock, shuddering as he came. Erin moaned as she felt him empty himself deep inside her, filling her completely. Her nails dug into his legs for support as she arched back against him.

When she was finally spent, Erin felt all her muscles relax. Abel's fingers tightened on her breasts as his forehead came to rest on her back. Exhausted, Erin slumped forward. Only Abel's strong arms kept her from toppling over.

Chapter Nine

As she sat there and drifted into a stupor, Erin became uncomfortably aware of the hot evening sun blistering her naked flesh. The heat was beating down upon them both as they sat entwined in the chair, but she was shading most of Abel's body with her own.

"I have to move." She said it out loud, hoping it would inspire her to action. "I really have to move," she repeated groggily. "My skin is burning."

"Damn it." Abel gingerly eased his cock out of her body and helped her to her feet. He looked closely at her prickly flesh. "I think you're going to have a slight sunburn."

Standing, he scooped her up into his arms and carried her towards the back door. "I'm sorry, honey. It never occurred to me that we were exposing virgin flesh to the sun."

His teasing made her laugh even though her backside was beginning to sting slightly. "You're just lucky that I sheltered you from the worst of it."

Abel tugged on the door handle and then used his shoulder to prop open the door as he carried her into the house. The cool interior was a welcome relief. "Where are you taking me?" She didn't care where they were going, but she was mildly curious.

Abel shifted her higher in his embrace, and she gave a little shriek as she threw her arms around his neck, gripping him tight. He took her straight through the kitchen and then started climbing up the stairs.

When he reached the top, he turned and padded down the hallway towards the bathroom. "I'm going to put you in a cool tub of water while I go and start the barbecue again. The coals have probably burned themselves into dust."

Cautiously, he deposited her on the side of the tub while he bent over and started the water running. Once it was partially filled and adjusted to his liking, he scooped her up and placed her in the tub.

Erin gasped for breath as the cool water touched her slightly baked skin. It stung slightly, but after a moment, the pain subsided and it actually began to soothe the abused areas of her body. A soft washcloth plopped into the tub next to her, and she grabbed it and laid it gently across her breasts. Sighing in relief, she eased back in the tub and rested her head on the cold enamel rim.

Turning her head slightly, she watched Abel as he laid out a large fresh bath towel and a bottle of aloe gel. He turned off the water and leaned over her, kissing her forehead. "You just relax and let me take care of everything. I'll be back with a glass of water for you as soon as I get the barbecue going again." He cupped her warm cheek with the palm of his hand. "I didn't take care of you properly. That won't happen again."

"I'm fine." Erin was surprised that Abel was angry with himself. She could see it in the set of his shoulders and the thin lines bracketing the lines of his mouth. "The sun was going down, so it wasn't that strong. It'll only be a slight burn and probably gone by the morning."

He shook his head in denial. "You rest, and I'll come and help you out before I put the steaks on the grill. I want to make sure you're coated in that gel so that maybe you won't sting quite so badly." Abel was up and gone before she could respond.

Allowing herself to relax, she lolled in the tub, feeling slightly better as the cool water revived her. It was strange to her just how quickly she'd become accustomed to being naked around Abel. She'd been hot and sticky all over when he'd carried her upstairs, and it hadn't bothered her in the least. And surprisingly enough, it didn't seem to bother him either.

It felt amazingly good to be so at ease with another person. Around Abel, she felt free to be herself. He not only accepted her, but he seemed to be honestly interested in her. The warmth inside her had nothing to do with sunburn and everything to do with the man downstairs.

Erin bit her lip and fought down the emotions that rose to the surface. She'd done exactly what she'd sworn to herself that she wouldn't do. She had gone and fallen head over heels in love with the man. It felt so right, but she knew that it was one-sided. Abel would be leaving at some point. He always did. His work would lead him to another town or city, and he would leave here without a backwards glance. But this time when he left, it would hurt her even more.

She wet the cloth and washed her face, scrubbing her eyes to keep the tears at bay. This was her problem. She was a mature woman and this was supposed to be an adult relationship. In truth, it was a summer fling. Abel hadn't promised her anything, and she had readily accepted his terms.

The last thing she wanted was for him to find out about her stupid feelings and regret their time together. He would end up feeling responsible and it would only make him feel bad. Erin was afraid if he sensed her deep feelings for him, his own personal code of honor might force him to put an end to their relationship to protect her from further hurt.

She loved Abel and wanted to spend as much time with him as she could get. It had taken her a long time to find a man to give her heart to, and she knew that she might never find another. A fierce need to protect him rose up in her. No, she had only one choice. Abel never had to know. They would enjoy a healthy sexual relationship that was based on mutual liking and respect, and she would happily set him free when it was time for him to go. Even if it killed her.

Hearing his feet on the stairs, she took a deep breath and rinsed her face once more. By the time Abel came through the door with a tall cool glass of water in his hand, she already had a smile on her face.

* * * * *

Erin sat back in her chair and rested her hands on her stomach, thankful that they'd cleared away the supper dishes before indulging in their dessert and coffee. "I can't eat another bite."

"Are you sure?" Abel pushed the cheesecake closer to her, grinning.

"You are totally evil to tempt me with more after the supper I've already packed away." The two of them were seated across from each other, at the patio table, with the remnants of their late supper scattered around them. She'd been impressed by the fact that not only had he cooked her a mouthwatering steak, baked potato and salad, but he'd also remembered dessert. And not any old dessert, but a rich, creamy cheesecake that had a swirl of chocolate through it and was topped with a thin layer of dark chocolate.

She eyed the cheesecake and wondered if she could squeeze in another tiny piece. Abel laughed and pulled the plate back closer to himself.

"You'll hate yourself if you do."

"I know, but I can at least think about it." Erin sighed wistfully, and contented herself with sipping her coffee instead.

"Come over tomorrow and you can have another piece." Abel was sprawled in a patio chair, the picture of a man totally at ease with himself and his surroundings. He hadn't bothered to get fully dressed after they'd made love, but had just pulled on his jeans. He'd opened the button on his jeans shortly after he'd started eating his dessert. His torso looked almost bronze in the setting sun, his muscles glistening beneath a light layer of sweat. Even though the sun was almost gone down for the day, the air was still hot.

"I'd really like to…" she trailed off, uncertain how to explain it to him.

"But you're worried about your brothers." The look on his face said that he was less than pleased, but he didn't say anything else about it. Instead, his expression turned thoughtful at first and then mischievous. "How about a picnic at three o'clock tomorrow afternoon at the old swimming hole?"

Abel's family was lucky enough to have a small pond near the far end of their property. As kids, they'd all snuck away from chores whenever they could and headed straight for the pond. Erin hadn't been there in years, but she'd spent many happy hours there with her brothers and Abel. "I'd love to. I don't know if I can be there exactly at three, but I'll be there."

"Good enough," he said.

They sat there in silence for a while, and it was a comfortable silence. The slight breeze felt good on her skin and she closed her eyes enjoying the sensation. Hitching the tails on the shirt she was wearing out of her way, Erin extended her long legs in front of her, trying to get more comfortable.

"Are you feeling okay?" The concern in his voice washed over her, making her feel very cared for.

He had probably asked her the same question a half dozen times since he'd helped her out of the bathtub. She opened her eyes and she gave him the same reply she'd been giving him all evening. "I'm fine."

Abel had returned to the bathroom just as she'd been about to climb out of the tub. He'd helped her out, carefully drying her slightly burnt skin for her, before applying a liberal amount of the aloe gel to her entire body. There had been no teasing comments as he'd stroked her breasts, belly and behind. He'd been totally absorbed in what he was doing and occasionally scowled when he reached a particularly red patch.

When he was finished, he'd held open one of his soft, white cotton shirts while she'd slipped her arms into the sleeves. Then he'd eased it over her shoulders and buttoned the shirt until it just covered her breasts. The long tail of the shirt hung down to cover the tops of her thighs much like a short dress. He'd escorted her back down to the deck seated her at the table, and proceeded to cook and serve her supper.

She couldn't seem to convince him that the burn wasn't serious and that she'd probably be fine in the morning. At least she hoped she would. Her breasts still stung slightly and it would be impossible to wear a bra if it didn't subside overnight. But there had been no harm done, and it had been well worth it, in her opinion.

Abel spoke again, drawing her attention away from her meanderings. "I started going through the boxes of Mom and Dad's stuff today."

Erin sat up straight and gave him her total attention. This was a big deal for Abel. After his parents' sudden death, he'd packed up all their papers and personal belongings and stashed them in several closets in the house before donating their clothing to charity. It had been too much for him to deal with as a young man, and it was only now that he was an adult, that he'd been able to even consider facing the painful task.

"I can help if you want." Her offer came straight from her heart, but she didn't want him to feel obligated to accept. "But I understand if it's something you want to do on your own," she hastily added.

"Thanks. I'll keep that in mind if I start to get bogged down." He moved his feet closer to hers and started to play with her toes. "So far I've been through a couple of boxes of old papers and shredded just about all of them." He laughed, but the sound held a touch of bitterness. "It's been so damned long that none of it matters anymore."

Leaning over, she wrapped her hand around his forearm, offering him what comfort she could. "It will always matter."

Abel stared at her for a moment before giving her a slight nod. He twisted his arm around until their places were reversed and he was gripping her arm in his hand. "Sit with me." He gave her a little tug of encouragement and she soon found herself ensconced in his lap with his arms wrapped around her.

"Let me know if I'm hurting your sunburn." He kissed the top of her head as she placed her head on his shoulder and got comfortable.

"I will," she promised softly.

They sat there until the sun was long sunk behind the distant hills. The night was alive with the sounds of crickets and various other insects. The air cooled slightly, and at one point Erin heard the hoot of an owl. It was only then that Abel stirred.

"Let's go to bed," he whispered in her ear.

Goose bumps slid down her spine as he placed a kiss on her neck. Erin slipped out of his lap and began gathering up the few remaining dirty dishes. Abel checked to make sure the barbecue ashes were all out and then held the door open for her as she carried the dishes inside.

"Just dump them in the sink. We're both beat, and I can do them tomorrow." Abel closed and locked the back door, and then waited patiently as she piled the dishes in the sink. She was sure he could hear the sound of her heart pounding over the clinking sound of the plates and glass as she stacked them.

Her stomach was filled with butterflies and her legs felt like jelly as she walked up the stairs to bed. Abel followed close behind her, his hand resting on the base of her spine. It was such a small thing, but it was very intimate, like the sort of thing a man did for his wife on the way to bed.

Erin experienced a sharp pang in her heart, yearning for that kind of committed relationship with him. If she let herself, she could easily imagine herself living here, and suddenly an image of a dark-haired baby popped in her head.

Enough, she warned herself. He'd already given her more than she'd thought any man ever would. Straightening her spine, she kept climbing straight up the stairs. She wasn't going to ruin this moment with regrets.

Erin was quick in the bathroom, and Abel went in when she was finished. She was brushing out her hair when he joined her

in the bedroom. Swiping the brush across her hair a few more times, she tossed the brush onto the dresser, and headed for bed.

Abel stopped her before she climbed into bed and undid several of the buttons before sliding the shirt down her arms and letting it drop to the floor. "You'll sleep better without it," he promised her.

Erin climbed gingerly into bed, watching Abel while he shucked his jeans. Her mouth watered as he casually eased his arms over his head and stretched. It was impossible for him to extend his arms fully given his height, so his elbows were bent. He was the perfect picture of masculinity. As she watched, his cock stirred and began to grow. Her breasts swelled slightly in response and she accidentally brushed them against the sheet. Caught off guard, she winced slightly. Her chest seemed to be a little sorer than she thought it was.

Abel, of course, noticed immediately. "I knew it was worse than you let on." He climbed into bed and carefully settled her into the warm crook of his arm.

Erin let her hand drift to his groin and grazed his growing erection. Her fingers had barely touched him before he gripped her hand and pulled it away. She looked at him, surprised by his action. "Why?" she questioned, lifting her head so she could see him. After all, he'd asked her to stay the night.

Cradling her face in his hands, he kissed her. Long and slow, it was a kiss that seethed with underlying passions. His tongue discovered every crevice of her mouth before he withdrew. He caught her lower lip between his teeth and nibbled on it for a moment before soothing it with his tongue. Placing one final kiss on her lips, he drew her body back down into his arms.

"I want you. Don't for one second think that I don't." His hand smoothed a lock of hair away from her face. "But not when you're not feeling well. If it can't be good for you, then it won't be good for me. Understand?"

His chest hair tickled her nose as she nodded, and she was glad for the excuse to rub her face. His declaration had touched her beyond belief. This action, more than anything else, reassured her that she'd made the right choice in loving this man. It showed her that he did indeed have feelings for her, and he cared about her well-being. That, plus great sex wasn't such a bad deal. Sighing contentedly, she snuggled closer to his chest.

She really tried to go to sleep, but her body was still humming with desire and she could feel his erection nudging her hand as it lay on his stomach. Casually, she extended one finger and brushed the tip of his penis.

He groaned and shuddered. "Baby, you're killing me here."

Erin grinned. She liked the idea that she could make him want her so much. It made her feel very womanly and powerful. Then she had a brilliant idea. "You know," she began, still stroking the bulbous tip with her finger. "There was a position in that magazine that we could do with no problem."

"Is that so?" he rumbled. "Tell me."

She licked her lips that were suddenly very dry. "We both lie on our sides, but my head is facing your feet." Trailing off, she glanced at his face, "It's called sixty-nine."

"It's a classic, but instead of our sides, do you think you could lie on top of me without hurting yourself?" His low sexy voice rolled over her, making her blood sizzle.

"I'm sure I could." At this point she didn't care if it did hurt. This was an opportunity not to be missed. Before he could change his mind, she twisted around in the bed until she was facing his feet, straddling him, and then she carefully lowered herself on top of him.

His large hands gripped her thighs guiding her backwards until she felt his breath on her already slick feminine folds. Taking his time, he adjusted her until he was satisfied with her position, and then his tongue snaked out and licked her entire length. Erin cried out, but his hands had clamped around her thighs, holding her in place so she couldn't move.

"I'm going to eat your pussy until you come." His words started a fire deep within her.

"Yes," she moaned and then lost her breath as his clever tongue curled around her clit, making her squirm.

Deciding that this worked both ways, she lowered her head to his cock, and with no warning, took him deep in her mouth. Now it was his turn to groan as she moved her mouth up and down his length, using her tongue to stimulate the sensitive flesh.

In retaliation, he stabbed his tongue inside her, thrusting it in and out as he used his fingers to stimulate her clit. It was almost too much for her to handle, but he wasn't finished. Replacing his tongue with his fingers, he thrust two of them deep inside her and began to move them slowly in and out. With his other hand, he traced the cleft of her behind, before using his teeth to nip at her ass cheeks.

Erin moaned and the sound vibrated along the length of his cock. Wrapping her hand around the base, she stroked him as she continued to lick and suck at the tip. She used her other hand to stroke and cuddle his testicles before moving to the sensitive skin just under them. His hips flexed as he tried to drive his cock deeper into her mouth. Taking him as deep as she could, she lost herself in the pleasure of the moment.

The smell of sex permeated the air, as he continued to stroke her clit and lick her flesh. She flicked her tongue over the tip of his cock, licking at the milky liquid seeping from the tip before she worked her way lower and sucked at his balls. Rubbing her nose against the hair of his groin, she inhaled his addictive scent.

His hips jerked, rubbing his cock against her cheek. Turning her face towards it, she rubbed her cheek across his hard length. His fingers dug into her ass cheeks and she could feel his heated breath on her pussy as he gasped for breath.

His arousal was driving hers even higher and she knew that she wouldn't last much longer. But this time, she wanted him to come first. She inched back until she could take his cock deep in her mouth once again. Letting it slid back as far as she could, she sucked hard, and when his testicles drew up close to his body, she knew he was close.

Redoubling her efforts, she used both her hands and her mouth, stroking, licking, and sucking. She was rewarded a moment later when he stiffened and came in her mouth. Erin didn't stop, but continued to pump his dick with her hand and suck on the tip until he made her stop. Rolling off him, she came up on her knees next to him, and looked him straight in the eyes as she swallowed and licked her lips.

"I'm not done with you yet." Abel was urging her closer as he spoke. "Sit on my face."

Erin didn't hesitate, but eagerly straddled his face. She ached with the need to come. She was so close. Raising her hands, she cupped her breasts carefully, as they were very sensitive. Using her fingertips, she teased her aching nipples. She licked her lips, and the taste of him made her inner muscles clench with need.

Abel didn't wait for her to settle, but pulled her pussy down to his face. His long fingers forged deep inside her as his tongue lapped at her wet lips and sucked her clit. Stroking hard and deep, her inner muscles clamped tight around them.

Abel rubbed his other hand over her pussy, coating it with her juices before using it to explore the dark cleft of her ass. She shrieked when she felt one of his wet fingers slowly, but steadily push its way inside her behind. It was a tight fit, and his finger stretched her. At first she wasn't sure she liked the sensation, but then he plunged two of his fingers deep into her vagina even as he pushed his other finger further up her ass. She felt so full, she just wanted to explode.

"It's all right, baby," he reassured her. "Just relax and enjoy." He withdrew his finger slightly before pushing it further inside her behind. "Your ass is so hot and tight, but you like this. Don't you, honey."

He moved his finger as he spoke and Erin moaned and gripped the headboard tight, giving herself up to the amazing new sensations coursing through her. When her inner muscles clenched around his fingers, she was almost afraid to move. "Yes," she hissed. She'd never imagined a man putting his fingers up her ass, but with Abel she found it exciting. She didn't think she could take much more. Her blood sizzled and her body was on fire.

When he inserted a third finger inside her pussy, she came on the upstroke. Exploding around his fingers, she came in a sudden gush.

Abel kept his fingers pumping and his tongue licking until she begged him to stop. Even then, he kept it up for a minute longer and Erin was shocked when her inner muscles contracted once again. This time the feelings were so intense that she screamed and arched back, letting her orgasm consume her.

She didn't remember moving, but when she came back to her senses a few moments later, she was sprawled across Abel's chest. Yawning, she snuggled against it, rubbing her cheek against the thatch of soft hair there.

"Sleep." She heard his voice as if from a distance, but couldn't summon the strength to answer him. The effects of her explosive orgasm, the long day, the sunburn, and the big meal all caught up to her, and she drifted off to sleep.

Chapter Ten

At the same time on the outskirts of town, Nathan Connors sat in his parked truck and stared at Carly Ames' little bungalow. A soft light still glowed in the living room window, but he couldn't see any movement inside. He didn't know why, but for some reason Nathan felt uneasy about Erin. His sister had seemed jittery this morning and slightly distracted tonight before she had gone out. Almost secretive. And that just wasn't like her.

He'd done his best to put it out of his mind, but it had done him no good. She'd been on his mind all evening long, and he knew deep in his gut that there was more to this evening than just a "girls only" evening. So here he was, just after eleven at night sitting outside of Carly's house trying to get up the nerve to go up and knock on the front door.

It was probably nothing but his imagination, but he knew he wouldn't sleep tonight if he didn't check on Erin in person. She'd probably get mad at him and accuse him of being as bad as Jackson, but it couldn't be helped.

Then there was Carly. Just the thought of her name made him sweat. With her short brown hair, pale blue eyes, and gamine face, she looked like a combination somewhere between an angel and a pixie. She was short, but she was rounded in all the right areas, especially her breasts and her ass. Nathan ate at the diner almost every day just so he could watch her ass as she walked away from him. He'd lusted after her for years, but had kept her at arm's length, because Carly was what was known as a good girl, and Nathan's taste in sex would probably shock her to death. Plus, she was his sister's best friend. There were unwritten rules about dating your sister's best friend, and a smart man avoided all contact if he knew what was good for him.

Nathan swore at himself and heaved himself out of his truck. For a man who had faced down drunks and armed men during his career as a deputy sheriff in this town, it was ridiculous for him to be nervous about facing two women. His boots echoed on the cobblestone walk as he strode purposefully up the driveway, climbed the three steps to the porch, and pounded on the front door.

A moment later, the outside light went on and he could see Carly's face in the window beside the front door. She looked shocked to see him. "Open up."

She hesitated for a moment before turning the locks and pulling the door open a crack. "What do you want?" A silky blue robe was wrapped around her body. She was obviously ready for bed.

Not exactly the warmest welcome in the world, but he hadn't really expected one. "I want to talk to Erin."

She shifted and stared directly at the center of his shirt, not meeting his eyes. "Erin's not available right now, but I'll let her know you stopped by."

The door started to close in his face and it was only instinct that made him shove his boot inside the doorframe to keep her from closing it. She glared at him, but said nothing.

"I want to see Erin. Now." The hairs on the back of Nathan's neck were standing on end, a sure sign that something wasn't right. If that wasn't enough to warn him that something was wrong, then the guilty look on Carly's face convinced him he was right.

Using his left shoulder for leverage, he muscled his way through the front door, and forced her to back up. He automatically scanned the entryway before closing the door behind him. The silence was deafening as they stood there and stared each other down. Nathan was determined to know what was going on, and Carly was staring at him with her arms crossed under her chest, a mutinous look on her face.

It really wasn't fair of her to cross her arms like that. The action pushed her sizeable breasts up even higher, distracting him from his goal. He could easily imagine himself uncovering her extraordinary tits and burying his face between them. Nathan groaned as his cock swelled and jeans grew far too tight for comfort.

"Are you okay?" Her soft words freed him from his enthrallment and he raked his hands through his hair, trying to regain control over himself and the situation.

"Where is Erin?" All signs of her concern for him vanished in the blink of an eye, and she once again appeared perturbed with him. His own temper began to flare. "If you won't tell me, I'll just look for her myself." Without waiting for a reply, he brushed past her and began a methodical search of the small bungalow.

"You can't do this." She was close on his heels, tugging on the back of his shirt.

"Watch me." He pulled away from her grasp and went through her home one room at a time until he reached her bedroom. The door was closed, but as he started to reach for it, Carly threw herself in front of it. Nathan barely managed to keep the grin off his face as he knew that would only infuriate her further. But it was ridiculous, almost to the point of being funny that this small woman thought she could keep him out of the room.

"You can't go in there. I forbid it." She stamped her small slippered foot against the hardwood floor as she spread her arms wide to block the door. Her robe slipped open slightly at the neckline and he caught a glimpse of her milky white skin and her bountiful breasts. When she widened her stance, the robe slipped away, exposing one of her firm, pale thighs.

It was far too easy to imagine wrapping his hand around the belt of her robe, and tugging until it came open. Instead of indulging in his fantasy, he bent over, gripped Carly by the waist, picked her up, and deposited her out of the way before opening the door. He strode into the room and came to a dead stop. Never in his life would he have imagined that her bedroom would look like this, and he had indeed imagined it many times in his life. In his dreams, it was soft, white, and feminine. This room was a study in rich vibrant colors and sensuality.

The four-poster bed was covered by a lush burgundy spread, which was turned back to expose matching sheets, and loaded down with pillows in a rainbow of jewel tones. The walls were a rich cream color, and a plush burgundy rug lay atop the hardwood floor. The furniture was all in a dark cherry tone and the drapes were the same material as the bedspread.

Carly rushed over to him, grabbed his arm and tried to haul him out of the room. "Get out of my bedroom before I call the cops."

"I am the cops," he said. Nathan didn't budge and finally she stopped pulling on him and threw up her hands in defeat. He was two inches over six feet and he wasn't moving until he had answers. "Where is my sister?"

Carly gave up all pretenses. "I don't know."

Her simple answer knocked the wind right out of him. "What the hell do you mean, you don't know?" he yelled. "She was supposed to be spending the night with you." Concern for his sister made him crazy and before he even realized what he was doing, he'd backed Carly up against one of the bedposts. Wrapping his hands around her shoulders, he shook her slightly.

"Stop it." She clawed at his hands. "Stop it."

The fear in her voice brought him back to his senses and shook him to his very core. Never in his entire life had he ever frightened a woman, and the fact it was the woman he'd wanted for years shamed him. He wrapped his arms around her and stilled her frantic struggles while crooning in her ear. "I'm sorry, honey. It's all right. Everything's fine." It took a minute, but finally she settled down in his arms.

She felt so good in his embrace, with her breasts pressed against his chest. His cock was nestled against her silky stomach, but there was nothing he could do about that. The fact was around this one woman, he had no control. It bothered him, but there was absolutely nothing he could do about it. He'd tried for years, but had long ago given up the struggle. He thought he'd died and gone to heaven when instead of pulling away from him, she snuggled tighter against him.

Unable to resist, he placed a small kiss on the top of her head while he took a deep breath, inhaling her unique scent. She always smelled of a combination of vanilla and something uniquely Carly. He gave her one more hug before forcing himself to step away.

She looked up at him with her big blue eyes, but he forced himself to ignore their plea. If anything else but his sister's safety was at stake, he'd probably be putty in the woman's hands.

"Please?" He said nothing else. All his years in law enforcement had taught him the value of patience.

She hesitated for a moment and took a step back before speaking. "I really don't know where she is. She asked me to cover for her because she was going on a date with a guy she's really stuck on. I don't know who it is, but I gather he's someone new. She promised to give me details tomorrow." Carly spewed it all out in one continuous stream, not pausing for breath. When she was finished, she heaved a sigh of relief. Her hands clenched the top of her robe tight, wrinkling the fragile material.

Nathan rubbed his hands over his face telling himself not to panic. So his sister was out all night with some guy he didn't know. He could handle this. Carly's soft hand patted his arm in comfort. "I'm sorry I can't tell you more."

Nathan nodded. He was totally convinced that she was telling him the truth. The sincerity of her words was all too real. "Did she give you any clues?"

Her brow wrinkled as she pondered, but finally she just shrugged and sighed. "I really can't think of anything." She hesitated for a second and thought some more. "But I got a feeling that although it's someone new, she knows and trusts him. Does that make any sense?"

Unfortunately for Nathan, it was beginning to make too much sense. A picture was beginning to form in his mind and he wasn't quite sure what he thought of it. Abel Garrett and his sister. It hurt his head to even think about it. It was one thing to intellectually know that your sister was a grown woman, but it was quite another to picture her in bed having sex with some guy, especially a guy you knew. He didn't know what he was going to say to Erin, but he was certainly going to pay a visit to Abel first thing tomorrow morning. Well, maybe not quite first thing. He'd damned well make sure his sister had left first.

Shifting closer to him, she rubbed his back with her hand, soothing him. "Trust her, Nathan. Your sister is a good judge of character and is capable of taking care of herself. You and Jackson saw to that."

He hung his head and tried to rub the tension out of the back of his neck. "I know you're right, but that doesn't make it any easier."

"I know."

Nathan didn't want to leave. He was basking in Carly's presence and the feel of her soft body pressed against his. But he'd done what he came here to do and it was time to leave. Turning abruptly, he headed for the front door. If he didn't leave now, he'd probably lock her in the bedroom and make love to her all night long.

"Thanks for everything." He tossed the comment over his shoulder as he neared the front door.

"Wait," she cried.

Nathan stared at the door. He was so close, but there was no way he could ignore her soft plea. He made himself turn around and face her. "What?" His answer was abrupt, but he was holding onto his control by a thread.

"Stay." Tugging on the belt, Carly opened her robe wide. Pushing it off of her shoulders, it pooled at her feet. She was totally naked.

Nathan couldn't take his eyes off her. Her skin was the color of cream and he longed to lap at every inch of it. Her spectacular breasts were even more magnificent uncovered. Her pink nipples were puckered tight, and a neat covering of brown curls covered her pussy. She belonged to him. She always had. But neither of them had been willing to admit it until now.

"Stay," she repeated.

Like a man finally coming home after being away far too long, he scooped her up in his arms and carried her towards the bedroom. "There's no going back." It was both a threat and a promise. She'd wanted him and she was getting all of him.

"I don't want to." Relaxing totally in his arms, she allowed him to carry her to bed.

Carly couldn't believe that it was finally happening after all these years. Nathan was in her bedroom, and he wanted her. She'd fantasized about this moment since she was fifteen and had seen Nathan working out at the farm without a shirt on. As she'd grown older, and gotten to know him as a man, the attraction had deepened. She'd never met a finer man in her life and knew that he was the one for her.

Until this moment, she'd been too afraid to take a chance, but a voice inside her head had urged her to grab the moment. Go for it, the voice commanded. The scariest thing she'd ever done in her life was to drop that robe to the floor. For a second, she'd really thought he was going to leave, but then he'd looked at her. Pure passion burned in the depths of his eyes, like blue fire. She knew she'd made the right decision when he'd snatched her up in his arms. She'd always dreamed of being carried off the bed and being totally ravished by him.

The door closed behind him with a solid thump, shutting the world outside. Nathan carried her to the bed and carefully placed her in the center. Stepping back, he searched her face as if looking for something. She reached out to him, but he stepped back from her.

"There are some things you need to understand before we go any further." He stood at the end of her bed, a large and unapproachable male.

Feeling slightly uncomfortable about lying there totally naked while he was still fully dressed, she started to pull a sheet over herself. "No." She stilled at his command and looked uncertainly at him. He crossed his arms over his chest and waited for her to comply. Slowly, she dropped the cover from her hands. Now she was more than a little nervous.

"I want you lying there naked, waiting just for me." Nathan prowled around the room as he spoke. "If we're going to have any kind of a relationship, then you have to accept that I'm in charge in the bedroom."

Carly was slightly appalled by his blunt statement even as she found herself being aroused by it. Images of her being at Nathan's every sexual whim filled her head and her breathing quickened. As if sensing her chaotic emotions, Nathan continued to explain.

"I respect you as a woman and an equal in life, Carly, but in here—" he swung his arm around to encompass the entire room, "—I'm in charge. You have to trust that I'll never do anything I know would hurt you or demean you. This is about pleasure, both mine and yours." His slow smile was filled with sexual promise. "I'll be good to you," he teased.

She was definitely intrigued by his proposition. She'd never pictured herself deferring to a man sexually. It sent a shiver down her spine, imagining what he would ask of her, what he would do to her. Even just lying here naked in front of him because he'd told her to was a huge turn-on. Her nipples were tight and she could feel the dampness between her legs.

Carly trusted Nathan implicitly, and knew that he would never ever hurt her. She wanted to please him, and if she was honest with herself, his very words had conjured images in her head that made her hot and achy. She'd always wondered what it would be like to be dominated sexually by a man, captive to his every whim, and Nathan was the only man she could ever trust enough to allow it to happen.

As if sensing her very thoughts, he walked to the side of the bed and looked down at her. "Spread your legs."

She hesitated for a moment before spreading them slightly.

"Wider."

He stood patiently beside her. Waiting. She sensed he was testing her resolve, so she opened her legs wider.

"That's a good girl," he praised her even as his fingers dipped between her legs and stroked her clit. Her legs started to tighten around his hand, but he withdrew it quickly. She moaned in protest.

"You've got to decide what you want. I know you're frightened, but you're also aroused and intrigued. I've stayed away from you for years because I didn't think you could handle my sexual demands, but you offered yourself to me and I'm not fool enough to turn you down." Nathan's face was grim as he watched her. "I love you, Carly, but if you can't accept me for who I am, then I'd rather walk out the door now than have you regret things later."

Her mind was reeling with his words. He loved her. The words rolled over and over in her mind. It was what she'd always wanted. Deep down, his intense sexuality frightened her a little, but she'd trust him with her life. She knew she'd loved him for years and had never been able to even look at another man. Faced with accepting him or losing him, there really was no decision to make.

"I love you too." Her voice was soft, but strong as she made her declaration. She could tell that he understood exactly what she was telling him by the sudden look of relief in his eyes, quickly followed by a flaring of passion.

Nathan walked to her dresser and began opening the drawers and rummaging around. He stopped when he got to the third one and took out two items. Curious, she tried to see what he had in his hands. Turning, he sauntered back towards the bed. A pair of black silk stockings hung from his large hands.

"I like your taste in lingerie, but I'll buy you some even better stuff that you can wear for me. Next time, I'll be better prepared, but this will do for now." Nathan sat on the side of the bed, leaned down and placed a soft, gentle kiss on her lips.

"Raise your arms and spread them wide." Carly inhaled a deep breath, told herself to be brave, and raised her arms over her head. Slowly she spread them wide, having a good idea what was coming.

Nathan kissed her again before wrapping one of the stockings around her right wrist and then anchoring it to the post of the bed. When he was finished, he walked slowly around the bed and did the same with the other. She never took her eyes off of him, but he was fully absorbed in his task. It was only when he was finished, and both her hands were securely tied to the bedposts, that he looked at her. "Does that feel okay?"

"I can't move them." Her voice sounded shaky and frightened to her own ears.

"I know you can't move them. That's not what I asked you." He stood silently, waiting for her to answer his question.

"It feels fine, I guess."

"Good. Don't pull on them and you'll be fine." He stood at the bottom of the bed and studied her for a moment. Her large breasts were thrust upwards, her nipples hard. She moved her legs restlessly on the bed under his intense scrutiny. He smiled as if pleased.

He reached behind his head and grabbed his cotton shirt with both hands before pulling it off over his head and dropping it to the floor. He yanked off his boots and tossed them aside before unbuttoning his jeans and pushing both them and his underwear to the floor at the same time. She drank in the sight of his large, hard body and her fingers itched to touch his skin and explore every inch of him.

Climbing up the end of the bed, he settled himself between her spread legs. "You are so damned gorgeous, you take my breath away." Totally enthralled, he used his hands to spread her legs even wider before bending over and licking the soft folds of her aroused flesh. "Mmm, you taste amazing."

Carly could feel the heat in her face at his words. No man had ever spoken to her in this way before. Nathan was very blunt and unabashedly sexual. "Thank you," she managed to squeak, not quite knowing what else to say.

Nathan laughed and crawled up over her until they were face-to-face. "You're welcome, but it's only the truth." He cradled her head in his massive hands, his eyes intense. "I'm the one who should be thanking you. You've given me my heart's desire."

Nathan's lips covered hers, sliding back and forth over them until she parted them, silently asking for more. His tongue eased inside, slowly tasting and teasing hers until they were both gasping for breath. "We'll keep it simple this time. I just can't wait."

His stark words thrilled her. She could feel his erection pressing against her stomach, and knew his desire for her was great. As he kissed his way down her neck, she could feel a trail of dampness being left on her skin as traces of his arousal seeped from the tip of his cock. Even though she couldn't move her arms, she felt powerful. As strong as he was, he couldn't hide the effect she had on him. It evened things out for her and she found it easier to give herself over to his particular style of lovemaking.

Nathan cupped her breasts in his hands and kneaded them slowly. The contrast of his dark fingers on her pale skin excited her. "Please," she gasped, and he bent his head and swirled his tongue over her aching nipples. First one and then the other received his undivided attention.

In spite of her resolve, she tugged at the silken bonds, wanting to stroke his body. "Let me touch you," she pleaded. Every time he licked her nipples, she felt an answering pulse between her legs. Her moist, hot slit longed to be filled by his cock.

"Later," he promised. His fingers skimmed down her stomach and straight between her legs where he slid two of them straight inside her. "I love that your pussy is hot and wet for me." Moving his fingers in and out of her, he continued to praise her.

"Your pink nipples are all tight and aching for my touch." He flicked out his tongue and rasped at one of her sensitive nipples. She writhed on the bed, moving her hips to drive his fingers deeper inside her.

"Come for me." His thumb pressed hard on her swollen clit even as his fingers continued to move in and out of her throbbing body. "Come for me." His voice was strained, and she shivered as he blew lightly on her damp breasts.

She could feel her orgasm building deep inside her and gave herself over into his keeping. Focusing on the sensations racking her entire body, she felt herself peak. Crying out, she came against his fingers. With his body wedged between her legs, she couldn't close them and Nathan kept moving his fingers until she collapsed back against the sheets, shivering and moaning.

Nathan quickly moved between her sprawling legs, sat back on his knees, lifted her hips, and plunged deep inside her. Unbelievably, she came again, convulsing around him. Her inner muscles clamped down hard on his cock, and he groaned, gripping his arm tight around her waist before pulling back and then thrusting long and deep inside her.

Carly was unable to take her eyes off his face as he continued to drive himself hard within her pussy. His eyes were closed and his concentration complete. She moaned again and managed to wrap her legs around his waist, drawing him even deeper inside her. Shuddering, he came. She could feel the power of his orgasm as he emptied himself inside her. When he was finally finished, he rested his head between her breasts.

Exhausted, her legs dropped back to the bed. Now that they were both spent, she noticed that her arms were feeling a little sore, but before she could summon the energy to ask him to untie her, he stirred. Heaving himself up, he untied both of her hands, lowering her arms carefully, and massaging her shoulders. Sighing, she allowed her arms to flop to the mattress beside her.

"It gets easier with practice," he promised her. His face was filled with emotion as he gathered her in his arms and pillowed her against his chest. "That was the most amazing experience of my life."

Carly rested one of her hands on his chest, enjoying the feel of his muscles beneath her palm. "Me, too."

"I didn't use protection," he pointed out.

"I'm on the pill," she told him, thinking to put his mind at ease. Instead, he heaved a huge sigh.

"You'd look gorgeous carrying my child, but I guess we can worry about that after we've been married a while. I'll admit, I'd like a few years of having you to myself." Nathan toyed with her hair as he spoke.

Carly was stunned by the ease with which he spoke about their future. "You're assuming a lot, aren't you." She knew that she loved him, but she was slightly perturbed by his easy assumption that she'd fall in line with his plans.

"No, I'm not." His voice was drowsy and filled with contentment. "You would never have allowed me to do what we just did if you didn't love me."

"So?"

"So, now that I've got you, I'm not letting you go." He dropped a kiss on the side of her forehead. "We're not kids playing games, Carly. There's a promise between us now, and if you're truthful with yourself, you know that it's been there for years."

"I know," she conceded. "But I don't want you to get the idea that you're always in charge."

"The only thing I want to be in charge of is your sexual pleasure." His wicked words made her shiver and the devil knew he'd aroused her again if his laughter was any indication. Her head shook as his chest rumbled with laughter. She didn't know if she should be peeved with him or amused. She chose to be amused.

"Hey, just to prove what an easy guy I am to get along with, I'll let you pick the wedding date."

Carly sat up in bed and swiped her hair out of her face. "Are you proposing to me?"

Nathan sat up next to her and took her cold hands in his. "Yes I am. Carly, will you do me the honor of becoming my wife?"

Tears filled her eyes and began to roll down her cheeks. Sighing, he released one of her hands and swiped the tears with his fingers. "Please tell me they're tears of joy."

"Yes," she said suddenly.

He froze at her words and searched her face. "Yes?"

"Yes," she nodded emphatically.

Nathan clutched her tight in his arms and held her against the frantic beat of his heart. Tilting her head back, he whispered one short phrase before proceeding to kiss her senseless. The sound of his simple, heartfelt "thank you" echoed in her ears as the passion overtook her once more.

Chapter Eleven

The feeling of something heavy lying across her chest awakened Erin the next morning. She lay there in bed, savoring the feeling of Abel's strong arm wrapped around her as if, even in sleep, he was unwilling to release her. Erin wished that he would never let her go, and that he would want to stay home with her for good. But that was just wishful thinking. As a crime writer, Abel always traveled extensively. It was necessary for his work that he investigated the crimes where they happened and talked to all the people involved. That meant living for months at a time in various parts of the country.

She shifted cautiously in the bed, testing to see if her skin was still sore. Peeking down at herself, she noted that her breasts were still slightly pink, but overall they looked better than she'd anticipated. She was just thankful that it hadn't been worse. The sight of Abel's strong, tanned arm rested against the softness of her pink belly made her feel soft and womanly. He was the only man who'd ever made her feel this way.

Turning, Erin buried her face in his chest, rubbing her nose against the fine covering of hair there. She fit comfortably in the curve of his body and felt more at home in his arms than she'd ever felt in her life. They suited each other well and not just physically. He was easy to be with, and she never felt like she had to be anything other than her real self. Abel seemed to like her for who she was, and that was the most precious gift anyone had ever given her.

As she lay there, she felt his heavy cock twitch against her thigh. Smiling, she waited to see how long it would take him to fully awaken. Even though they'd made love after they'd gone to bed, she expected that Abel would wake up with a hard-on. She could feel his arousal lengthening and thickening, and she pushed her hip against it. Her own body answered his and she could feel the moisture between her legs as her own arousal grew. She stretched sinuously against him, enjoying the heavy feeling in her breasts and the ache between her legs. It was amazing how quickly her body responded to his.

A low rumble escaped him as his hand slid up her belly to cup her breast. "How do you feel this morning?"

Arching into his hand, she all but purred. "I feel wonderful this morning."

Fondling her gently, he tweaked her nipple between his thumb and forefinger. "You certainly do."

Erin laughed, feeling happy. She'd never spent the night with a man before, and found it extremely intimate to sleep wrapped around this one and wake up in his arms. It would be very easy to become addicted to his touch and his presence.

Turning onto her side, she faced him and slung her leg over his hip. His hand drifted down to her behind where he squeezed gently. "Are you too sore?"

Erin knew that if she said yes, he wouldn't make love to her, but there was no way she was going to let him get away with that. "Not if we do it a certain way."

His eyes were filled with a combination of lust and indulgence when he looked at her. "What do you have in mind?" His hand continued to lazily trace circles on her butt and she gasped when he trailed his fingers in the dark cleft between her ass cheeks. His index finger traced the outline of her anus before going lower and slipping into her vagina.

Erin gasped as a second finger joined the first inside her and he began to move them in and out in a lazy rhythm. "I want to fuck you until neither one of us can think straight, but I don't think you're up to that yet." He continued to stroke the inside of her body. "But I think we'll have to take it slow this morning. You should be feeling much better later today or tomorrow."

Biting her lip was the only way Erin could keep from begging him to fuck her now. She wanted him hard and hot inside her. "Scissors," she blurted.

He froze, his fingers deep inside her. "What?"

Erin would have laughed at his dumbfounded expression except she was much too aroused. Her body was on fire for his and she was tired of waiting. "I don't want scissors. It's a position from the magazine, remember?"

Relief spread across his face and she felt his body relax once again. "I guess I conveniently forgot that one. For a second there, you had me worried." Leaning down, he kissed her on the forehead. "You have got to show me the article in that damned magazine. Now, what do I do?"

Doing her best to picture the position, she realized that they were perfectly aligned already. Hoisting her leg higher onto his hip, she wrapped her arm around his shoulder to give her some support. "You slide inside me and use your hands on my butt for leverage."

Abel shifted, spreading the folds of her labia wide as he squeezed his cock into her. Her slick vagina welcomed him, and her muscles clasped greedily around him. She clung to his shoulders as he got a firm grip on her behind. Keeping her bottom leg braced against his, she rotated her hips in little circular motions, moaning as his cock seemed to swell even larger inside her.

Flexing his hips slightly, Abel's thrusts were short and quick. The pace was maddening for Erin and she wanted more. Frantically, she rubbed her breasts against his muscular chest, but the rasp on her engorged nipples against his chest hair served to arouse her even further. "I need more." Erin could feel herself poised on the edge of an orgasm, but not able to make it happen.

Abel's hand on her bottom moved and he once again slid his fingers into the cleft. When he reached the spot where they were joined, he slowly inserted one of his fingers inside of her vagina to join his throbbing cock. The movement stretched her even further, causing her to cry out. At the same time, he stroked the opening of her ass, inserting the tip of his thumb slightly into her anus.

Erin exploded. Abel filled every part of her until there was room for nothing else. Her convulsions were almost violent as she shook from head to toe. Abel continued to stroke her with his fingers and cock until she collapsed against him, totally spent. When he carefully removed his hands from her she shivered, already missing the intimate contact with him.

She knew that he hadn't come and expected him to keep thrusting, but instead, he gripped her bottom and rolled until she was lying under him. His cock was still rock-hard inside her and she could feel it pulsing deep within her. Pushing her knees back towards her head, he gripped her knees and spread her legs wide. The move left her legs spread wide open and him in total control. A bead of sweat rolled down his temple as he began to thrust once again.

He plunged into her over and over, harder with each stroke. Even though she'd just had an amazingly intense orgasm, she felt her body spring to life once again. Every time he drove into her, he ground himself against her clit, until she wanted to scream. She urged her hips up to meet his downward thrust, wanting him to be deeper, wanting him to push harder.

"Harder," she moaned. "Deeper."

His nostrils flared and the lust in his eyes boiled over. Dropping her legs, he gripped her hips, and rammed himself into her. She could feel his fingers biting into her hips, and feel the frantic beat of his heart as he drove himself into her. His breathing was harsh as he thrust so hard that her entire body slid upwards on the bed. Erin wrapped her legs around his hips and locked her ankles behind him. She was so close.

He pushed one final time and shook as he emptied himself into her. The feel of his hot semen spurting deep inside her caused her to come again. She cried out as Abel thrust several more times before collapsing on top of her. Digging her heels into his ass, she kept him deep inside her. Her inner muscles continued to milk his cock making them both shake with desire.

Little aftershocks rocked her as she lay there covered by Abel's large body. She could feel his cock getting smaller with in her, but refused to let him go. Keeping her arms and legs wrapped tightly around him, she held him tight.

It was Abel who moved first, easing back so that she had no choice but to drop her legs back to the bed. He rolled onto his back and settled her onto his chest. Erin shimmied until his semi-erect cock was back inside her before sighing contentedly and resting her head on his chest.

Neither one of them spoke. Their feelings were still too raw, too intense. Both of them were totally exhausted, but clung to each other, refusing to let go of the moment.

Erin finally made herself look at the clock and knew she no longer had any choice. It was already seven o'clock and she had blueberry fields waiting for her. She started to move, but Abel held her with his arms, refusing to let her move. She allowed herself to enjoy the sensation for a moment before she tried again.

"I've got to get up."

"I know." Reluctantly, he let her go.

Leaning over, she kissed him, enjoying the feeling of his lips against hers. "Good morning," she whispered against his lips.

"It certainly is." Abel gave her a quick kiss before lifting her off him and rolling up to sit on the side of the bed. "If we don't stop now, you won't get to work today." He inspected her skin more closely. "And you're still a little sore."

Erin felt totally comfortable sitting on the bed naked while he looked her over. "It doesn't really hurt."

"Doesn't matter. I'll make some breakfast while you shower." Snagging a pair of jeans off the floor, he tugged them on. Standing, he zipped them, but didn't bother to button them.

Holding out his hands to her, he helped her off the bed. "Make sure you use some more aloe gel on your skin before you get dressed."

"Yes sir." She saluted him smartly, making him smile. Tiny laugh lines bracketed his beautiful green eyes as he gave a little laugh.

"Smart-ass." He smacked her playfully on the behind as he shooed her towards the bathroom. Erin hurried to get showered and dressed, already anticipating breakfast.

* * * * *

Abel was relaxed and mellow when a knock came on the door an hour later. Erin had left just a few minutes ago after agreeing to meet him at the swimming hole later this afternoon. With any other woman, such a domestic scene would have left him with an uneasy feeling in his gut, but with Erin, he felt content. He had taken pleasure in cooking her a breakfast of bacon, eggs, and toast. She'd eaten with an obvious enjoyment that had left him smiling. His woman didn't pick at her food. She had a healthy hearty appetite in every aspect of her life.

Thinking Erin must have forgotten something, he continued stacking the dirty dishes on the counter. "It's open," he shouted. "Did you forget something, honey?"

"No, sweetheart." The male voice was mocking with an underlying hint of anger. "I didn't."

Abel had been afraid that this would happen. In spite of Erin's belief that she could keep their relationship a secret, he knew better. Neither of her brothers was stupid, and it was only a matter of time before one of them or both of them found out. That it was Nathan didn't surprise him. The man was a cop, after all, and was trained to be observant.

Turning slowly, he crossed his arms across his chest, leaned against the counter, and tried to gauge the extent of Nathan's anger. "Say what's on your mind."

Nathan stood there with his feet spread, his hands on his hips and a scowl on his face. "I sat in my truck and watched my sister leave your house this morning."

"Would you believe it if I told you she was just here for breakfast?" Abel never took his eyes off Nathan.

"Is that what you're telling me?" Nathan's blue eyes narrowed, and the expression on his face grew even blacker.

"Nope." Abel was tired of pussyfooting around the truth. Pushing away from the counter, he took two mugs out of the cupboard, and filled them both with coffee. "Sit down." He motioned to Nathan to have a seat and placed one of the mugs on the table in front of the vacant seat. Pulling out his own chair, he sat and spread his long legs in front of him.

Nathan stomped to the table, hauled out the chair, and sat. His two hands were clenched into fists as he stared across the table at Abel. "I know that Erin is a grown woman, but there's just some things a brother doesn't want to think about his sister."

"I can imagine." Abel picked up his mug and took a sip of the hot, steaming brew. Nathan was obviously doing his best to be open-minded about the whole thing, so Abel let him take his time and gather his thoughts.

"What bothers me the most is that she lied to me and Jackson." Nathan toyed with the handle of his mug before picking it up and taking a large swallow.

"That wasn't my idea," Abel felt compelled to point out. "Nothing I said could convince her differently." Taking pity on the other man, Abel did his best to explain. "Erin is afraid that my relationship with both you and Jackson would change for the worse if you found out that we were sleeping together."

"Well, she's right about that." Nathan's whole body was tense now as he placed both palms on the table and leaned forward. "I can't stop her from doing whatever she wants because she's a grown woman. But that's my baby sister you're messing with and if you hurt her, I'm going to come back here and beat the crap out of you. Understand?"

Abel had no doubt that he could win a fight against Nathan. It would be a close one, even though he had half a foot on the man. There was nothing meaner than a pissed-off older brother, especially one who had special training in hand-to-hand fighting. Abel had expected nothing less from him, and would have been disappointed in him otherwise.

"I understand. It's what I'd do in your position." Sighing, he scrubbed one of his hands over his face. "It's complicated."

A reluctant grin appeared on Nathan's face. "It usually is with women."

"That sounds like the voice of experience." Now he was intrigued. He hadn't been aware that Nathan was seeing anyone special.

"How do you feel about her?" Nathan relaxed back in his chair, but Abel wasn't fooled. There was still a readiness about his posture that told Abel that he could explode at any moment, and very well might if the answer to the question wasn't one that he liked.

"Erin is the most special woman I've ever known," he answered honestly. "I don't know where this is leading, if anywhere. I don't even know if I'm gonna stay here." Abel held up his hand to stop Nathan from interrupting him. "But Erin knows all this. Hell, man, I tried to discourage her, but she's got a mind of her own, and she knows what she wants. I've never lied to her and never will. She's happy with where we are now and so am I."

Nathan sighed and tilted his head back and closed his eyes. "But what about when you leave?" The question sat there between them like a ticking bomb.

"If and when I leave, it will be between me and Erin." Abel kept his voice low and firm. "I'm not out to do anything to hurt her. In fact, I'd want to pound anyone who harmed her in any way. I don't know what the future will bring, but Erin is more than just a fling for me."

Nathan opened his eyes and stared at Abel for a moment as if searching to see if he was sincere. He seemed to find whatever it was he was looking for because a moment later, he held his hand across the table. Abel extended his towards Nathan and they shook hands in mutual understanding.

"I'm curious, though." Abel sprawled back in his chair once more. "How did you find out?"

Nathan snorted. "I went to Carly's to check on her last night. Erin seemed too excited and nervous about a normal girls' night out." A slow, sensual smile covered his face. "Carly put up a good front, but that woman can't lie to save her life."

Abel noted that Nathan's clothing looked a little rumpled and began to form a picture of his own. After all, investigating situations and putting together the facts was his stock in trade too. "I'll bet you had a good time interrogating little Miss Carly."

Nathan was a blur of movement as he reached out, grabbed Abel by the shirt and yanked him halfway across the table. "Don't you ever insinuate that she's anything less than a lady."

Without backing off, Abel held up his hands in mock surrender. "Relax. From what little I know about her, she seems like she's a great lady. Erin obviously thinks the world of her." He was very impressed at how fast Nathan had moved in his defense of Carly. His respect for the man was growing in leaps and bounds.

"Fuck." Nathan let go of Abel and dropped back into his chair. "I suppose I deserved that after the way I came in here asking about your love life this morning."

Abel just picked up his coffee mug and grinned. "Women. The most complex creatures on the face of the planet." He saluted Nathan with his mug and then took a swallow of coffee.

"Yeah, well, she's my woman now." His whole face shone with pride. "And as soon as she's ready, the whole world is gonna know."

Swallowing hard, Abel was filled with the twin emotions of envy and longing. It surprised him, as he'd never thought in terms of settling down with one woman before. Being home and being with Erin were beginning to change him. He wasn't at all sure he was ready for any of it, as the question of his career was already a big problem for him to deal with.

Pushing all of it to the back of his mind for now, he stood up and extended his hand once again. "Congratulations, Nathan."

"Thanks." Nathan stood and shook his friend's hand. He had the look of a very satisfied man. "A word of advice." He paused and made sure that he had Abel's full attention. "Sometimes the best thing in your life is right in front of you and if you're not careful you'll miss it because you're looking somewhere else. Don't make that mistake."

Abel ignored the obvious implications and changed the subject. "Have you told anyone else yet?"

"No. So don't tell Erin when you see her later. Carly will kill me if someone else tells her before she gets a chance to." Nathan paused for a moment. "I won't tell Jackson about your affair because I think that it's your and Erin's decision, but don't wait too long. The man isn't a fool and if he finds out on his own, he's gonna blow his stack." Nathan strolled to the back door and opened it. "But don't forget that I'm watching you."

With that, he was gone. Abel stood in the middle of his kitchen pondering the strange twist his life had taken in the last week. But for the first time in months, the burning in his gut was gone and he felt lighter than he had in years. Shaking his head, he dumped the rest of his coffee in the sink and went to tackle the boxes of papers in the den.

Chapter Twelve

Erin ambled towards the pond, feeling slightly guilty for playing hooky from work. She justified her time off by reminding herself that in less than a week, her blueberry fields would be ready for picking and she'd be working nonstop until all the berries were harvested for the season.

Usually, she loved this time of year. It was the thrill of bringing in her crop and seeing all her hard work finally pay off that pleased her most. But this year, she found herself just a little resentful of the time it would force her to spend away from Abel, especially when she had no idea when he would be leaving. He said he was staying for the summer, but she knew that could change at a moment's notice.

It was a perfect July day. The sun was shining, but a light breeze kept it from being too uncomfortable. The bees were buzzing and the occasional bird song could be heard. There was a stillness hovering over the fields as most of the insects and birds sought the shade through the hottest part of the day. Later tonight, they would be much more active.

Erin enjoyed the feeling of the sun's rays on her face, shoulders and legs. This time she was ready for it, as she'd coated her entire body with waterproof sunscreen. Parts of her were still a little pink, and she didn't want to take any chances. She wanted nothing to keep them from enjoying each other's bodies whenever the mood arose.

Her day had been wonderful so far. Waking up in Abel's arms had filled her with a sense of rightness. It had convinced her, that no matter what happened in the end, she'd done the right thing by pursuing a relationship with Abel. Some of her muscles ached slightly from the unusual positions she'd been put it in, but they felt good now as she stretched her arms and legs.

Erin was more aware of herself physically than she'd ever been in her entire life. The softness of her skin, the hollows and curves of her body, and an innate sensuality that she hadn't even known existed, all delighted her.

Up until now, she'd seen her body as a source of aggravation and sometimes disappointment. She'd despaired at her height and lack of breast size. At best, she'd seen her body as a well-oiled machine that enabled her to work hard. She'd taken pride in her strength. Very quickly, she was coming to see her body as an instrument of sensuality and pleasure, and she was starting to view it with pride. Her time with Abel was certainly changing her perceptions of herself for the better.

When she'd dumped her stuff off at home, Jackson was out mowing the grass in the orchards and Nathan had already left for work. It was lunchtime before she'd had to deal with Jackson and he'd been in a hurry to eat lunch and get back to work, so she hadn't even had to answer any questions about her "supposed" evening with Carly. She was glad for that, because she hated lying to either of her brothers, even if she only considered it a little white lie to keep anyone from being hurt. It would be easier for her if the subject never came up. Hopefully by suppertime, last night would be the furthest thing from anyone's mind.

Now it was midafternoon, and she was headed to the pond to enjoy the rest of the afternoon with Abel. Her stomach gave a loud rumble, announcing it was hungry. It was her own fault as her nerves had kept her from consuming more than a few mouthfuls of lunch. She only hoped that Abel had brought food and that her stomach would behave itself until she was able to finally eat.

The short path through the trees was well-worn from years of use and Erin enjoyed the shade from the leafy branches. She shivered slightly as her skin cooled. Goose bumps dotted her arms as she neared the end of the path, whether from the cool shade or anticipation of what was to come, she couldn't say. It was probably a combination of both.

When she finally stepped into a lush field of grass and wildflowers, the sun was so brilliant that she had to shade her eyes with her hands. At first she didn't see him and wondered if she was early, but as she scanned the area around the pond, a flash of color caught her eye. Stretched out on a blanket under the shade of a maple tree, he looked like a pagan warrior come to life.

Creeping closer as not to disturb him, her eyes got even wider. Naked. The man was totally *naked*! His skin glistened as a light sheen of perspiration covered his entire body. His hands were stacked under his head, the muscles of his arms chiseled like a sculpture even though he was obviously relaxed. Because his eyes were closed, she felt free to enjoy the view.

Up close, she became aware again of just how large Abel was. His long, thick legs were like tree trunks and most men would envy the hard six-pack that rippled across his stomach. The planes of his face were prominently etched in his high cheekbones and square jaw. The only softening on his entire face was the fullness of his lips. Even his neck looked strong, and his shoulders were a mile wide.

Her gaze drifted lower once again, and her eyes were drawn to his groin area. The man was extremely well-built and his penis was no exception. Even semi-erect, as it was now, it was rather impressive. Abel was a large man, and his equipment was built on the same grand scale as he was. Erin grinned, for once glad that she was woman enough to take all of him inside her. She licked her lips as she imagined his cock deep inside her. The sensations made her shiver and she inched closer for a better look.

As she watched, his cock began to stir and grow. Her eyes flew to his face and he lay there with his eyes half-open and a sexy grin on his face. He looked tousled and much too handsome for her peace of mind. "Like what you see?" His comment sent the heat flowing to her cheeks.

Trying to be nonchalant, she allowed her eyes to flow over him in a slow look of perusal that encompassed his entire body. "Yeah, I like it just fine."

"Why don't you join me?" The carnal look on his face and his growing arousal sent heat flaring to her own groin. Her panties were already wet, as her body was ready for him instantly.

Taking her time, she pulled her shirt over her head and tossed it towards him. He caught it in one large hand before bringing it to his nose and inhaling deeply. "God, you smell hot."

Erin knew she was blushing, but couldn't seem to stop herself. She was no match to him when it came to sexual banter. He was just so darned self-assured and relaxed with his sexuality, but there was no way she was stopping now. Reaching behind her back, she unhooked her bra, leaned forward, and allowed the straps to slip down her arms. The scrap of cotton fell to the ground at her feet. Her breasts dangled free, and she intentionally jiggled them as she straightened once again. His eyes scorched her bare flesh worse than the sun ever could.

"Don't stop." His command was deep and guttural, his jaw tight.

Erin slowly unzipped her shorts and pushed them down over her hips. When they hit the ground, she carefully stepped out of them. Turning sideways, she removed her sneakers and socks, and put them to one side. Hitching her fingers in the waistband of her panties, she slid them along the band but didn't lower them at all.

Abel's eyes narrowed as they followed the movement of her fingers. "Do it."

A sultry smile covered Erin's face and she allowed her hands to leave her panties and slide up her stomach to cover her breasts. Plumping them up in her hands, she skimmed her thumbs over her nipples, making the hard nubs even tighter.

"It's not nice to tease, sweetheart." Slowly, he raised himself to a seated position. "There's always a price to pay."

"Maybe I'm willing to pay that price." Erin had never participated in this kind of sexual banter before, but her whole body felt energized and every nerve ending in her body tingled in anticipation.

He smiled a slow wicked grin before unhurriedly getting to his feet. "I'll bet your pussy is nice and wet for me. Isn't it?"

"Yes," she whispered.

"You want me hard and deep inside you. Don't you?"

It never crossed her mind to deny him. "Yes."

"Maybe I'll have to teach you a lesson about being a cock-tease." He ran his hand down the length of his penis. "Maybe you'll have to convince me you're sorry before I let you have what you want."

"Maybe I won't," she countered. In one motion she whipped her panties off and flung them at him.

He grabbed them out of midair and rubbed them over his lips. "You want my lips on your hot pussy, lapping at your juices. Don't you, baby?" he taunted. "I can smell your heat."

Erin couldn't take any more. If she didn't cool off, she'd burst into flames on the spot. Pivoting, she raced for the water's edge and dove deep. The cool water of the pond felt good on her skin, but instead of calming her arousal it seemed to stimulate her even further.

Strong arms enveloped her from behind and she was hauled to the surface. Both their bodies broke the surface, each gasping for breath. Erin only had time to take one mouthful of air before Abel's mouth slammed down on top of hers. She couldn't breathe as he consumed her with his kiss. As they both were sinking below the surface, he continued his ardent assault. Gripping his hair in her hands, she clutched him tight, trying to get even closer to his body.

When her own breath ran out, he gave her his as they rose to the surface of the water again. Erin's heart pounded in her chest as her lungs worked hard, trying to provide her with air. If it weren't for Abel's strong grip, she would have sunk back down to the depths below. As her breathing slowly returned to normal, she noticed that Abel was having as much trouble breathing as she was. Raising her head, she looked at him and smiled.

Abel swore softly and once again lowered his head to hers. His lips covered hers, but this time, the kiss was softer, gentler. He trailed a line of heated kisses down her neck and shoulder. Gripping her bottom in his hands, he easily hoisted her higher in the water as he continued his downward path. He kept lifting her upwards until her breasts were level with his mouth.

"Please," she whispered.

Abel groaned and began to lick the moisture off her breasts. He tasted every inch of both of them before he finally rasped his tongue across one of her nipples. Erin's breath hitched in her throat, and she wrapped her legs tight around his back, locking her ankles behind him. At his leisure, he suckled each nipple, one at a time. He seemed enthralled with her breasts and her reactions to his ministrations.

Erin could feel the tip of his cock at the opening to her vagina, but he held her out of reach, continuing to pleasure her breasts. She squirmed against him, wanting him inside her. One of his hands left her behind and inched forward to trace her opening. "Hot, little pussy," he whispered against her breasts.

Erin retaliated by reaching one hand down into the water and wrapping her fingers around the very tip of his cock. She rolled her fingers around the tip, allowing one of them to stroke the very top.

Abel thrust two fingers deep inside her and suckled one of her nipples. Hard. She wavered on the edge for a moment, but he pushed his fingers to the front of her vagina as he withdrew them. She felt the contractions begin deep inside her and when he thrust his fingers in once again, she came apart in his arms. Waves of pleasure washed over her and she rode them to the very end.

Contentedly, she lolled in the water, enjoying the slight lop of the waves against her skin. She could feel the tip of Abel's cock brushing against her and realized that he hadn't come. It took her a moment to gather her strength, but she finally managed to raise her head to look at him. Drops of water beaded on his skin and rolled down his neck and shoulders. Cupping his face in her hands, she brushed a kiss across his full, sensual lips. "Thank you," she murmured.

Tenderly, he used one hand to brush the hair out of her eyes and carefully tuck it behind her ear. His other hand still supported her weight in the water. "You're very welcome."

It was the look on his face as he spoke that brought an ache to her heart. He looked pleased with himself, but there was gentle warmth in his eyes as he watched her. She felt her own eyes begin to well with tears, but they never got a chance to come to the surface. Abel suddenly laughed and allowed himself to fall backwards in the water, taking her down with him.

Erin broke away, sputtering and spitting as she swam to the surface. He brushed by her leg and tugged her back under the water. The game was on in earnest then, and they spent the next five minutes playing underwater tag, chasing one another around the confines of the pond. Erin tried her best to keep up with him, but she was beat after the late night and the hard work of the day. Giving up, she closed her eyes and relaxed, floating on the surface of the water.

Suddenly, he rose next to her and scooped her out of the pond. The water streamed off both of them as he carried up the grassy bank and deposited her on the blanket. He came down between her legs, spreading her thighs wide with his hands. "I'm not through with you yet. I don't think you learned your lesson about being a tease."

She levered herself up on her elbows, trying to sit, but fell back again the moment his lips traced her opening. He stroked the soft, pink flesh with his tongue, teasing her. Spreading her legs wider, she tilted her hips higher, encouraging him. He ignored her offering and used his thumbs to push back the folds of her labia until her clitoris was totally exposed to him. Taking his time, he made a circle around it without touching it.

"You beast." She tried to move her legs, but his hands kept them clamped open.

"It's your own fault for taunting me, honey. Now you've got to pay." His fingers lightly stroked her already sensitive flesh as she continued to thrash on the blanket. Nothing she did helped. She was totally aroused, but he kept her perched on the edge. His tongue flicked and his teeth nibbled her clit, but the moment he sensed her starting to come, he stopped. Once she was calmed down, he began again. The sensual torture seemed to go on forever.

"Please," she moaned.

"Please what?" His fingers dipped carefully in and out of her, stroking lightly, leaving her feeling empty and aching.

"I want you."

"What do you want me to do?"

"Make love to me," she wailed.

"That's not what you really want," he countered.

She looked at him now, confusion evident on her face. His tongue pressed down on her clit making her moan again. "That's too tame for you now. What you really want is for me to fuck you. Hard."

"Yes," she hissed through her teeth. Anything to end this torture.

"I warned you if you teased me, I'd make you beg for it."

Erin's eyes narrowed. Two could play this game. She remembered the one position the magazine said was a man's absolute favorite. There was no way that she was letting him hold back on her any longer.

In one motion, she lifted one of her legs and flung it right over his head. The unexpected movement caused his head to jerk back, and this allowed her to roll up on her knees. Planting her hands and knees firmly on the blanket, she spread her legs wide, and turned her head over her shoulder to look at him. "Fuck me."

His hands covered the cheeks of her ass, but he didn't move. Instead, he stroked his hands over her behind, his fingers kneading her flesh. "You still need to be punished for teasing me." One of his hands moved from her behind and came back down with a stinging slap.

Erin reared up, but he planted one hand in the middle of her back to keep her in position while his other hand spanked her bare bottom again. Abel rubbed her bottom and then slid his fingers inside her pussy again, chuckling when his fingers were coated in her juices. "I knew you'd like it."

The first slap shocked her more than anything else. Abel certainly hadn't hurt her, but it had felt strange to have his large hand smacking her bottom. She could feel the blood rushing to the area, and it only served to heighten her arousal.

The sound of Abel's hand landing on her behind once again made her moan. Her bottom and pussy were on fire and she could feel her juices sliding down her inner thighs. Erin was no longer in the mood to play. She wanted him now.

Shoving her bottom back towards him, she spread her legs as far as they would go, offering herself to him. "Fuck me, Abel," she demanded. "Now."

For a moment he didn't move, and then he exploded in a flurry of movement. Grabbing her waist, he shoved her legs even wider with his own, and then plunged deep inside her. Erin cried out as he filled her completely. Her head fell between her shoulders and she froze, trying to absorb the sensations.

"Oh, God, did I hurt you?" Abel's forehead was resting on her back and his arms were wrapped tight around her waist. His breathing was harsh, and she could feel the tension in his body.

She felt him start to withdraw from her and arched her back against him. "No." He couldn't stop now. She needed him.

"No, what? Talk to me, honey." He remained motionless, not wanting to hurt her.

"Love me, Abel." Her own voice was strained as desire built inside her. Her breasts felt heavy as they hung in front of her, and she longed for him to touch them again.

As if he'd read her mind, he moved his hands to her breasts and cupped them in his large hands. Slowly and carefully, he began to move inside her. As his cock slipped in and out of her moist body, the friction aroused her further. From this position, he filled her completely, and she loved it. With his wide stance behind her, he was totally in control of how deep and hard he thrust. There was something very hot about making a man totally crazy for you and then being at his sexual whim.

Even when Abel was as primed and ready as he was, he took his time pleasuring her. He stroked in and out of her for what seemed like forever, all the while fondling her breasts and gently rolling her turgid nipples between his thumbs and forefingers. Erin bucked back against him, needing him harder and deeper.

One of his hands slipped back between her legs, while the other one cupped her breast once again. His thrusts became harder and faster as he stroked his fingers against her clit. He plunged into her again and again, and this time as his fingers touched her, she came, powerfully and deeply, shaking her entire body to its core. Abel gave a hoarse cry as he came. He emptied himself deep inside her as her muscles clamped hard around his cock, wringing him dry.

Lowering them to the blanket, they both lay there, unable and unwilling to move. Still inside her, he was half on, half off her body. His torso covered her back and his face was buried in her hair. Slowly, the sounds of the afternoon penetrated her foggy brain. She could hear the soft sound of his breathing near her ear and feel the slow thump of his heartbeat against her back. The water lapped quietly at the shore and the low buzz of various insects wafted through the still afternoon heart.

Erin stretched her entire body. Although, she didn't want to, she needed to move. Abel stirred behind her and withdrew himself from her. Flopping to his back, he pulled her against him, unwilling to let her go. She snuggled contentedly for a few moments before she began to feel hot and sticky.

Sighing, she sat up, and avoided his attempts to pull her back down with him. "I need to clean up." Her stomach chose that exact moment to give a gigantic growl.

Abel chuckled and sat up next to her. "After you're done, I'll feed you. You need to keep your strength up."

Erin ducked her head and pressed her hand against her stomach, willing it to stop. Before she could become too embarrassed, Abel cupped her chin in his hand and kissed her. Thoroughly, he caressed every part of her lips before he pulled back from her. By the time he was finished, her toes were curled and her fingers were clamped around his shoulders. The man certainly knew how to kiss. Her stomach chose that moment to rumble once again.

Abel shook his head, stood, and offered her his hand. "We've definitely got to feed you."

Together they waded into the pond and took a quick swim to clean themselves off. Abel was back on the blanket and spreading out lunch by the time she climbed out of the water. Wringing out her hair, she plopped down next to him, totally unconcerned about her nudity.

The feast on the blanket was simple but inspiring. Fresh grapes, slices of peaches, strawberries and chunks of melon were piled high in a bowl. Another container lay open, revealing several types of crackers and chunks of various cheeses. But the thing that caught her immediate attention was the two slabs of cheesecake set to one side. She reached for the cake as he filled a glass with iced tea. The ice cubes were almost melted, but the tea was cold and refreshing as she took a sip from the one he handed her.

"Dessert first?" He propped himself on one arm and reached for his own piece.

"I thought we'd already had dessert?" She batted her eyelashes playfully at him.

"We certainly did." Desire flared in his eyes and his cock began to stir again.

"You're impossible," she informed him before taking a large forkful of cheesecake. She allowed the flavors to roll across her tongue before slowly chewing and swallowing it. Carefully, she licked the fork clean before reaching for another bite.

Abel groaned. "Not impossible at all. In fact, very likely if you keep that up."

Erin grinned, and scooped up another bite. "Eat first. I don't want to wear you out."

He waited until she'd finished her cheesecake before urging her to lie flat on her back. Erin settled comfortably and watched him as he removed several containers from a thermal bag. Leaning over, he leisurely kissed her lips. "Close your eyes," he whispered as he kissed both her eyelids shut. Erin relaxed and waited to see what he would do.

The only sound was the one of containers being opened. Then she felt something cool and light on her breasts. Her eyes twitched, almost opening, but she caught herself before they actually opened. The sensation was arousing and she squirmed on the blanket.

"Open your mouth." She opened her mouth and felt the soft slide of something sweet on her lips. The sweet scent of strawberries tickled her nose, and she flicked her tongue out to taste before she took a bite.

Abel groaned, but held another one to her lips. She took that one from his fingers, pausing to lick the sticky tips before chewing and swallowing the luscious fruit. Strawberries had never tasted this good before. With her eyes closed all her senses were heightened and she was eagerly anticipating what would come next.

Her lips parted, waiting for another strawberry. She gasped when she felt Abel's lips on her breasts, licking at whatever he had coated them with. His lips came up to graze hers and she tasted fresh whipped cream. "Umm, that tastes good." The combination of strawberry juice, fresh cream, and Abel was better than anything she'd ever imagined.

Abel returned to her breasts, licking the cream from her flesh. His teeth flicked the hard nubs of her nipples before swirling back over the plump mound. Every inch was suckled until all the cream was gone. Erin just lay there, lost in the wicked sensations. Being unable to see him, and not knowing what he was going to do next, aroused her to new heights.

He kissed a trail down her stomach, pausing to nibble on her hipbones before continuing down to her pussy. She could feel him shifting as he spread her lips wide with one hand and poured something onto her skin with the other. Thick liquid oozed slipped down her folds, making her shiver.

Abel nuzzled her pubic hair before lowering his lips to lap at her slick folds. "Honey, sweet and thick," he murmured as he sucked her clit. "But not as sweet as the honey from your body." His tongue plunged deep inside her pussy making her cry out with desire.

"Abel," she groaned, not quite knowing what she wanted.

"You're so sweet." Abel's tongue was all over her pussy, licking and sucking the honey from every crevice of her body. His fingers slipped inside her, stroking her, as he continued to pleasure her with her mouth.

Her entire body was on fire now as she clenched her eyes shut and rode the waves of pleasure that racked her body. She was just about to come, when Abel moved. "No," she cried, reaching out her hands to pull him back to her.

His hands gripped her hips as he plunged his cock deep into her pussy. Erin almost cried the relief was so great. There was no more teasing now as he slammed into her, his strokes getting harder and deeper with each thrust. Erin could feel her muscles clench and then she was soaring as she came.

Her eyes popped open as she screamed her release. Abel was like some dark warrior between her thighs, taking what was his. His eyes were closed, his face a mask of concentration as his large body strained for completion. He gave one long, hard thrust and then he came, his entire body jerking as he grunted and continued to drive into her, prolonging his orgasm.

He slumped to his forearms, still buried in her depths. She could feel him still pulsing within her and her own body responded by clamping down hard around his cock. Erin was feeling wonderful, but sticky, and although she would have liked to stay as she was, she desperately needed to rinse her body. She pushed at his shoulder, but it was like trying to move an immovable object.

"Abel, we're going to attract ants if I don't get cleaned up." That thought made her glance around the blanket. So far, so good, but that wouldn't last if she didn't get cleaned up.

Abel raised his head, and a huge grin split his face. Easing his cock from her body, he reared back on his knees, hauled her over his shoulder, gained his feet, and sauntered towards the water.

Erin laughed as she hung upside down and took the opportunity to ogle his tight butt. He gave her no warning, but suddenly flipped her over and dropped her into the pond. His wicked grin was the last thing she saw before the water covered her head and she began to sink.

Planting her feet on his stomach, she pushed off and felt smug when she heard a very satisfying splash as Abel fell backwards into the water. She tried to swim away, but his large hand wrapped around her thigh, pulling her backwards. Erin didn't even try to fight, but instead allowed him to pull her to the surface.

Abel hauled her tight against his chest and kissed her, deep and long. Flinging her arms around his neck, she returned the heated embrace. Then her stomach growled again.

Abel laughed and tugged her out of the water behind him. "Obviously, we haven't fed you enough."

Erin allowed him to lead her back to the blanket where they both collapsed and began eating their picnic feast.

The next hour flew as they ate and talked. She told him about the upcoming harvest and Abel told her that he was halfway through his parents' papers. He popped a cracker topped with a piece of cheese in his mouth before offering her one. They'd been taking turns feeding each other. He chewed and swallowed before taking a sip of iced tea.

"I found an old journal of my mother's. It seems to be quite old."

"Really." Erin was intrigued. "Are you going to read it?"

"Of course," Abel replied. "Giving my chosen profession, how could you think that I wouldn't?"

"That's right," she teased. "You're a professional snoop."

Abel didn't take offense. Instead, he popped a grape in her mouth. "I think it's from the year I was born. It's a chance to maybe understand what she was thinking and feeling at the time." He ate a fresh strawberry before continuing. "It's strange to see your parents as people in their own right and not just as your parents."

"I imagine it would be. I know I've never really thought about it before." Erin's mind drifted to her father and her brothers, as well as to the mother she'd never really known.

They fell into a comfortable silence until Abel began to put away the remains of their picnic. "As much as I hate it, you have to get ready to go if you're not going to be late for supper."

Reluctantly, Erin stood and began to search for her clothing. It took her awhile to find most of it, but she couldn't find her panties anywhere. Finally, she gave up and hauled her shorts up over her bare butt. When she'd retied her sneakers, she shook out the blanket and handed it to Abel. He placed it on the top of the satchel he'd brought and turned to her. She slipped easily into his arms, not wanting to ever let him go.

"Thank you for this afternoon." She nuzzled her nose against his chest, loving the feel of his hot skin. He hadn't buttoned his shirt and she was taking full advantage of that fact.

"You're very welcome. But I should be thanking you." He kissed the top of her head before he took a step away from her.

"Go, before I change my mind and keep you here with me." From the look on his face, Erin could tell he was only half kidding.

"I'll be over first thing tomorrow morning." With that, she turned and ran towards home. She never looked back, afraid that if she did, she'd never find the strength to leave him. He was fast becoming the most important thing in her life and she didn't want to imagine what her life would be like after he was gone.

He watched her until she totally disappeared from sight before he reached into his back pocket and withdrew a bundle of white cloth. Shaking it out, he rubbed the soft fabric against his cheek and inhaled the rich perfume of a woman's arousal before placing it back in his pocket. It was a way of keeping her close even when she wasn't here, and he rationalized, she wouldn't miss one pair of panties.

Chapter Thirteen

Erin cautiously opened Abel's back door the next morning, holding her breath as it creaked slightly. Last night had dragged on forever as she'd wanted desperately to spend it with Abel. Instead, she'd sat through supper with her brothers enduring their banter and small talk about work, crops, and town gossip. Nathan had watched her constantly. She'd wondered if he'd suspected something when he'd casually asked her if she'd talked to Carly.

She'd managed to talk to her, but it had been brief as Carly had worked a double shift yesterday when one of her waitresses had called in sick. Her friend had sounded tired but excited. Erin figured if they didn't talk soon, Carly would show up at the house and drag her upstairs until she spilled her guts about everything. She might be small, but she was tough. Erin grinned as she imagined Carly grilling her about her "mystery" date.

Finally, she eased Abel's back door open and let herself inside. She didn't want to wake him if he was still asleep. In fact, she was hoping he was still sleeping so she could hop in bed and surprise him.

Instead, she found him already sitting at the kitchen table, slumped over a cup of coffee. "Well, darn. I was hoping to surprise you." She walked to the counter, grabbed a mug, and poured herself a cup of coffee from the mostly full pot.

There was silence behind her. No teasing reply or quick comeback. Only silence. Concerned, she turned back towards the table. He hadn't moved a muscle. Leaving the coffee on the counter, she hurried over to the table to his side. "Abel?" Her voice shook slightly. His unnatural silence was beginning to scare her.

When he raised his head, she was appalled at the stark look of despair in his bloodshot eyes. His clothing was rumpled and his face unshaven, suggesting that he hadn't slept at all last night. Tortured was the word that popped into her head. He looked like a man trapped in absolute anguish, and it was this look that had her wrapping her arms around him and hugging his face to her chest. "Whatever is wrong, I'll help you through it."

The sound of her voice seemed to penetrate his misery. "Erin?" Like a man coming out of a trance, he tugged her into his arms and gripped her so tight she could barely breathe. His desperation was a living, breathing thing. Every muscle in his body was tense and she could see the strain on his unnaturally pale face.

"Should I call Jackson or Nathan?" She didn't have any idea what could have upset him like this, but she was ready and willing to mobilize everyone she knew to help him. She started to ease out of his arms so she could use the phone.

"No," his voice was raw. "Stay."

Erin cupped his face in her hands. "I won't leave you, but tell me what has happened."

He shook his head and looked away. Determinedly, she brought his face back around so he was forced to look at her. "You're scaring me, Abel. If you can't talk to me, will you talk to Jackson or Nathan?"

Abel opened his mouth and closed it. He swallowed hard and tried again. "Mom and Dad," he began.

"What about them? Was it something you found in their papers?" She couldn't begin to imagine what he could have found that would have upset him so. All those papers were at least fourteen years old or more.

"They're not my parents."

"What?" Erin couldn't believe what she was hearing. "You're adopted?" She could understand why that would shock him. But he was more than just shocked, whatever he'd discovered had wounded him deeply.

His laugh was harsh and angry. "Adopted. I wish." He rubbed one of his hands over his face and sighed. "I was purchased for cash from another couple."

Erin was too stunned to speak for a moment. "Isn't that illegal?"

"Yeah."

Abel closed his eyes and tipped his head back. She could see he was fighting down the emotions that welled up inside him. "How did you find out?" If she could pull together all the details, then maybe she could help him work through this.

"I found the bill of sale. Look for yourself." He leaned forward and plucked a piece of paper off the table and handed it to her.

Erin glanced nervously at the document, but she was determined to read it. Perhaps Abel had misunderstood what he'd read. Even as she had that thought, she was discarding it. Abel was a top-notch investigative writer, and he would have checked and double-checked his facts before believing them.

Her hand was shaky as she took the seemingly innocent sheet of yellowed paper from him. Amazing to think such a simple thing could cause such huge problems. Scanning it quickly, she noted the sum of ten thousand dollars was paid to a Mr. and Mrs. Benjamin for the adoption of their son, Abel.

"I don't believe this." She felt her anger rising. Erin had loved Abel's parents, but especially his mother, Sarah, who had taught her so much. If she felt their betrayal so deeply, she figured it must cut Abel right to the very marrow of his bones. "I'm so sorry, Abel."

A part of her still wanted to believe that this was all just some kind of horrible mistake. "You're sure there's no mistake?"

"None." He gestured to the journal sitting on the table. "I read it in her diary after I found the papers. Part of it was around the same time they got me. Same dates. Everything matches…"

"Tell me," she encouraged as his voice trailed off and he started to stare absently off into space.

Gathering himself for a moment, he launched into his tale. "Apparently, she miscarried when they were traveling through Illinois on a holiday. She ended up in the same hospital as the Benjamin family. Mom was despondent and the Benjamins were poor and couldn't afford two children, so they sold their youngest one. Both couples went home with a child and everyone lived happily ever after."

Bitterness filled his voice, but Erin focused on the most appalling part. "What do you mean they couldn't afford two children?"

Abel continued to stare at the table, so she grabbed him by the front of his shirt and shook him. He barely budged and was hardly even startled by her physical outburst. "Tell me!" she yelled.

"I have a twin brother." His voice broke on the last word and he buried his face in his hands. "All these years I've been alone and I have a brother. How could they do that?" He swiped at his eyes and looked at her as if she had the answers for him. "How could they not tell me?"

"Oh, sweetheart, I don't know." Wrapping her arms around him, she rocked him gently, trying to soothe some of the pain in his heart. Betrayed by those who supposedly loved him best. Desperately, she tried to find something to help him. "Perhaps they meant to tell you on your eighteenth birthday, but never got the chance. They were killed just two weeks before. Remember?"

"You really think so?" Like a drowning man, he grabbed onto the lifeline she threw him.

"I do." She nodded emphatically. "I might not approve of what they did, but your parents loved you more than anything. Like most of us, they probably figured they had all kinds of time to tell you. And besides, they probably knew you'd want to find your brother right away, but until you were both of legal age, it's possible his parents could have kept you apart."

Abel nodded, more thoughtful now. "I didn't finish reading everything, but I got the feeling that the Benjamins were at their local hospital that night. They probably lived close by." She could see the wheels beginning to turn in his head. Now that he had something concrete to focus on, it seemed to give him new strength.

"I'll bet you can find them in no time."

"I don't give a damn about them." His voice was harsh and condemning. "But I want to find my brother. Even if nothing ever comes of it, I want to meet him face-to-face."

Abel buried his face in her neck and hugged her tight. "I'll do whatever I can to help you," she reassured him. He was such a strong, independent man so all she could do was offer her assistance and hope that he took whatever he needed.

"Thank you." His voice was muffled against her neck, and a moment later, she felt his lips nibbling the sensitive skin behind her ear.

She could feel his cock pressing against her side and knew that he was channeling all his emotion into sexual energy. Sex was something he could deal with and it would help him vent some of his frustrations. She sensed he was holding back until she gave him the okay, and her heart melted. This was the man she loved and she would gladly give him anything. Right now, he needed the mindless release of wild, hot sex and she was more than willing provide him with just that.

Slipping from his arms, she stood next to the chair and held out her hand. "Let's go upstairs."

"You're sure?"

She smiled at him and gently tugged him to his feet. "Very sure."

"I don't know if I can be gentle right now." She didn't know if he was trying to warn her or himself.

"Be gentle later then," she told him. "I can wait."

Swooping down like a marauding Viking, he scooped her up into his steely arms and carried her towards the stairs. His mouth came down on hers hard and desperate. Their tongues met in a frantic duel and Erin sensed he was near the breaking point. Kneading her hands against his chest, she met his tongue stroke for stroke.

Abel stopped on the landing halfway up the stairs and shifted her so that her legs were on either side of his waist. Pushing her back against the wall, he jammed her there and yanked at her shirt. He released her mouth long enough to tear the shirt over her head, and then ground his lips against hers once again. Erin gripped his sides with her knees for support, trying to give herself more stability. The move pushed her pelvis right against his erection, causing her to moan with pleasure.

Abel pushed her legs downward, ripped her shorts open, and tore them and her underwear off in one motion. Before she could even comprehend what he'd done, she was back in his arms. His desperation was fueling her own growing arousal and she was quickly becoming as frantic as he was. Her hands tugged at Abel's shirt, pushing her hands beneath it so she could touch his warm flesh. Leaning forward, she licked and sucked at the throbbing pulse at the base of his neck.

His fingers groped between her legs as she hung in the air with her back against the wall and her legs locked around his waist. He sucked in a deep breath when he found her pussy already damp and willing. The moment his fingers stroked her slick folds, she arched her head back against the staircase wall and moaned. Her whole body burned for his touch.

Abel shoved her bra out of his way, covered one of her nipples with his mouth and suckled hard. "Yes," she hissed as she tugged him even closer.

Suddenly, he reached between their bodies and jerked open his own jeans. Shoving them and his underwear down far enough to release himself, he drove his hard, pulsing cock deep inside her.

Although she was ready and eager, the shock of his sudden entry made her cry out. She could feel his desperation as he drove himself into her. He felt large and thick inside her as he held her pinned against the wall, ramming his cock into her. With each thrust, she tried to relax her body until the uncomfortable feeling was gone and the pleasure began to grow. She clung to him, unable to do anything, but allowing him to take whatever he needed from her.

She could feel her own arousal growing as he gripped her behind in his hands and drove his cock deep. But Abel was already too far gone and, on the next stroke, he came deep inside her. Erin squeezed her inner muscles tight around him, giving him everything that she could. Finally, he stopped pumping into her and slowly slid to the floor with her still gripped tight in his arms.

Partially lying on the landing and partially sprawled on the stairs, they remained locked in each other's arms. Erin was uncomfortable as she was partially crushed beneath his much larger frame, but she didn't move. Abel needed the comfort of her body at the moment, and she offered it to him without hesitation or restriction. After a long moment, he stirred in her arms.

He shook his head as if trying to regain his muddled senses. Erin was unable to stifle a groan when he shifted one of his legs. His laser green gaze pinned her to the spot where she lay flat on her back against the hard floor, with her legs trailing down over the stairs. Shrugging her shoulders, she gave him a tentative smile. "Sorry, but the position is a little awkward."

Abel swore and pulled away from her. She lay on the landing in front of him in a tangled mass of clothing. Too tired and worn out to move, she promised herself she'd only rest for a moment and then she'd get up.

Abel stared down at Erin and felt bile rising in his throat. He'd fucked her like some mad animal in heat with no regard for her pleasure whatsoever. While he was still completely dressed, she lay almost totally naked beside him, except for her bra, which was twisted, around her chest.

Her hair was a tangled mess, her face pale, and her eyes closed. He didn't blame her. He didn't think that he'd be able to look at himself either. God, he'd all but raped her against the damn wall. Shaking his head to try and regain his senses, he realized that she hadn't been ready when he'd plunged into her. Her pussy had been slick, but nowhere near ready for what he'd demanded of her.

All she'd wanted to do was help him, and he'd hurt her. Swallowing hard, he pushed his anger and loathing at himself to one side. Right now, all that was important was Erin. Somehow, he had to make things right with her. He couldn't bear to lose her from his life.

It came to him then, as clear as crystal, that he loved her. It was a fine time to realize that after he'd mindlessly fucked her. If she could manage it, she'd probably run from him. He almost dreaded for her to open her beautiful blue eyes. Abel didn't think he could endure it if she looked at him with either fear or loathing.

He staggered to his feet, tugged his shirt down, and hitched his jeans back up over his hips. Bending down, he carefully eased his arms under Erin and lifted her into his arms. She felt slight and delicate in his massive arms. As he climbed the rest of the stairs, she said nothing, but snuggled closer to him.

Sighing in relief, he carried her into the bedroom, and although he didn't want to relinquish her, he forced himself to place her on the bed. He left her for a moment to go to the bathroom and wring out a soft washcloth with warm water. The least he could do was try and make her more comfortable.

Sitting beside her on the bed, he gently eased her legs apart and pressed the cloth against her abused flesh. Her eyes fluttered open and she stared at him.

"I'm sorry," he began.

A look of concern crossed her face. "What for?" She seemed confused.

"I took you like a damned rutting animal." There, he had said it and it was now out in the open between them. "Forgive me?"

Erin reached out her hand and placed it again his cheek. Her soft skin felt good against his face and it helped soothe his anger at himself. "There's nothing to forgive." She gave him a perplexed look. "You didn't take anything I didn't give you."

His heart pounded heavily against his chest. The more time he spent with this woman, the more his love and admiration for her grew. She gave so freely of herself and not just physically, but emotionally as well. He could tell by the way she was looking at him, that she really meant it when she said there was nothing to forgive.

She might feel that way, but he knew that he had a lot to make up for, and if she wasn't too sore, he was determined to begin right now. "How do you feel?"

Stretching like a cat, she moved her arms and legs. "I feel good." At the skeptical look on his face, she tried to reassure him. "Really, I do."

By some miracle, Erin wasn't upset by what had just happened. Perhaps she was still too stunned by what had transpired to think clearly about the whole thing. Now was the time to consolidate his position before she had a chance to change her mind. Her bra was still pushed up over her breasts, so he unhooked it and slipped it off her, hoping to make her more comfortable.

Her skin was flushed, as she lay sprawled across the crisp white sheets. She looked so damned good, he just wanted to eat her up. Her red hair was spread across his pillows and the lush pubic hair between her legs left no room for doubt that Erin was a natural redhead. He sifted his fingers through the curls, loving the way they wrapped around his fingers as if trying to trap them there. The lush color looked even brighter against his dark skin.

Plucking up a pillow, he guided it beneath her hips. She watched him intently but never once moved to stop him. Pushing himself off the mattress, he stood beside the bed and started to strip off his own clothes. Yanking his t-shirt over his head, he dropped it to the floor beside him before shoving his jeans down over his legs. Bending down, he tugged his jeans and socks off and kicked them away.

He knelt on the bed and positioned himself between her legs. Wrapping his hands around her knees, he then slid them upwards over her silky skin, spreading her thighs wide as he went. Leaning forward, he kissed the inside of her knee before leaving a string of kisses up her long, pale thigh.

When he reached the top of her thigh, he traced the crease with his tongue before performing the same delicate ritual to the other thigh. Erin gave a startled laugh and then groaned. "Ticklish, are you?" He gave her a wicked grin.

She reached down and swatted at his hand. "I won't be responsible if I accidentally kick you," she warned.

"I'll take my chances." Abel wanted to make this good for her. No, he needed to make it great for her. He wanted her to remember only pleasure when she thought back to this day and not the harsh way he'd taken her on the stairs.

Gently, he skimmed the juicy pink folds of her labia. She shuddered and her thighs opened even further. Pleased, he stroked her until he could feel her arousal growing once again. Using one hand to open her wide, he gently teased her clit until Erin was moaning and arching her hips.

"I've got to taste you." Unable to resist, he bent his head and took a deep breath, inhaling the musky scent of her arousal. "God, you smell hot." His tongue lapped at the folds of her vulva, tasting her exotic flavor.

Erin got tired of waiting and grabbed him by the hair, tugging him to where she wanted him. Abel allowed himself to be pulled higher until his mouth was over the nub of her arousal. Taking his time, he blew gently on her, loving the sound of her voice as she cried out. His tongue flicked out to stroke her clit. Back and forth and round and round he went. Erin's hips were pumping higher now, her heels digging into the mattress.

He drew the nub into his mouth and sucked as he slipped one of his fingers inside her wet channel. The feeling of her moist pussy closing around his finger made his already growing cock stand completely at attention. Closing his eyes, he sought some small measure of control. He had to have her again. His cock was as hard as stone again and throbbing for release. But, this time, she had to come first.

Easing another finger inside her, he stroked in and out, pressing on the front of her vagina as he did so. Keeping her clit captive between his teeth, he flicked his tongue over the hot button as he moved his fingers deliberately within her.

Her head thrashed from side to side, and she cried out as if in pain. She was so close. He could feel her orgasm rising within her as she mindlessly arched her hips against his hand. Abel worked his fingers in and out of her pussy, moving them faster and driving them deeper.

Erin let go a long, thin scream as she came long and hard. Her thighs clamped tight around his head and he could feel her body pulsing around his fingers. His cock pulsed in time with her inner muscles and he pushed himself hard against the mattress to try and ease some of the painful pressure.

They rode out the storm together and when it was over, Erin's thighs relaxed once again and dropped open. Her hands fell to the sheets beside her, and her body sank deep into the mattress. Abel sat back on his heels and just stared at her. She was the most erotic creature he had ever seen. The way she responded to him was amazing. A man could certainly become addicted to this.

His own arousal was clamoring at him as she opened her eyes and smiled at him. It was a sleepy, sultry smile that made his cock twitch violently. Abel clenched his teeth and swore under his breath, but Erin smiled her sultry, siren's smile and held her arms open. "I need you," was all she said, but it was everything to him.

Picking up her feet, he placed one against either shoulder. She looked startled for a moment and then, slowly but surely, intrigued. Abel needed to give her a sense of control this time because he didn't know if she was sore from earlier. He wanted this to be about mutual pleasure. Wrapping his hands over her waist, he bent forward and eased his cock inside her. Her wet warmth welcomed him immediately and he shuddered as he forged his way inside. Her inner muscles were still swollen, but she was so wet he was able to seat himself to the hilt with no problem.

For a moment, he just sat there, content to be inside her. Her breasts heaved as her breathing deepened, and he enjoyed the way they moved. Her nipples were large and red, and he reached up and ran his thumb across one of the taut peaks.

"Abel." Her voice was low, husky, and pleading. He felt himself swell even larger within her.

"Tell me what you want." He continued to feather her nipple with his thumb.

"I want you hard and so deep that I'll never forget what it's like to have you inside me." Her eyes blazed with passion as she spoke.

Abel was aroused but slightly angered by her words. Jealousy rose within him at the thought of her forgetting him, or worse, having another man inside her. Gripping her waist once again with both hands, he pulled back and plunged deep within her. "You're mine now and you damn well won't ever forget me."

He withdrew again and drove himself hard against her again. "I'll fuck you until you can't remember how it ever was without me." He meant his words as both a threat and a promise. No matter what it took, he decided, he would find a way to bind Erin to him. "You'll want me whenever you're not with me."

He thrust harder and faster. "You're mine." He could feel his testicles pulling tight against his body and knew he was close to release. Wrapping one arm tight around her, he moved the other one between their bodies and stroked her clit. He needed her to come with him, but more than that, he needed her to give herself to him totally. "You're mine," he told her again.

"Yes, I'm yours." The softly spoken words sent him over the edge and he came hard. He continued to stroke inside her, not wanting to let go of the intense feeling of release. She came a moment later, her body shuddering and shaking against his. Abel closed his eyes and threw back his head as the powerful wave washed over his entire body. It had never been this good before.

When he finally came back to his senses, he was slumped forward, half on top of Erin. Her legs were bent back towards her head, keeping him from crushing her. Easing himself back and out of her, he straightened her legs before collapsing next to her.

Wrapping her in his arms, he tucked her against his body until her ass was tight against his dick and her head was tucked under his chin. Tired mentally and physically, he released the tension of the morning and allowed himself to drift off to sleep.

Chapter Fourteen

Erin wanted to sleep. She felt tired and slightly battered from their intense lovemaking, but was unable to stop thinking about the situation with Abel. It was impossible to imagine the shock and turmoil that he must be experiencing right now. Even she was shocked by the secrets his parents had kept. They had been such a normal family and such doting parents, it was beyond belief to think that they had kept the fact that Abel was adopted from him for all those years.

On one hand, she could understand them wanting to keep his adoption from him, considering it wasn't a legal one. Indeed, it was more of a sale than an adoption. But on the other hand, Abel had the right to know that he had a not just a brother, but a twin.

Even as a child, Abel had seemed lost sometimes, as if he was looking for some part of himself. She even remembered one occasion when Abel had been playing with Nathan and Jackson, and he'd suddenly grabbed his back and yelled. Abel had fallen to the ground, rolling around and screaming in agony. Erin remembered the incident vividly because it had scared her to death. His parents had seemed worried, but when the doctor had reassured them that nothing was wrong, they had passed it off as psychosomatic. Now Erin wondered if it might have something to do with this unknown twin of his.

So many questions and no answers. Knowing she wouldn't sleep, Erin carefully eased her body from Abel's grasp. It wasn't easy, as he seemed disinclined to let go of her. His arms started to pull her back so she quickly stuffed a pillow in his arms in her place. He frowned in his sleep, and she held her breath, fearing he might wake, but he moved around for a moment before settling back to sleep. When his breathing evened out again, she scooted from the bed.

Her body ached all over, but it was no wonder considering the wild sex they'd had. Sensing that Abel had needed the physical release in order to cope with the mental turmoil within him, she was just glad that she'd been able to give him some peace from his torment. Looking down on him, she fought the urge to crawl right back in bed with him.

Plucking up her bra from where it was hanging off the corner of the bed, she went in search for the rest of her clothing. She shook her head in disbelief as she picked up her shorts and panties on the stair landing and her shirt almost at the bottom. Shaking the wrinkles out of her shirt, she draped it over her shoulder and went back upstairs to take a quick bath. The hot water would ease her sore muscles and give her time to think. There had to be some way she could help Abel find his brother, even if it was only moral support.

All while she soaked in the hot tub of water, and even now when she was fully dressed and back in the kitchen, Erin's mind remained on Abel. She knew that finding his brother meant that he would be leaving once again. The thought almost brought her to her knees with despair, but her love for him was bigger than that.

Right now, he would need to find this unknown brother and reconcile his parents' behavior in his own mind. She loved him enough not only to support him while he did this, but also to let him go in order to do it. That's what real love was all about. Erin could only hope that when he was through with his quest that he might find his way back home to her.

Erin started a pot of coffee and then rummaged through the cupboards for something to eat. She was starving and knew that Abel would be too when he finally woke up. A foray into the fridge uncovered a variety of cold cuts, cheese, lettuce, and tomatoes. Humming while she worked, she made a large stack of sandwiches, putting some on a plate for herself and wrapping up the rest for Abel for later. Pouring herself a cup of coffee, she pulled out a chair at the table and devoured one sandwich.

The documents on the table taunted her as she ate, so when she started to nibble on her second sandwich, she pulled them over in front of her. Wiping her hands in her shorts, she took her time and studied each one carefully. It was all laid out in black and white. The stark reality of his so-called adoption and the fact that he was one of a twin. Even though she was reading it, Erin could still hardly believe it was the truth.

The clock measured the passage of time as the morning disappeared. Erin was engrossed in the diary that Abel's mother had left. There was no doubting the love she had for her son, but there was also the underlying fear that Abel would find out someday and hate her for what they had done. Sighing, she closed the book and set it aside. There really was no new information to be gained from reading anymore. The hospital in Illinois was the key to finding the Benjamin family. They would have records of the birth of the twin boys.

"Did you find anything useful?" Erin turned in her chair, glancing guiltily at the journal she'd just finished. She knew she didn't really have the right to read it, except that she loved Abel.

Tilting her chin defiantly, she met his gaze. "No. The key is obviously the hospital records, but you already knew that."

"Yeah." He sauntered across the kitchen, his bare feet making no sound on the hardwood floor. "I missed you." Bending down, he kissed the top of her head.

Erin closed her eyes and sighed in relief. He didn't seem mad at her that she'd read his private documents. She felt slightly bereft when he moved away and headed to the counter.

"I could use a cup of coffee." Pulling down a mug, he poured himself some of the bitter brew. Leaning against the counter, he sipped it slowly.

He hadn't bothered to get fully dressed and had just pulled on his jeans. They were zipped but they weren't buttoned and Erin could see the dark line of hair disappearing down into his jeans. She didn't think he was wearing any underwear, but she couldn't tell for sure. Just the thought was enough to make her skin flush.

Jumping out of her seat, she hurried to the refrigerator. "I made sandwiches." Grabbing out the plate, she laid it on the table and unwrapped it.

"Thanks. I'm starved." Carrying his coffee to the table, he pulled out the chair next to her, and sat down. Hauling the plate over in front of him, he wolfed down two sandwiches before he stopped to take another mouthful of coffee.

"I already sent out a request to the administrator of the hospital." Abel turned the coffee mug in his hands, absently watching the remaining coffee swirl about.

Erin swallowed hard. "Already?" She knew that Abel would investigate quickly, but she'd thought she'd have a little more time.

"Yeah. I didn't want to talk myself out of it or waste any more time. I implied that I might implicate them in an illegal adoption case if they didn't give me the information."

"No hospital wants that kind of publicity." Erin knew that Abel would have answers sooner than later. She just hoped he was ready for the answers he got.

Abel was a massive man with great strength, but his physical prowess was no help to him now. His mind was his greatest asset, and he used it like the well-honed machine that it was. Erin had no doubts that he would have found his brother within a matter of days. He had always been a self-contained loner, dealing with the world on his own. But sitting there at the table with his hands clenched around his coffee mug and the furrow of worry between his brow, he needed her strength right now. She could offer him her moral support and also her body for him to lose his worries in. Both were given freely.

Scooting back her chair, she came around the table and stood next to him. He pulled her into his lap, as she'd known he would. Taking advantage of the situation, she wrapped her arms around his broad shoulders and gave him a hug. "How about you check your e-mail and then come on over to the house for the rest of the day?" When he looked uncertain, she brought out the big guns. "I'll make you an apple pie and cook you supper. It will give you an opportunity to tell Jackson and Nathan if you want to. Nathan might be able to give you some help if you need it."

Abel hesitated for a second before nodding slowly. "Okay. Supper is good, but I've got to think about what I want to tell your brothers."

"Fair enough." She slipped from his lap and held out her hand. "Let's check your mail and then you can come help me out in the fields for an hour or so before we head over to my place for supper."

"I have to work for my supper, is that it?" His smile was halfhearted, but Erin was more than glad to see it.

"That's right, buster." Placing her hands on her hips she gave him a mock scowl.

Slinging his arm around her shoulder, he guided her towards the office. "You drive a hard bargain, but I'm up to the challenge."

Erin leaned into him and stayed by his side as he turned on his computer. Holding her breath, she watched as his mail came in.

* * * * *

Looking up from the counter where she was placing the finishing touches on a large pan of lasagna, Erin watched Abel. He seemed engrossed in his conversation with Jackson and Nathan as he told them about his being adopted. She noticed that he gave them the basic facts only and kept most of the details quiet.

Both her brothers had been surprised to see Abel at the house when they got home from work, but both were quick with support when they discovered what had happened. Both had listened intently and Nathan had promised to do whatever he could to help. Jackson had been his usual solid self, offering Abel his support in whatever way he could. That had come as no surprise to Erin, but she was still pleased by her brothers' offers of help.

Nathan had been quieter than usual and had causally mentioned that Carly was coming over for dessert. Usually Erin wouldn't have given it a second thought, but she hadn't talked to her friend in almost two days now. Something was definitely up, but she figured she'd find out what it was soon enough.

For now, all her attention was focused entirely on Abel. She longed to be able to walk up behind him and slip her arms around his neck and kiss him. Keeping their relationship a secret was beginning to wear on her nerves more than she'd thought it would. She had to satisfy herself with short glances every time her brothers were looking in another direction.

By the time they finished eating supper, Erin's patience was near the breaking point. She could tell that talking about his adoption had been hard on him, and all she wanted to do was sit on his lap and wipe the look of frustration and anger from his face. Sex was exactly what he needed. Mind-blowing, hot, sweaty sex. That would certainly take his mind off his troubles and put him in a better frame of mind.

As she cleared away the dishes and poured the coffee, she plotted how she planned to sneak out of the house tonight. No way was she going to let Abel be alone right now. A bang on the door startled her, and she jerked her hand, spilling some of the coffee from the pot.

"Damn," she swore as she replaced the pot and began mopping up the coffee spill.

Abel jumped from the table and hurried over to the counter while Nathan went to answer the back door. "Did you burn yourself?" He cradled her hand in his and bent his head over it, checking for redness.

"No." Her voice caught on a sob as she lied. The coffee had missed her, but she had indeed been burned by their relationship. Scorched was more like it, and her heart would be left in embers when he left her. "I'm fine," she croaked.

"Are you sure?" His eyes were soft with concern, but when he looked at her the passion flared and sizzled between them. Erin felt the moisture pool between her legs as her body made her well aware how much she wanted him.

"Hi everyone." Carly's cheerful voice broke the spell. Giving herself a mental shake, Erin carried filled coffee cups to the table and handed them to Carly and Nathan. Abel followed quietly behind her, carrying two more.

"Hey," Erin said as she returned to the counter to slice the apple pie. She could hear everyone talking behind her, but she wasn't really listening to the conversation. It was taking all her concentration to make her heart stop pounding. Right now, all she could think about was grabbing Abel by the hand and dragging him off to the nearest bedroom where they could be alone.

Erin served up huge slabs of pie and gave everyone a piece before returning to sit at the table. She sipped her own coffee and tried to catch Carly's attention with her eyes, but the other woman was openly staring at Nathan. The look in her friend's eyes was one she recognized only because she'd seen it so often lately on her own every time she happened to glance in a mirror. Carly was obviously lusting after Nathan. And why not? They were both young and healthy.

Nathan surprised everyone when he plucked Carly right out of her chair, plunked her in his lap, and proceeded to kiss her soundly in front of them all. Like a man who had discovered water in the desert, he drank from her mouth. Erin couldn't take her eyes off of them. Any minute now, she expected to see smoke coming out of their ears. She fanned her face with her hand, feeling slightly jealous of their obvious passion for one another. Then she felt mean and petty for begrudging them their obvious happiness.

"Enough." Jackson's roar made them all jump. "Just what in the hell is going on?" Resting his large hands on the table, he glared at his younger brother who ignored him. "For God's sake, Nathan, show a little respect for the woman." Jackson shook his head, obviously exasperated with his brother.

Nathan took his time, planting one last kiss on Carly before easing away from her. Carly had a dreamy look on her face and snuggled contentedly in his arms. Grinning like a fool, he wrapped his arms tighter around the woman in his arms before making his announcement. "Carly has agreed to marry me."

"What!" Erin jumped out of her seat. "When? How? I mean, I didn't think you guys had even had a date." She was totally confused.

"It happened Wednesday night." Nathan stared pointedly at her as he spoke, and Erin sank back into her seat again.

She fought the temptation to bury her face in her hands and hide. Nathan knew that she hadn't been at Carly's that night. She risked a quick look at Abel and noted that his jaw was clenched tight. Oh lord, it was obvious to her that Nathan had already talked to Abel about it. Why hadn't he mentioned anything about it to her? She scowled at Abel, letting him see her displeasure, and not caring who saw.

"Congratulations." Jackson reached across the table and offered his hand to his brother. "I'll kiss the bride-to-be later," he teased.

"Over my dead body," Nathan retorted.

"Erin?" Carly's soft questioning voice brought her back around. Her friend was giving her a pleading look from across the table, and Erin realized that she was frowning.

The reality of the moment washed over her. Her brother was marrying her very best friend. Squealing, she jumped from her chair and raced around the table, plucking Carly out of Nathan's lap.

"Hey!" he protested. Both women ignored him. They were much too busy jumping up and down and hugging each other.

"This is fantastic." Erin swiped at the tears in her eyes and laughed as her friend did the same.

"I promised myself I wouldn't cry." Carly wiped her face with the back of her hand and laughed when Nathan hauled her back into his lap and dried her cheeks with the tail of his shirt.

"Congratulations to you both." Abel offered up his own best wishes and then sat back and allowed the conversation to flow around him.

Erin was torn. She was so happy about Carly and Nathan's news, but right now it was hard to enjoy it, knowing just what was on Abel's mind at the moment. The evening passed quickly and, before long, Nathan was excusing himself and Carly. When he announced his plans to follow her home in his truck, Erin knew that her brother wouldn't be home until late.

All the better for her. Nathan was the one with the good ears and would be sure to hear her when she tried to sneak out of the house to be with Abel. Not that she cared about being caught any longer. He certainly couldn't say anything about where she was spending her nights considering where he was spending his.

Abel left soon after, but she didn't get a chance to tell him she would be over later. Jackson had taken it upon himself to walk Abel out so that they could have a chance to talk to one another. She heard Abel's truck pulling away about twenty minutes later. Sighing, she finished cleaning up the kitchen and headed upstairs. Jackson wouldn't settle down for hours yet. It was going to be a long night.

Chapter Fifteen

"I was hoping you'd come." Abel's low whisper broke the silence of the night. There was a rustle of movement just before the bedside lamp clicked on, temporarily blinding her with its light.

Blinking to adjust her vision, she kicked off her sneakers as she walked into the room. "I didn't get a chance to talk to you before you left. Then I had to wait for Jackson to fall asleep." Erin pulled her t-shirt over her head and tossed it over the chair in the corner.

Abel scowled. "I'm sick of this sneaking around. Either you want to be with me or you don't." Stretched out on the bed with only a thin sheet covering him, his arousal was just as evident as his bad temper.

"You know I want to be with you." Her heart was pounding in her chest, but she retained her composure and continued to undress. She shucked her jeans and socks, and strolled to the side of the bed, clad only in her white cotton bra and panties.

Abel shrugged his massive shoulder and stacked his hands under his head, watching her with an inscrutable gaze. His jaw was tight and his eyes were narrowed as he watched her undress. There was no encouragement or gentle humor in his voice, and certainly nothing lover-like in his actions. Erin almost lost her nerve, grabbed her clothes and ran from the room because this was beginning to feel very much like the beginning of the end.

Stripping off the rest of her clothing in the face of his cold demeanor was one of the hardest things she'd ever done. Only the memories of the magical week they'd just spent together enabled her to get through it. Reaching behind, she unhooked her bra and tugged it off. She hooked her fingers in the waistband of her panties, but hesitated.

"Don't stop now." His voice was slightly mocking. "You came for the sex, you might as well have it." Flipping back the sheet he exposed his fully erect penis. "After all, it would be a shame for this to go to waste."

Erin struggled against her conflicting emotions. Something deep inside her recoiled at his harsh, cold words, while another part of her was instantly aroused by the sight of his naked body, obviously ready and waiting for her. "Why are you acting like this?" she asked, fighting the impulse to cover her naked breasts with her hands.

"Like what?" he countered. "I feel like nothing more than a stud service, but if that's what you want then have at it."

Erin licked her dry lips as she stared at him. His legs and arms were thick and strong. Muscles rippled with every movement he made. His shoulders were wide and his chest was covered in a light dusting of hair that tapered down to his groin. There was no doubt that he was an extremely fine specimen of manhood, especially with his hard cock jutting out in front of him. But there was more to him than that. Much more.

Abel was a man of principles and lived by his own code of ethics and honor. And right now, she knew that he felt that he was dishonoring them by sneaking around with her. It was worse now that Carly and Nathan had announced their relationship at suppertime. His anger was probably much deeper now because of his own betrayal by his parents.

Right now, he was every inch the wounded beast. Wounded by the deceitful revelation about his family and by the secret she was forcing him to keep. It was up to her to try and soothe his anger at himself and the world.

Determined now, she pushed her underwear off and stood naked in front of him. He just cocked an eyebrow at her, but said nothing. Slowly, she knelt on the bed by his feet.

"What are you waiting for? Suck it or fuck it, I really don't care which." Abel didn't move, but every muscle in his body appeared tense as he waited to see what she would do.

Erin felt her own temper rising along with her arousal. If he didn't care, then she'd do both and please herself. Crawling between his legs, she pushed them apart until she was comfortable. Reaching out her hand, she traced the vein on the top of his penis with her finger. It jerked underneath her touch, but Abel didn't move, didn't speak.

With her other hand, she gently cupped his testicles and rolled them between her fingers. She felt Abel stiffen and smiled to herself. Moving her fingers, she rubbed the underside of his sac where it attached to his body. This time Abel couldn't contain the moan of pleasure that broke from him.

Pleased with herself, she continued to manipulate his testicles as she wrapped her other hand around the top of his cock and began to pump her hand up and down. Using her thumb, she rubbed and pressed it against the bulbous head. When a pearly white drop seeped out of the tip, she used her thumb to spread it over the head.

Bending forward, she nuzzled his heavy sac with her nose, loving his musky scent. She sucked the sacs with her mouth and tongue while continuing to pleasure it with her fingers. Abel's hand shot out and tangled in her hair, holding her in place.

Erin laughed and licked her way up the sides of his penis and then swirled her tongue over the tip. His entire body jerked, and he thrust his hips towards her. Smiling, she took him into her mouth. Slowly, she swallowed him whole, until she had taken as much as she could. Using her tongue and teeth, she teased the sensitive flesh of his cock.

Abel's fingers tightened around her skull, and he used his grip to hold her head in place as he flexed his hips up and down. His cock slid almost out of her mouth, hovering at her lips for a moment, before forging its way back in again. Since Abel was controlling the rhythm, Erin wrapped her hand tight around the base and continued to pump up and down. She could feel his testicles pulling tight to his body and she knew that he was getting close to coming, but she wasn't ready to let that happen yet.

Easing her head back, she allowed his cock to pop out of her mouth. Abel groaned and guided her mouth back to him. Shaking her head, she moved up over him, but he didn't release his grip on her hair. Erin was filled with the need to touch and taste him everywhere until there was no part of him left explored.

Her tongue and fingers traced every muscle of his torso. Her forefinger circled one of his brown male nipples before her tongue flicked out to lick it. His fingers flexed, easing the grip on her hair, until he was cupping her head in his hand, urging her closer to him. A low rumble came from deep within him as she continued her heated exploration.

Running a string of kisses up his neck, she finally brushed a light kiss on his lips. "I'm sorry." Her apology, though spoken in a husky, sensual voice, was heartfelt and deep.

"I know, but that doesn't change the fact that what we're doing is wrong." His green eyes were serious as he looked at her. "Nathan already knows, and I sure as hell don't want Jackson to find out by accident. I'm telling him tomorrow." His voice was implacable, his decision final.

"*We'll* tell him tomorrow." There was no way she was letting him face her brother alone.

Every muscle in Abel's body seemed to relax as he sighed deeply and sank back onto the pillows, and it was only then that she realized just how tense he had been. He smiled, and his eyes crinkled with delight. His entire demeanor changed in a heartbeat and Erin understood then just how wrong she'd been to make him lie about their relationship.

At first, it had seemed necessary to her to keep their affair a secret because it was just supposed to be a quick summer fling. What had started out as just fun had grown into something much deeper and richer. Her love for Abel was real, so what did it matter if other people knew about them. She wasn't ashamed of it, or him, and didn't want him thinking that for even a second. If he wanted their relationship public, then that was fine with her, and to hell with what her brothers thought. Consequences be damned.

His hands slipped from her head and skimmed down her back to cover her rump, bringing her back to the moment in a hurry. Grasping a cheek in each hand, he squeezed, his fingers molding her flesh.

"Now that that's out of the way, whatever shall we do?" His light teasing tones filled her with delight.

She pretended to ponder the situation for a moment. "We could get a good night's sleep."

Abel shook his head. "I don't think you're tired yet. I'll have to wear you out." Grasping her waist, he dragged her body upwards until her knees were on either side of his head and she was straddling his face. He pulled her down so that she could feel his hot breath on her pussy. The sensation made her shiver with delight.

"God, you're so beautiful." His voice was low and reverent as his tongue snaked out and wrapped around her clit.

Erin moaned and grabbed the headboard for support. Abel continued to lick and suck at her swollen folds. "I love eating your pussy." He smacked his lips. "So tasty."

Laughing and groaning at the same time, she rocked her hips against his face. Her breasts felt heavy and achy so she reached down and grabbed one of his hands and placed it on her breast. Abel murmured against her and the vibrations sent shivers though her entire body. His hand cupped her breast, rubbing his palm against the straining nub. Erin could feel her entire body tightening.

"I want you inside me." Grabbing his hand, she held it tight against her breast. "Take me inside you." Desperate now, she raised herself up on her knees so he couldn't quite reach her.

Abel lifted her back and pulled himself into a seated position with his back against the headboard. His thumbs skimmed her face as he feathered kisses down her cheek, across her lips, and down her neck. Outlining her ear with his tongue, he eased it inside and swirled it around. "Ride me," he whispered.

Shivers ran down her spine as he nipped at her earlobe, and she eagerly reached for him, guiding his engorged penis inside her. Her pussy wrapped around his cock like a tight-fitting glove. Sitting back, she squirmed around trying to get comfortable and drove him even deeper inside.

Abel laughed and groaned. "Go easy on me, honey."

Unable to resist, Erin wiggled around some more. Growling, Abel buried his face against her breasts and raised his knees so that she was surrounded by him. One of his fingers slipped between her legs and stroked her clit while his tongue lapped at her engorged nipples. Closing her eyes, she gasped for breath, almost dizzy with passion.

Erin felt wanton and eager. Her breasts were heavy and sensitive, and the light scratch of the day's growth of his beard heightened the sensations even more. Her entire body was buzzing with pleasure, and all her concentration was focused on coming. Her hips rotated in a slow sensual motion as she ground herself against him. Erin alternated that with a slight up and down motion, enjoying the solid feel of his thick cock as it slid up and down the inside of her snug channel.

"Come for me." Abel punctuated his command by gently nipping one of her nipples with his teeth.

Her eyes popped open, and she basked in the erotic picture he made, pleasuring her breasts. Her inner muscles clenched tight around his thick cock as he fucked her. His entire body was tense, ready to come any second. Erin wanted this moment to last forever, wanted him to always be this deep inside her.

Abel thrust hard, gripping her waist with his hands and pulling her down hard on his cock. For a moment she froze, and then her whole body shook as her climax washed over her. Clutching at his shoulders for support, she could feel her body tightening and relaxing around his as the pleasure pulsed through her. Crying out, she tightened her inner muscles wanting him to join her.

Growling, he thrust into her one final time, and she felt him let go then. Jerking and heaving, his entire body shook as he came deep inside her.

Erin slumped forward, snuggling against his chest. Abel raised his knees higher and wrapped his arms around her, unwilling to let her go. The long, tiring day caught up to her and she drifted off to sleep with him still locked deep inside her. She could feel him playing with her hair, his long fingers sifting through the tangled mass. Totally contented and relaxed, she drifted off to sleep. Her final thought as she drifted off was that she loved him.

Abel froze, unable to believe his ears. "What did you say?" His voice sounded hoarse to his own ears. Erin remained silent, so he tilted her head gently to look at her. He couldn't believe she would tease him like this.

But Erin was sound asleep, her mouth slightly parted as little puffs of breath caressed his skin. Had he really heard what he'd thought he had? He was sure that she'd whispered that she loved him. Or maybe, he was so tired himself, that he'd only imagined it, his fertile writer's mind creating the words he longed to hear from this beautiful woman curled in his embrace.

Although he wanted to shake her awake and demand that she repeat what she'd said, he sat there with her cradled in his arms knowing that he would never be able to let her go. No woman had ever fit him as well as she did. She seemed to understand his moods and not hold them against him. He'd been surly and angry when she'd arrived under cover of darkness, but Erin had managed to put him back in good humor within a matter of minutes. The woman was truly a wonder.

He'd expected more of an argument with her over making their relationship public, but instead of a fight, she had calmly agreed with him. He knew it wasn't because she particularly wanted to tell her brothers, but because she sensed that he needed to. Sexually, she pleased him in every way. She was totally open and giving when it came to their sex life, but he felt as if she was holding back a part of herself from him. But he was determined to have all of her, and he was patient enough to wait.

Carefully, he eased her onto her side and pulled out of her. She muttered in her sleep, but didn't wake. He'd been keeping her busy this last week and it seemed as if he'd finally worn her out. He was glad she was asleep and couldn't see the satisfied male smile that covered his face. The sight of her lush curves and long limbs had his cock stirring once again. Amazing. He hadn't gotten it up this fast or this quick since his teens.

But she needed some sleep. He consoled himself with the fact that he could always wake her later. Drawing the sheet up over her naked flesh, he draped it so that she was totally covered, her gorgeous form outlined against it. She sighed and snuggled into his pillow. Doing his best not to jiggle the bed, he rolled off the mattress and headed to the bathroom.

He was energized now and decided to work for a few hours. Some information had come in via e-mail earlier, and he had plans to do a little bit more digging tonight. It was amazing what information a man could dig up with a little bit of perseverance and a bit of charm. Call in a few favors that were owed him by certain people in privileged positions, and Abel was sure he'd had located his brother within a day or two, tops. He wasn't an award-winning investigative writer for nothing.

After a quick shower, he checked in on Erin before padding down the stairs to make a pot of coffee. She was curled on her side with her hands tucked under her chin, snoring softly. He'd have to tease her about that tomorrow.

While the coffee perked, he leaned against the countertop wondering how long it would take Erin to put together a wedding. There was no way that they could live together. Her brothers would kill him for defiling their baby sister, and rightly so. But, he wanted her by his side each day and in his bed every night, and he wasn't willing to wait much longer to make that happen. He could manage it for a couple of weeks. That would give him time to sort out this whole mess with his newly discovered brother. If he was truthful with himself, he wanted to tie Erin to him in every way possible. Dealing with all the big changes in his life would be much easier with her beside him.

Yeah, a couple of weeks sounded about right. Filling his mug with coffee, he carried it to the study where the computer was humming patiently in wait for him. Abel put his coffee on the desk and promptly forgot about it as he pulled up his chair to the screen and noted that he had several e-mails. Taking a deep breath, he clicked open the first one and started to read.

Chapter Sixteen

When Erin awoke she was alone. She knew it was still night, as the room was dark. The digital clock radio by the bed told her that it was just after three in the morning, but Abel was nowhere to be found. Crawling out of bed, Erin stretched as she went to Abel's closet and pulled out one of his soft, cotton shirts. Slipping it on, she rubbed her face against the material, and breathed in his unique scent that still clung to the fabric as she did up four of the buttons before going in search of him.

He wasn't in the bathroom, so she crept down the stairs. There was a light on in the study, so she headed in that direction. Her bare feet were silent on the hardwood floor, and she stood in the doorway to the study and observed as he worked in the glow of his computer screen. His entire concentration was focused on whatever he was reading. She propped herself up against the doorframe and waited. Five minutes later, he sat back with a satisfied smile on his face. As if sensing her presence, he turned to her and his smile deepened.

He beckoned her in with a wave of his hand. "How long have you been standing there?"

She pushed away from the doorframe and ambled across the room towards his open arms. "Only a couple minutes." He tugged her into his lap and she went easily, relaxing against his chest. "I woke up and you were gone."

"Miss me?" he teased.

"Yes." She was in no mood to play games. "I'm getting used to having you sleep next to me."

"Good." He brushed a lock of hair back from her sleepy face and kissed her lips softly.

"Mmm," she moaned and opened her mouth to admit him. The kiss was long and leisurely and Erin gave herself over to the rising passion. Abel slipped one of his hands inside her shirt to fondle her breast as he continued to plunder her mouth. She was breathless when he finally pulled away. "Let's go back to bed." Slipping out of his arms, she stood beside the desk and waited for him to join her.

"Just let me close this down for the night." Swiveling the chair back around, he started closing down files.

"Did you find out anything yet?" Erin admitted to herself that she was too curious to wait for him to volunteer the information. Leaning forward, she glanced at the screen and then at Abel.

Abel stopped what he was doing and sat back in the chair, clasping his hands behind his head. "I found him." His simple words belied the enormity of what he had done.

She didn't know whether to laugh or cry. Of course she was happy that he'd found his brother, but that meant that he would be leaving her. And soon. "How?"

"It was easier than I imagined. I did a bit more digging through Mom and Dad's files and found my original birth certificate. With that, I traced my birth parents' address and found that the property was up for sale. I checked with the real estate company and they told me the property is being sold by a company called E. S. Investors." He paused and took a deep breath. "I researched the company on the net and found that it is owned and operated by one Cain Benjamin."

"That's amazing." Erin clasped his hand tight in hers.

"No, it was lucky." Abel raised her hand to his lips and kissed her knuckles. "The man is a recluse and I couldn't find a picture of him anywhere, but I do know that he lives in Chicago and was recently married. This was the easy part. Now, I have to go to Chicago and try to meet a man, who by all accounts, doesn't see anyone."

Swallowing hard, she asked the question that she really didn't want answered. "When will you be leaving?"

"I thought about flying out tomorrow." He watched her carefully as he spoke, likely wondering what her reaction would be. "I figure, there's no need to wait."

Well, she'd known going into their affair that it would come to an end and it was up to her to make this easy on him. She wouldn't cause a scene and she would save her tears for when he was gone. "That's great." She tried to infuse some enthusiasm in her voice, but her words just came back to her, hollow and flat. "Don't worry. I'll keep the house up while you're gone and it'll be here when you decide to come home again."

"What the hell are you talking about?" His voice was tight with anger, and his whole body had suddenly stiffened.

Erin wiped her sweaty palms on her legs. Her nerves were beginning to fray. Why was he making this so damned difficult when she was trying to let him off the hook? "I'm just saying that I'll take care of things."

His expression was as dark as a thundercloud. Gripping the arms of his chair until his knuckles whitened, he glared at her in total disbelief. "You don't think I'm coming back, do you?"

She backed away from him, frightened by his growing fury. "When we agreed to have an affair, it was understood that you wouldn't be staying." Her own voice grew shriller and louder with each word, and she struggled to find some control.

"The hell with that." In one single motion he was off the chair and grabbing her by the arm. His hand was clamped tight around her upper arm, keeping her chained to him. She tried to pull away, which seemed to infuriate him even further.

Reaching out with his free hand, he swiped everything off the end of the desk. Papers and books flew everywhere, making Erin gasp at his unexpected violence. But he wasn't finished. Pulling her close, he picked her up like she was no more than a rag doll and draped her over the top of the desk. Her legs hung over the end and he stepped between them. When she tried to sit up, he held her down with one hand. He froze her to the spot with his heated gaze, and like a cornered animal, she was afraid to move, fearful that any movement might set off a storm of violence.

Grabbing the edges of the shirt she was wearing, he ripped it open. Buttons flew everywhere and Erin's hands automatically reached up to cover her breasts. But that was entirely the wrong thing to do.

"Oh, no, you don't." He grabbed both her hands and raised them over her head, holding them easily in one of his. His other hand gripped her chin. "You're not getting rid of me that easily. Do you understand me?" She didn't, not really, but she nodded anyway. Anything to calm him.

Towering over her, he looked like some conquering barbarian, capable of just about anything. Deep in her heart, she knew that he wouldn't hurt her physically, but her heart pounded frantically as she realized just how much at his mercy she was at the moment. She was a tall, strong woman, but Abel was beyond huge. He was massively built and all of it was pure solid steel.

All Erin knew was that she'd somehow hurt Abel with her words, and now he needed to reestablish the connection between them. She knew she could stop him with just a word, but her woman's heart wanted to give him whatever he needed, and her body, as always, yearned for his.

Reaching down, he unzipped his jeans until his cock popped free. Then in one motion, he positioned himself at her opening and drove himself deep inside her.

Erin arched off the desk as he filled her. It was a little uncomfortable as she hadn't been ready for him, but her body was used to the pleasure he gave her, and as he remained seated deep inside her, her muscles began to relax and her body began to welcome him.

Dragging her bottom to the very edge of the desk, he began to pump into her. "You are mine," he repeated over and over as he continued to fuck her relentlessly.

There was a desperation in him that called to her, and she lifted her hips to meet each stroke wanting to be closer to him. "Yes," she answered him again and again, wanting to reassure him in any way possible.

Ignoring the uncomfortable hard wooden surface beneath her, she raised her legs, wrapping them around him, and digging her heels into his butt. She clawed at the edge of the desk, desperate for something to hold onto, anything to help anchor her in this storm of passion.

As the frantic pace drove her closer to the edge, he leaned over and plunged his tongue in and out of her mouth in a parody of the sex act. "Tell me you love me," he ordered.

How did he know? she wondered desperately. She'd done her best to hide it from him, but he'd somehow found out her secret, and now he wanted her to lay her soul bare to him. She shook her head, trying to deny him, but he was relentless.

"Tell me." He bit her neck as he continued to pound in and out of her. Her pussy was wet and full, and the pleasure threatened to overwhelm her until she could deny him nothing.

"I love you. I love you." It rose up from the depth of her soul, and came spewing out of her in a torrent of emotion that she could no longer control or stop.

"Yes!" he shouted as he drove hard into her one last time. Erin felt him explode into her and then she was coming apart herself. Her orgasm shook her to the very core of her being. Abel slumped on top of her, releasing her arms and gathering her close to him. Her heart pounded against her chest as they both gasped for breath.

Emotionally and physically drained, she lay there on the desk unable to keep the tears from seeping out of the corners of her eyes. Her legs slipped from around his waist and dangled against the side of the desk. She felt naked in every way possible, and she was too worn out to care.

"Don't cry, honey." Abel used his thumbs to wipe away the tears that fell from her eyes. "Everything is going to be fine now."

She shook her head, unwilling to believe him. "Yes, it is," he assured her. "How could you think that I could ever leave you?"

Erin still was not sure she could believe him. "But you're going away," she quietly reminded him.

Abel smiled the soft sexy smile that she loved so much. The one that made his green eyes smolder with passion. "You're coming with me...if you want to?"

"I am?" she blinked at him in confusion.

"Yes you are," he calmly informed her. "Then we're coming back here to settle down. I figure we can have the wedding in a couple of weeks."

Erin sputtered. "Marriage. Who said anything about marriage?" It was hard to follow the conversation as she could feel Abel swelling inside her again.

Cupping her breasts in his hands, he traced the hard nubs with his thumbs making her moan. "Marry me? I'll make you happy."

"Why?" she managed to spit out between groans.

"Because you make me happy." He leaned over and flicked one of her nipples with his tongue. "Because we're absolutely compatible sexually." Closing his mouth over the tip, he nibbled it. "Because I admire and love you and want to spend my life with you." He suckled her breast hard and Erin thumped her feet against the side of the desk, unable to form a coherent thought.

"Say yes," he prodded her. "I'll just torture you until you do."

"What will you do if I say yes?"

She was moved to tears by the look of love and lust on his face as he answered her. "I'll spend the rest of my life loving you."

There was no way she could refuse him. "Yes." Reaching up, she pulled his head down to her. "Yes, I'll marry you." As joy bubbled up inside her, she felt herself crying once again, except this time they were tears of pure happiness.

Abel traced her lips with her tongue, and gave her teasing little kisses. When he felt one of her salty tears on his mouth, he cupped her face in his hands and used his thumbs to wipe away the fresh tears. "Don't cry, honey."

"But I'm happy," she wailed, unable to stop the tears.

Abel gave up trying to stop her crying and instead diverted her attention. "Wrap your legs around my waist and your arms around my neck." When she'd done so, he stood up and placed one hand under her bottom and the other around her shoulders. The motion drove his cock deeper inside her and she cried out in desire.

"I want you again." Nuzzling his neck, she placed hot kisses down his neck before biting his shoulder. She then licked away the sting, savoring his salty taste on her tongue.

Abel leaned against the desk and got his balance for a moment before he began to walk. With each step he took, he drove his cock deeper inside her. The motion drove her mad, and she quickly found that she was totally aroused again. She could feel her inner muscles tightening and knew she was perilously close to coming.

Abel, the devil, knew it too as he sauntered towards the stairs. Slowly, he walked up the stairs, one step at a time. With each step, his cock thrust to the depths of her molten core. She was so close. Digging her fingers into his shoulders, she tried to get leverage enough to move.

He laughed and pushed her back against the wall on the landing. She gave a cry of protest when he pulled his cock from her body, but he ignored her and went down on one knee in front of her. His long, thick fingers explored her wet sensitive flesh, before slipping inside her pussy. Her cream coated his fingers as he worked them in and out of her.

Burying his face in her pussy, he lifted her legs over his shoulder as he licked and sucked her clit. Withdrawing his fingers from her slit, he rubbed them gently over her anus, slowly pushing one of his fingers into the tight little hole.

Carefully, he worked one finger inside her ass. She could feel the tight muscles squeezing his finger, which felt huge inside her. It hurt slightly, but it was a pleasure-pain combination that left her breathless. With her legs spread wide over his shoulders, she couldn't move away from him, and Abel continued to suck and tease her pussy as he carefully withdrew his finger from her ass before thrusting it deeper than it was before. Erin moaned as he continued to work his finger in and out of her behind.

"I want to be able to fuck that beautiful, tight ass of yours, baby." He inserted the tip of a second finger inside her.

Erin sucked in her breath at the burning sensation. His fingers slid easily as they were coated in her cream, but the fit was still extremely tight.

"I know it hurts a little, but once you get used to my fingers, you'll be able to take my cock." Now he had two fingers inside her ass. "Wouldn't you like that, baby?"

"Yesss," she hissed. Having his fingers buried in her ass was a complete turn-on. It did hurt a little, but there was also pleasure. It felt so damned good. She was willing to do whatever it took to be able to take him inside her in any way he wanted.

She moaned in pain and relief when he finally withdrew his two fingers. Abel coated his fingers with more of the cream from between her legs and rubbed it over the puckered little hole. She found herself moving against his fingers, wanting them back inside her.

Abel laughed as he slipped her legs off of his shoulders. "Soon, baby," he promised as he stood, lifted her up, and impaled her on his cock once again. Pressing her against the wall, he began to thrust his cock deep. Her pussy wept, she was so close now.

"Come for me, baby," he encouraged her as he gripped her ass tight. He traced the cleft of her ass with one finger, before pushing it inside. This time her ass accepted him more easily. He kissed her then, his tongue thrusting into her mouth.

Erin had never experienced anything like this in her life. Her mouth, pussy, and ass were all filled by him. Totally out of control now, she bucked against him, needing even more.

Tearing her mouth from his, she grabbed his head in her hands. "Move," she commanded. Running her fingers through his hair, she kissed whatever part of him she could reach. His chin, lips, nose, and forehead were peppered with hot, little kisses before she worked her way around to his ear and nibbled on his earlobe.

"God, I love your ass and your pussy and your tits," he whispered as he flexed his legs and drove himself inside her. "I can't wait until we're married and it's all mine," he grated out as he continued to work his finger in her ass.

"I already am," she whispered in his ear. "But you're mine too. And I love the feel of your cock deep inside me, your finger in my ass, and your hard arms wrapped around me."

Her words moved him to action and she could hear the slapping sounds as their flesh met, thrust after thrust. Tilting back her head, she clung to him as he pounded into her. "Harder. Fuck me harder."

Abel grunted and groaned as he rammed himself into her. Erin gasped, almost lightheaded as she struggled for breath. Her whole body was on fire, demanding release.

Erin didn't know how close he was to coming, but she could hold out no longer. Crying out, she came with her legs wrapped tight around his waist and her heels dug into his hard butt. She ground her pelvis against his as hard as she could and pulled him close with her feet.

Abel slammed into her once more, gave a hoarse yell, and came in a hard rush. When he had emptied himself inside her once again, he leaned into her, propping her back against the wall to hold them both up as they struggled to recover.

A minute passed before he pulled out of her. She felt bereft without him inside her, but he scooped her up into his arms and carried her up the rest of the stairs. Stumbling into the bedroom, he tumbled them both into bed, and tucked her into his arms.

"We'll talk to your brothers in the morning and fly out tomorrow night." It was said as a statement, but she sensed that he was looking for her approval.

"That's fine with me." Wiggling her behind until she was settled comfortably against him, she sighed when his hand came up to cup her breast, and she drifted contentedly off to sleep.

Chapter Seventeen

It was both physically and emotionally harder than she'd imagined it would be to make herself step into her home early the next morning. Jackson was seated at the kitchen table, sipping a cup of coffee, as he scanned a newspaper. He glanced up when she entered, and the look on his face quickly changed from one of confusion to one of anger as he noticed Abel behind her and the proprietary hand he had rested on her shoulder.

Jackson pushed his chair back from the table and slowly came to his feet. His hands were fisted at his sides and his face went from a stark white to an enraged red in a matter of seconds. Although she wasn't afraid of her brother, she was very glad to have Abel's massive, protective body behind her for moral support.

"What the hell is going on here?" His quiet tones made Erin flinch. The angrier that Jackson got, the quieter he became. This was definitely not a good sign. She hesitated for a moment, trying to find the right words.

"Garrett?" Jackson's laser gaze was now focused entirely on Abel and the fact that he'd called him by his last name put them both on notice that Jackson was feeling less than friendly at the moment.

She sensed Abel shifting behind her and knew she had to speak. "Sit down, Jackson. I want to talk to you." She had created this mess, so it was up to her to deal with it.

Striding forward, she pulled out a chair at the table and arched her eyebrow at her brother. He never took his eyes off Abel, but he slowly sank back into his seat. Reaching out, she grabbed one of her brother's hands and tugged on it until he turned and faced her.

"You want to tell me what's going on?"

Erin felt herself flush at his question, but refused to feel shame for what she'd done. She was a grown woman, not a child. Only Jackson had the ability to make her feel like a little girl being scolded by a parent.

"Abel and I have been seeing each other." The clock on the wall ticked off the seconds as she waited for his reaction. Its ticking and the heavy sound of breathing were the only sounds she could hear above her pounding heart.

"You mean you're sleeping together." Jackson's voice was little more than a harsh whisper as he studied her face intently. He tugged his hand free from her grip, and Erin clenched her hands helplessly in her lap.

"It's much more than that, but yes, we are sleeping together." Erin opened her mouth to begin to explain things to her brother, but it was already too late.

"You bastard," Jackson roared as he erupted from the table. The chair fell backwards and slammed onto the floor as he charged across the room towards Abel who had been standing quietly, waiting just inside the doorway.

"Jackson, no!" Erin screamed and jumped from her seat, but Jackson was past listening to reason, and there was no stopping him.

Abel stood his ground, not moving when Jackson reared back and landed a hard right hook. Staggering backwards, he landed heavily against the wall, shaking the very foundation of the house. The kitchen clock fell off the wall and smashed to the floor, shattering in a dozen pieces.

Jackson pulled back his arm to land another blow, but this time Abel caught his hand in mid-swing before it landed. Both men strained, but Abel held Jackson's arm in an iron grip. "The first one was free because I deserved it, but from now on I'll fight."

Jackson's face turned even redder as he yanked his arm away and turned on Erin. "How could you?" he yelled.

She stood her ground, determined not to flinch from his fury. She'd freely admit that it was her own deception that had led to this scene, but enough was enough. "How could I what?" she yelled back. "How could I act like a grown woman who wants a relationship with a man? How could I grow up and want more out of life than living at home for the rest of my life? How could I want to be loved, rather than grow old and dry up like some old maid?"

Erin was on a roll now as years of her pent-up frustration spewed forth. "How could I want you to treat me like an adult, rather than a child? You're not my father, Jackson, you're my brother. I want your blessing, but I don't need it."

Her head was spinning, as she gasped for air. The coffee she'd had earlier was threatening to come right back up. Taking a deep breath, she held her hand out to him, wanting desperately for him to understand. "This is my decision to make and no one else's." When she finally ran out of steam and finished, she didn't feel any better. Instead, she felt slightly ill. She didn't want to fight with Jackson.

Her brother paled and staggered backwards as if she had landed him a fatal body blow. She reached out her hand to him again, willing him to understand. "I love him." Her voice grew quieter as she continued. She glanced at Abel for support as he came to stand beside her before turning back to Jackson. "I really love him."

Erin closed her eyes and swallowed back her tears when Jackson turned to leave the room without saying another word. He didn't even look at her as he headed towards the back door.

"You can't run away from this." Jackson froze with his hand on the back door as Abel spoke. "Why don't you ask me how I feel about your sister?"

"It doesn't matter how you feel." Jackson didn't turn around, but continued to face the door. "It's a proven fact that you never stay."

"Maybe Erin will go with me when I leave." Jackson tensed at his words. "Or maybe we'll both stay. That is, if we're welcome." Abel's words, stark and bare, lay between the two men.

Jackson slowly turned and faced them, his face like granite. "Well, which is it?"

It slowly dawned on Erin that Jackson had already suffered the loss of his best friend over the years that Abel was gone, but he was now afraid of losing her as well. He was like a parent faced with the fact that his child was grown up and leaving home. Yes, he was her older brother, but he'd been the one to take care of her since she was a child. He was the one who'd bandaged her bloody knees, read her bedtime stories, and it had been Jackson who'd taken her shopping to buy her first bra.

Over the years, he had been the one constant in her life. It was Jackson who'd attended all her school plays and made sure she had a costume at Halloween. He had made sure that birthdays were celebrated and that she and Nathan had presents at Christmas. But now, she was moving onto adult things like sex and relationships and these were things she had to do on her own. Jackson could not protect her woman's heart from harm.

The knot in her stomach dissolved as she realized that he wasn't judging her, but was afraid for her. Afraid that she might be hurt. Afraid that they might not be as close anymore. Erin reached out and gave Abel's arm a squeeze before she slowly walked across the kitchen towards her brother.

Though he was standing as stiff as a board, she eased her arms around him and hugged him tight. "I love you, Jackson. That will never change."

Jackson swallowed hard as his hand came up to pat her awkwardly on the back. "I know." Suddenly, she was enveloped in a huge bear hug as he hauled her into his arms and held her as if he would never let her go. Erin didn't know how long they stood clasped in each other's arms or how much longer they would have stayed if they hadn't been interrupted.

"Come back to the table so we can talk." Abel picked up the chair that had fallen to the floor and placed it back beside the table. Using his boot, he shoved the larger pieces of the shattered clock close to the wall and out of the way.

Erin stared at the remains of the clock before giving Jackson a little grin. "I always knew you didn't like that clock."

When he gave her another quick squeeze before releasing her, she heaved a sigh of relief. It would take time, but she was now confident that they would work things out. The worst of the storm was past. Taking his hand in hers, Erin led her brother back towards the table and waited until he was seated before sliding into a chair between him and Abel.

"Does Nathan know?" She'd hoped that Jackson wouldn't ask her that, but deep down she'd known that the question was inevitable.

"Yes." Abel answered the question for her. "He paid me a visit as soon as he found out."

"Well, that's just great," Jackson retorted. "Does everyone in Meadows know except me?"

"No." Nathan stepped out from the hallway from where he'd been watching the scene unfold and into the kitchen. He ran his gaze over all of them, and when he was satisfied that no one had been hurt, he pulled up a chair. "It got too quiet. I figured I should come down and investigate." Once he was seated, he turned to Jackson. "I know because I went looking for Erin the night that she supposedly went to Carly's house."

"If you knew, why the hell didn't you go drag her out of there?" Jackson glared at his younger brother.

"Because our sister is an adult. And besides—" a pleased masculine smile covered his face, "—I was otherwise occupied."

Abel obviously decided that he'd sat back long enough. Sitting forward, he laid both his hands on the kitchen table and addressed both brothers at once. "I know you love your sister, but I love her too." He reached towards Erin and caught up her hand in his. "I asked her to marry me." Raising it to his lips, he placed a tender kiss on her knuckles. "She said yes."

Jackson nodded his head in silent resignation while Nathan slapped Abel on the back and offered his hand in congratulations. "That's great news. I can't wait to tell Carly the news. She won't believe it."

Jumping up, he came around the table and reached down to hug Erin. "Congratulations, Sis," he whispered in her ear as he tenderly kissed her cheek.

"Thanks." She returned his hug eagerly, clutching him tight for a moment before releasing him. She'd known that Nathan would be happy for her and accept her relationship with Abel, but she really didn't know what to expect from Jackson.

Abel had accepted Nathan's well wishes and handshake, but his focus was obviously still on Jackson, waiting to see his reaction to their news.

"Congratulations." The word was little more than a croak and Jackson cleared his voice before continuing. "So when are you leaving?"

"Later today, but we'll be back in a couple of days." Abel reached out and pulled Erin into his lap before continuing. She leaned against his chest, grateful for the support, as she was still feeling a little shaken. It was the most natural thing in the world for her to wrap her arms around his neck and settle her head in the crook of his shoulder.

"Look," Abel continued. "I'm set financially and I own the farm, lock, stock, and barrel. I can live anywhere, but I know that Erin is happy here." Leaning down he kissed her softly. "I want her to be happy, so we'll be settling here."

"But what about your work?" Erin was surprised, but touched by his declaration.

"Well," he began slowly. "I've been meaning to talk to you about that."

"So talk," she urged him.

"I've had enough." He gave a short laugh. "That's an understatement. I'm burnt out and I don't want to spend the rest of my life writing about the horrific side of mankind."

"So what will you do?" Jackson asked him.

"I'm a writer," he shrugged. "I thought I'd try my hand at some fiction. Probably a mystery. Heck, I know just about everything there is to know about police work and forensic science. I might as well put it to good use. But this way, the story can end the way I want it to."

"Are you sure that's what you want?" Despite being cautious, she was almost bursting with relief.

"Yes," he nodded emphatically. "I'm very sure."

Jackson heaved a huge sigh and slowly came to his feet looking directly at Erin. "Does he make you happy?"

"Extremely." She didn't feel the need to add anything else. That one word had said it all.

Slowly Jackson turned to glare at Abel, his face hard. "I'll be watching you." His hands were clenched at his sides, and it took an obvious effort for him to open his fists and relax his hands.

"You wouldn't be the man I thought you were if you didn't." Abel met his stare unflinchingly. Erin glanced from Abel's hard features to her brother's harsh face, pleading silently with him to accept Abel into their lives.

Jackson stomped around the table and plucked her out of Abel's arms, giving her a huge hug that pulled her right off her feet. Abel had tensed when Jackson had first grabbed her, but he'd relaxed when they began to hug. Erin offered Abel a watery smile as Jackson kissed her on the forehead before he moved her to one side.

He stood there, silently with his hands on his hips for a moment and searched Abel's face intently. Whatever it was he was looking for, he obviously found it, and a moment later, he finally raised his hand and offered it to Abel. "Welcome to the family."

Abel reached out and took Jackson's hand, accepting the offer of acceptance. No one said a word as the men shook hands. Suddenly, Jackson let go a string of curses that shocked them all, and pulled Abel to his feet, giving him a quick manly hug before slapping him hard on the back.

Erin grinned as she watched them. They were both as stiff as trees as they embraced and mostly just pounded each other on the back before stepping apart.

"I just love a happy ending. Don't you?" Nathan made mock sniffing noises as he wrapped his arm around her shoulders.

"Don't be an ass, Nathan," Jackson admonished before reluctantly smiling at his brother. "I know you can't really help it, but try."

"I'm so misunderstood," Nathan bemoaned. "That's the plight of the middle child, you know." He gave Erin a hangdog look.

"Save it for Carly." It was hard, but she just managed to contain her smile.

"You're absolutely right." He nodded as he tugged on her braid. "Now," he turned to Abel, all business once again. "What's this about you two leaving today? Where are you going, and when will you be back?"

Erin elbowed her brother in the ribs, and he flinched, shooting her a wounded look. "What? I'm just asking the obvious questions."

"Why don't I make some breakfast while we talk?" Erin didn't give anyone time to disagree, but went to the cupboard and started pulling out the ingredients for pancakes. The three men were still standing there looking at her. "You can't tell me you're not all hungry, because I'm starving." They all nodded their heads at the same time. Erin bit the inside of her lip to keep from laughing at them. "Sit. Abel will fill you in on the details."

There was a generally shuffling behind her as they pulled up their chairs to the table and settled themselves comfortably.

When she turned back to the counter, she allowed herself a smile, knowing they couldn't see her face. God, she loved them all so much and she was an incredibly lucky woman to have such wonderful men love her back. Happily, she set to work putting on a pot of fresh coffee before she started cooking pancakes.

Behind her, Abel filled them in on all the details of her search and their planned trip to Chicago. It was fascinating to listen to them interact together. Jackson was the listener. He didn't have much to say, but when he did speak, what he had to say was worth listening to. Nathan, on the other hand, was full of questions and keenly interested in the simple techniques that Abel had employed to find his brother.

Erin mostly listened, only now and again adding details and the occasional bit of commentary. By the time all of them had eaten their fill of homemade blueberry pancakes, Jackson was already on to practical matters.

"What do you want to do about the berry fields? They'll be ready for harvest any day now." Jackson leaned back and took a large swallow from his mug of coffee.

"I know, but hopefully I won't be gone too long." Her mind was already busy making to-do lists and organizing tasks. "I've already hired my pickers, and some of them have been with me for years. If something happened and I don't make it back in time, they know what to do." She hated not being here for the harvest, but being with Abel when he confronted his brother was more important. Besides, she trusted her young employees.

But Jackson was already shaking his head, making tentative plans to take over her berry harvest if she had to be gone longer than anticipated. "They're good kids, but I'll supervise the picking if it comes to that. Nathan can help me with the orchards and I'll take on extra help for a week or so if I have to."

It was at that moment that she realized that he was okay with her marrying Abel. In his own way, he'd just given them his stamp of approval. Catching his eye from across the table, she smiled at him. He nodded and winked at her before turning his attention back to the conversation between Abel and Nathan.

In a very short time, she'd come a long way from the woman who'd sat at the end of the table reading her magazine. Oh my God, the magazine! She made a mental note to pack it for the trip, as she'd never actually showed it to Abel yet. They always got sidetracked before she could bring it up. She flushed at the images that thought conjured up, but decided that it was probably too late anyway. As far as she could remember, they'd already covered every single position in the article. But it was probably better to pack it, just in case.

Chapter Eighteen

Erin held Abel's hand tight as they stood at the back entrance of the older stone building. From what Abel's contact at the police department had informed him, Cain Benjamin lived in the penthouse apartment here. They had no idea if he was home or if he would even see them. Chances weren't good, since the man preferred to isolate himself from the rest of the world. Abel raised his hand to knock, but the door flew open before he had the chance.

A slender, athletic-looking woman suddenly appeared in the doorway, her short brown hair spiked around her head in tousled disarray. She almost barreled headfirst into them before coming to a dead stop. "I'm sorry..." she glanced up, an apology left half-spoken on her lips. Her blue eyes widened as she got a good look at them, and she took a hasty step backwards.

"Wait." Abel stepped forward before she could close the door in his face. "Can you tell me if Cain Benjamin lives here?" Abel's voice was calm and deep, but Erin could hear the underlying urgency.

The woman continued to stare at him. "Yes." She seemed at a loss for words and said nothing else. She glanced at Erin for a moment, but then her gaze returned to Abel and seemed to focus entirely on him.

Erin knew that the last thing he wanted to do was frighten this woman, who obviously had access to Cain's apartment. Abel softened his voice, and tried his best not to look intimidating, which was impossible for a man of his size. "I'd like to see him if that's possible."

Abel's shoulders were tense, obviously braced for disappointment. Erin gave his hand an encouraging squeeze and almost yelped out loud as his grip on her hand tightened almost to the point of causing her pain.

The woman shook her head, as if coming out of a trance. "I imagine you would," she slowly replied. She stared at them for a moment longer before seeming to come to some internal decision. Taking a deep breath, she stepped forward and offered her hand. "I'm Katie. Who are you?"

"Abel Benjamin Garrett." He took Katie's hand gently in his much larger one, and was careful not to hold it too tight.

"And this is Erin Connors." The grip on Erin's hand lessened as he introduced her, until he finally let go of it altogether. Erin casually flexed her fingers by her side as she nodded her own greeting.

Katie held Abel's hand for a moment before dropping it and holding the door open wide. "Follow me." She beckoned with a nod of her head before turning and leading the way.

Abel placed his hand on Erin's back, as he ushered her through the door. He glanced down and made eye contact with her, as they followed Katie into the dimly lit parking garage. His face was a mask of determination, and Erin gave him a smile of encouragement as they crossed the threshold of the building.

The door slammed shut ominously behind them. There was no going back. Erin had no idea where this stranger was leading them, but they were one step closer to meeting Cain Benjamin. The door to the fortress had been opened, and neither of them was about to question their good fortune.

They swiftly followed Katie across the garage to a private elevator, the sound of their shoes echoing throughout the cavernous space. Katie pressed a red button on the wall, and the door immediately slid open. Nobody spoke as they all climbed inside the waiting elevator.

As the door closed behind them and they started to ascend, Erin blurted out the question she knew that Abel wanted answered. "Will he see us?"

"Yes," she nodded decisively. "I believe he will." The elevator lurched to a halt, the bell rang, and the door glided opened before Erin could ask Katie anything more.

Katie swiftly exited the elevator, digging a key out of her pocket as she went. They hurried down the short hallway behind her, unwilling to let her out of their sight for a moment.

Erin shot a quick look at Abel. His jaw was clenched tight, and his eyes were grim, but determined. Mentally crossing her fingers, she hoped for the best. But whatever the outcome, she was glad she was there to support him. As if he knew what she was thinking, he glanced down at her and smiled. It was an intimate smile that made her body tingle and her heart melt.

Katie didn't stop at the front door, but unlocked it, and went straight into the apartment, yelling as she went. "Cain!"

They quickly followed her through the open apartment door, but stopped suddenly as a huge dog that appeared to be a wolfhound of some sort bounded out of nowhere, barking for all it was worth.

"Gabriel, down." The dog ignored Katie's command and kept on coming towards them.

Erin found herself looking at Abel's broad back as he grabbed her arm and thrust her safely behind him. Abel glared down at the beast when it skittered to a stop in front of him. "Sit," he commanded.

The dog ceased barking and turned its head to look at Abel. After a moment, Gabriel sat and waited expectantly, his tail wagging behind him. Slowly, Abel extended his hand and allowed the dog to sniff it.

"Sorry about his bad manners," Katie said before making the necessary introductions. "As you probably already gathered, this is Gabriel." Erin inched out from behind Abel and held her hand out to the large but seemingly friendly dog.

"What the hell is going on out here?" Erin's head jerked up at the sound of the voice. For a moment, she'd thought that Abel had spoken. It took her a few seconds to realize that Abel's gaze was fixed on a dark figure standing imposingly at the end of the hallway. The dog gave a happy woof and padded towards this new voice.

"Cain, there's someone you need to meet." Katie held out her hand and the man walked towards it, never taking his eyes off Abel. When he reached Katie, he pushed her behind him and fisted his large hands on his hips.

"Who the hell are you?" At the stranger's surly tone, Erin found herself once again gazing into Abel's back, and she was forced to stand on her toes and peek over his shoulder.

The resemblance between the two men was amazing. The only difference was that Abel's twin wore his dark hair long and had a patch on his eye that had scars radiating out from it. They were the same height and build, and their voices were uncannily alike.

"I'm Abel Benjamin Garrett." Abel's reply was calm and steady. "And I'm your brother."

"I don't have a brother," came the quick reply.

"Obviously you do," Abel replied, his tone now as cold as Cain's. The similarity in their tones of voice made Erin shiver. She could barely take her eyes off of Cain. It was like looking at a slightly distorted view of Abel. Katie seemed to be as fascinated by the two men as she did, and watched them just as intently.

"It's a long story, but suffice to say, we were definitely born to the same parents." Abel waited for a moment, but Cain stood like a statue in the hallway with his arms crossed, all but ignoring him.

Erin could feel the frustration and anger radiating from Abel, but he continued to speak evenly. "I have documented proof if and when you're ever interested." Reaching into his pocket, Abel drew out a white business card and held it out to Cain. When Cain made no move to accept it, he placed it carefully on a small hall table. Abel clenched his hand into a tight fist as he withdrew it.

"I'm not looking for anything from you, except maybe some answers. Just think about it." Abel's frustration was obvious as he waited, and waited. The silence was almost deafening. "But since we're obviously not welcome, we'll leave."

Abel grabbed her by the arm and began to tug her towards the door. Erin glanced over her shoulder, pleading silently with the other woman.

Katie hesitated for a moment, looking from Cain to Abel and back again. "Wait!" she cried out.

Erin planted her feet and refused to move. Short of dragging her all the way to the elevator or picking her up and carrying her, either of which was a distinct possibility, Abel was forced to stop. She heaved a sigh of relief when he came to a halt a few steps from the door.

Abel kept his back to them all, refusing to give an inch. She knew he felt that since he'd made the first move and been rebuffed, it was up to Cain to make the next move. Male pride could be such a pain in the ass at times like this.

Erin was trying to think of what to say to break the tension when Katie did it for her. It was all Erin could do not to laugh when the smaller woman turned on Cain and poked him in the chest.

"What's wrong with you? I know you've only got one eye, but it's obvious that this man is your brother."

Cain heaved a sigh. "Katie…" he began, but she cut him off.

Katie ignored him and turned back to Abel. "Please don't leave." Her voice was soft and pleading. "I, at least, want to talk to you."

Erin could see Abel's resolve softening at Katie's request. It faltered completely when she placed her hand on his arm and surprised him even further. "I'm your sister-in-law."

Erin held her breath and waited to see what Abel would do.

Abel looked down at the small hand resting on his arm. Her strength was nothing compared to his, but she held him prisoner with a simple touch. It was almost too much for him to take in. He had a brother and a sister-in-law. Blindly, he sought Erin, needing her advice. When she looked at him and gave him a slight nod, he knew he had to see this through to the end or he'd regret it for the rest of his life.

Reaching out, he tugged Erin under his arm and felt better immediately with her by his side. "Erin and I are getting married in a couple of weeks, so I guess you'll be sisters-in-law."

Katie grinned with delight. "How wonderful! We've only been married a few months ourselves."

"I don't mean to break up the family reunion." Cain's laconic voice made them all turn towards him. "But what proof do you have that we're related?" He crossed his arms across his chest and pinned them with his laser glare. "I find it interesting that you waited so long to find me. Perhaps it had something to do with my recent wedding announcement and the fact that they listed some of my various business assets in the article."

His brother wasn't giving an inch, and oddly enough, that reassured Abel. He'd have done the exact same thing in his brother's position. It gave him a respect for the man who was his brother. It was time for an explanation.

"My parents were killed when I was eighteen, but it was only a week ago that I started going through their papers. Imagine my surprise when I found out that I was adopted and that my parents had purchased me from a couple who'd had twin boys. You're older, by the way. They sold their second born." He laid it all on the line and held nothing back. He heard Katie gasp, but he was more interested in Cain's reaction. "As for your money, I have more than enough of my own."

"Abel's a very successful writer," Erin put in hastily. Abel glared at her, but she just glared back at him, totally unrepentant.

"Were your parents good to you?" Cain stood stiffly, his head cocked expectantly to one side.

Cain's question took him by surprise. It was not the response he was expecting. "Yes, they were." Abel wondered where his brother was going with this.

"Then you were the lucky one." Cain shook his head and sighed deeply. "Nothing those people did would surprise me."

Abel swallowed back the emotion that rose within him. It had never occurred to him that his brother's childhood hadn't been as good as his, and he was slightly ashamed for only thinking about himself. Anyone who could sell one of their children to strangers was indeed capable of anything.

"I'm sorry." Abel didn't know what else to say. Then a horrible thought occurred to him. "They didn't have anything to do with your..." He didn't quite know how to phrase his question.

"My deformity?" Cain seemed to have no problems addressing his appearance. "No, that was a fire when I was in college, but that's another story. As for my childhood, that's all water under the bridge." He shrugged off the concern. "Life is good now and that's all that matters." As Cain spoke, Katie went to her husband and wrapped her arm around his massive frame.

"Why don't we all go into the living room and get acquainted?" Katie said.

Cain nodded and seconded her invitation. "I'm afraid you're going to have to do a little more convincing, Garrett. But I'm curious to know how you found me."

Abel grinned at his brother as they all walked into the living room. "Didn't I mention that I'm a true crime writer? Investigation is what I do best."

Cain gave a snort of laughter, but it quickly died when Abel reached into his pocket and pulled out his mother's journal and the documents that both their parents had signed. He took the documents without saying a word and walked towards the window before opening them.

Abel stood in the middle of the living room with his hands in his pockets, waiting to see what his brother's reaction would be when confronted by such irrefutable proof. Now that he'd met Cain, he felt connected to this other man. It would be a hard thing to swallow if Cain decided he wanted nothing to do with him. Cain was the only remaining family he had.

Then again, no, that was no longer true. He could feel Erin waiting patiently beside him, and just her mere presence soothed his battered soul. Erin and her brothers were his family now. As long as he had Erin, he didn't need anyone else, but he really wanted the opportunity to know this stranger who was his brother.

Cain finished reading the papers and then took another minute to flip through the journal before closing it. Tilting back his head, he closed his eye and swallowed hard. Katie went to him and laid her hand on his chest, and Cain gathered her into his arms. It was an intensely personal moment, and Abel felt like an intruder. He felt himself backing away from the other couple, but Erin stopped him simply by placing her hand on his back.

Cain bent down and planted a tender kiss on Katie's forehead, and she clung to him for a moment before releasing him. Turning, he walked back across the room and handed the documents back to Abel. "So, where do we go from here?" Cain gave no indication how he felt about the situation or even if he believed they were indeed twins.

Abel hesitated before gradually extending his hand. "I'm Abel Benjamin Garrett, and I'm your brother."

Cain looked at Abel's hand and swore softly. A second later, he wrapped his arms around his brother and held him tight. The sight of the two strong men embracing each other brought tears to Erin's eyes. Katie swiped at the tears running down her face and gave Erin a watery smile. It was a good beginning.

Chapter Nineteen

Abel was still wired late that night as he stood in front of their hotel window and gazed out the window. They had made plans to meet Cain and Katie for lunch tomorrow, and Abel was surprised at just how excited he was about spending time with them. Erin and Katie had already made tentative plans for Cain and Katie to come to Meadows for the wedding. It seemed that he and his brother were alike in at least one way. They both would do whatever it took to make their women happy.

Erin chose that moment to roll over in bed. Her eyes sought him through the darkness. "I can hear you thinking all the way over here, and it's keeping me awake." Climbing out of bed, she padded silently across the carpet and cuddled up next to him.

"Sorry." He absently kissed the top of her head.

"For a first meeting, I thought everything went really well." Erin began to trace circles around his nipples as she spoke, distracting him from his thoughts.

"Yeah, surprisingly enough, it did go well." He still had a hard time wrapping his brain around the fact that he had a twin brother. It was one thing to know it intellectually and quite another to be faced with a physical mirror image. "I wonder if he'll ever tell us the whole story about how he came to lose his eye. He said it was in a fire, but there's obviously more to the story than that."

"Katie said that he'd got burned in an apartment fire when he was in college. He got trapped inside after going back to help rescue some other people." Erin continued to caress Abel's chest. "He was a real hero that day, but he doesn't talk about it at all."

Abel looked down at her in amazement. "When did she tell you that?"

"When I asked her to show me some of her paintings." Erin shot him an amused smile. "Her work is really amazing. She said she can't wait to visit us in Meadows, because she'd always wanted to paint nature scenes. Katie also promised that I could pick out one of her paintings for a wedding present."

"You and Katie certainly seemed to have packed quite a bit into the ten minutes you spent in the den by yourselves."

Erin grinned. "You have no idea."

Abel wasn't sure he liked the sly smile on Erin's face. "What exactly does that mean?"

"Don't you worry. I didn't tell her any secrets. We just talked about men in general." She bent forward and playfully nipped at his chest. "We now have not only an author, but an artist in the family as well."

Abel laughed and tugged playfully on her hair. "Brat. How did she come to tell you about Cain?"

Erin shrugged. "I asked her."

Abel shook his head in amazement. He should have known because of his years of research, but he was still surprised at how much more easily women communicated than men. He had so many questions about his brother, but they would have to wait until tomorrow.

Right now, he had more pressing issues on his mind, like how damned good Erin felt pressed against him. His mind might have been distracted, but his dick was as hard as a rock, clamoring for attention.

"It's amazing how alike you both look, but you're obviously the more handsome of the two." Erin's hand left his chest and began to inch its way towards his erection.

"Obviously you're biased," he teased, sucking in a breath when her fingers skimmed the length of his cock.

Erin ran her fingers up and down his shaft several times before wrapping her hand around his cock and stroking it. "Obviously," she readily agreed.

"I love you, Erin." He needed her to know how much it meant for him to have her with him, not only today, but also every day.

"I know. I love you too," she told him. He could tell by the tone of her voice that she understood what he meant without having to explain himself.

Capturing her lips with his own, he stroked his way into her mouth with his tongue. Taking his time, he kissed her thoroughly. She rubbed her breasts against his chest, and he loved the feel of her hard nipples against his skin.

Pushing her hips forward, she spread her pussy lips with her hand, and snuggled his cock between her spread legs. Wrapping her hands around his neck, she began to slide her moist sex up and down his length. She moaned as she stroked her clit against his throbbing dick. Her obvious pleasure made him even harder.

He grabbed her ass and ground her against his cock, pulling her up on the tips of her toes as he did so. Her nails dug into his shoulders for support as she arched against him. Abel gripped her with one hand, reached out, and pushed the curtains open all the way so he could see her better. The bottom of the window was at knee level so the light caught her writhing body in it pale yellow glow.

Erin squealed and hid her head against his chest. "Close the curtains before somebody sees us."

"No. I don't care who sees me fuck you. You're mine and I want the whole world to know it." She stiffened, but he could feel the slick wetness of her pussy against his cock and knew she was aroused by the thought.

"Turn around and face the window." She peeked up at him uncertainly before turning around. "Place your hands on the glass and spread your legs wide."

Erin hesitated for a moment before turning and spreading her legs. Her hands automatically braced against the window for support. Abel eased her slightly backwards until she was at more of an angle with her ass thrust backwards, and then pushed her legs further apart so that she was spread wide for him.

"Perfect." Stroking between her legs, he found her pussy was wet and dripping for him. He eased one finger inside her and slowly pulled it back out. Erin moaned and pushed her ass back towards him.

"Stay just like that." Abel walked away and left her there, totally exposed to anyone who happened to walk by and look up at their bedroom window.

Erin stood with her hands pressed against the cool glass, totally naked, with her legs spread wide. She felt totally exposed and vulnerable as she waited for Abel to return. Today had been hard for him, and she knew that he needed her tonight more than ever. It was if he was trying to stake his claim on her, to assure himself that she was his.

She could hear him rummaging around in his overnight bag, and then he was back, standing behind her. He slipped his fingers over the cleft of her ass, and she could feel something cool slide across her flesh before he pushed one finger inside the tight opening.

He spread the cheeks of her ass with one hand while he worked his finger deeper. "I told you I wanted to fuck your tight ass." A second finger joined the first one, sliding in easily, stretching her. "Will you let me?"

Erin sensed Abel's need to possess her completely. She could feel her cream coating her inner thighs at the thought of him taking her like that. Her pussy pulsed and clenched and her breasts ached with arousal. She pushed her ass against his fingers, taking them deep. There was a slight burning sensation, but she wanted this, and she knew that he needed the words.

Taking a deep breath, she gave herself over to this new experience, trusting him to make it good for her. "Fuck my ass, Abel." Her voice was a low, seductive purr.

His finger stilled within her, before he withdrew them totally. "Don't worry, honey. I'll use plenty of lubrication and take it slow."

Erin nodded, shivering slightly in anticipation as she waited for him to prepare himself. Cool gel coated her cleft and then he was behind her again, spreading her wide and pressing his cock against her opening. In spite of herself, Erin clenched her cheeks tight in anticipation.

Abel chuckled and thrust two fingers of his other hand into her pussy. Erin moaned and moved against them, loving the way his thumb scraped her clit. The moment she relaxed, Abel pressed the tip of his cock inside her ass. She gasped as he stretched her wider than before. It was uncomfortable, bordering on painful, but she wanted this for herself and for him.

With their height difference, he had to bend his knees slightly as he guided himself inside her. "Relax, Erin," he whispered as he continued to stroke her pussy.

"I'm trying," she panted. The sensations were almost overwhelming. The combination of pleasure and pain almost too much to bear. Erin tried to focus on the pleasure that radiated from her clit, and block out the slight burning in her behind.

Abel gripped her waist with both hands and flexed his hips slowly. His cock forged deep into her waiting heat, and she could feel her ass muscles tighten around him, gripping him tight. By the time he was all the way inside her, she didn't know how she felt. The burning in her behind was tempered by her growing arousal. He flexed his hips, thrusting her upwards, and she was forced to stand on her toes. She tried to move, but was unable to stroke him.

He laughed. "I control your pleasure now, my love." One hand moved up to cup her breast, tweaking her nipple between his thumb and forefinger, while he used his other to toy with her clit.

N.J. Walters

Erin cried out and tried to reach one of her hands behind her to make him move. Her pussy clenched painfully, and her entire body cried out for release.

He ignored her cries and continued to pleasure her. His fingers shaped her firm breasts before teasing their nubs. "Can you see your reflection in the window? Look at how beautiful you are."

It was faint, but she could see her outline in the window and knew that he could too. The bottom part of the window was open and the sounds of people walking through the parking lot drifted up to them. "Imagine if they looked up what they would see." She stiffened for a moment at his words, but he stroked her clit hard and she melted against him once again.

She glanced down at the parking lot and saw that a man had come to a complete stop in the middle of the lot and was staring up at their window. "Someone is watching us," she hissed.

"Let him watch." Abel rubbed his palm over both of her breasts before pinching each nipple tight. "You look so fucking beautiful."

Erin cried out as his fingers moved over her body. The man in the parking lot slowly drifted away as his buddies called him to join them. He glanced up towards the window one last time before hurrying after his friends. Their voices gradually faded as they walked away.

He could feel her ass muscles grabbing his throbbing dick and he knew she was close. "I don't even have to move for you to come for me, do I?" He nipped the back of her neck and then licked the small sting away. "You're almost there."

Her breath grew short, and a tingling sensation began deep inside her. He fondled her breast and pressed hard on her clit at the same time he stood just a little taller and lifted her off her feet. His cock was thrust even deeper up her ass.

"Omigod," she screamed. She could feel the beginnings of her orgasm as her ass clenched around his cock. Her pussy pulsed and contracted at the same time. The sensation was incredible, but not quite enough.

"Abel," she wailed, needing something more to push her over the edge.

Gripping her waist tight, Abel pulled his cock almost all the way out before driving himself into her. A high keening sound came from deep within her. She jerked in his arms and her orgasm erupted as he continued to thrust deep into her ass.

Wrapping his arms around her, he lifted her up and drove her back against him one last time. He shuddered and yelled as he came, emptying himself in her tight ass. Abel stumbled slightly, and she cried out, grabbing the window frame for support.

Gently, Abel eased his pulsing cock out of her behind, and steadied them both. They both moaned at the separation, and Erin swayed in his arms. He half-carried, half-dragged her back to the bed and tumbled them both to the mattress where they lay trying to catch their breath.

Abel muttered an oath as he rolled off the bed. "I've got to clean up." Not waiting for her to answer, he padded to the bathroom. A few minutes later he dropped back onto the bed next to her.

Erin gave a small cry of distress and buried her face in the pillow. Abel pushed her hair back, trying to find her face under the mound of red hair. After a moment he gave up and lay on his back next to her.

"No one saw us," he soothed her, as if guessing the source of her discomfort.

She rolled over and whacked him with her pillow. "How do you know? I saw several guys cross the parking lot and I'm almost positive that one of them looked straight at me."

Abel made a grab at the pillow as she continued to hit him with it. She could tell he tried to contain himself. He really tried, but he began to laugh. That made her even angrier, and she grabbed another pillow and started to pummel him with both of them.

"It's not funny," she wailed, even as her lips started to tilt up in a small smile.

Grabbing her, he rolled until she was under him, her legs trapped under his. She struggled against his hold, but he stroked her face and kissed her. "It was too dark for them to really see anything, honey."

"Promise?" Erin lifted her head, reaching for his kiss.

"I promise." Abel stroked his tongue across her lips before forging inside her welcoming mouth. When she started sucking on his tongue, he moaned, but didn't stop kissing her.

By the time he withdrew from their heated embrace, Erin was once again totally relaxed and mellow. He rolled both their bodies onto the other side of the bed so that she was now lying on his chest. "I peeked at your magazine while you were taking a shower earlier."

"I figured we could look at it tomorrow if you wanted to." Erin rested her hand over his heart, and he could feel the warmth of her hand on his chest.

"By my reckoning we've already covered all the positions they listed, and then some." He tried to keep the smugness out of his voice, but she could hear his satisfaction.

She heaved a sigh and started toying with his chest hair. "I thought so too. Whatever shall we do now?"

Abel laughed and started tickling her sides until she began to squeal with laughter. "Stop it!" she shrieked.

Abel flipped her onto her back, capturing her hands in his and restraining them over her head. He threw one of his muscled legs over hers to keep her still before lowering his lips closer to hers. "We can always buy another magazine, or we can explore together."

Erin's entire face radiated the love she felt for him. "Together," she whispered.

"I want to shop for a ring tomorrow. I want the whole world to know that you're my woman."

Erin knew that it was more than that. He wanted her to have a symbol of the love he felt for her. It was for that reason that she agreed easily. "Okay, but nothing too fancy," she told him.

"Whatever you want," he promised her.

Tugging her hands out of his, she cupped his face in her hands and smiled at him. "I'll hold you to that promise." Sliding her hand lower, she stroked his erection before guiding him inside her once again, knowing once and for all that he was more than just her summer lover, he was her forever love.

Chapter Twenty

The sun was barely peeking over the horizon when Erin eased the back door open and snuck into Abel's kitchen. It was a beautiful September morning and Erin had walked through the fields rather than driving over in her truck. The blueberry bushes were almost all bare now that the season was coming to a close. Her hard work was behind her for this year, but she was already looking forward to next year's crop. On the other hand, the apple harvest was in full swing, the trees heavy with ripe fruit. She'd enjoyed both the brisk early morning walk and the solitude. It had helped calm and settle her for the hectic day ahead.

She knew that she shouldn't be here, but she desperately wanted to see him. The thought of Abel lying naked, tousled, and alone in his bed was too big a lure to resist. They hadn't had too much time together in the last few weeks as she'd been running from sunup to well past sundown while her blueberries were harvested. Many nights, she'd tumbled into bed too tired to do anything but collapse facedown in the pillow. She missed making love with him, sharing her body with him as he enjoyed hers. But that was all about to change.

The kitchen was empty, so she crept up the stairs and down the hallway until she was just outside his bedroom. Standing in the doorway, she stared as the sunlight drifted into the bedroom, bathing Abel in its golden light. Her heart clenched as she watched him sleep, and she gave a contented little sigh. She could still hardly believe that he belonged to her. And as of today, she would officially belong to him.

Her sneakers made no sound as she tiptoed across the floor to stand beside the bed. Abel filled the bed completely, his feet sticking out over the end. Erin was glad that the king-sized bed they'd ordered had arrived yesterday. There were plenty of things they could do in a bed that big, and her heart sped up as erotic images of the two of them, their bodies entwined as they made love, popped into her head.

Groaning, she shook her head, reminding herself of why she'd risked sneaking over here this morning. It was a morning much like this just two months ago, that she'd snuck into this very room. But this time she didn't strip off her clothing. Instead, fully dressed she stretched out beside him, propped her head on one hand, and reached out with the other to stroke his hard abdomen.

His skin was firm, and his muscles rippled under her fingers as she slid them upwards, kneading his firm chest. His chest rumbled, much like a large lion purring, as his green eyes opened and captured her in their gaze. Wrapping his large hands over her shoulders, he dragged her on top of him and pulled her head down to his.

Seizing her mouth with his, he rubbed his lips back and forth over hers until they parted. Thrusting his tongue inside, he stroked every inch of her mouth, exploring every crevice. Cupping her face in his large, warm hands, the man kissed her senseless. Erin enjoyed the erotic sensations of her tongue dueling with his. Her toes curled in her sneakers, and her body tingled with growing arousal. Erin sucked on his tongue, and was rewarded when he moaned.

She was totally breathless when he finally pulled away. "Good morning," she gasped.

"It certainly is." Abel's voice was deep and low as he stroked her back and bottom with his hands.

Erin could feel his cock growing beneath the sheet, pressing into her belly. She slipped her hand down and cupped his hard length through the thin sheet, squeezing and shaping it as she stroked up and down. "I'm not supposed to be here."

He gripped her hand in his, pushing it harder against his erection. "I won't tell if you won't."

Leaning down, Erin nuzzled his chest, loving the crisp feel of his body hair against her nose. She nipped at his chest playfully, biting and licking his hard muscles, before lapping at one of his small male nipples. Abel wrapped his hand around the back of her head and held her there as she used her tongue to tease and delight him.

She tightened the hand that she had wrapped around his cock, gripping him hard as she began to move it up and down. Slowly at first, and then harder and quicker.

"Why do you still have clothes on?" he muttered as he tugged at her top.

Laughing she released him and rolled off him, standing up next to the bed. Gripping the ends of her top, she flipped it up to give him a glimpse of the soft skin beneath.

"Don't tease me, honey." He threw back the sheet exposing his engorged cock. "I'm a man in need."

Erin licked her lips and Abel groaned. A pearly drop of fluid seeped from the slit at the tip of his cock. Her panties were already soaked, her pussy soft, wet and ready for him.

Lying naked on the bed, disheveled, and totally aroused, Erin thought he was the most gorgeous man in the world. The early morning stubble of his beard, and his heavy-lidded green-eyed gaze made him look sexy as hell. She could almost come just from looking at him. Her breasts ached with need and she cupped them with her hands, rubbing her fingers over the pointy tips that were visible from beneath her shirt.

"Strip for me, baby." His command made her even hotter, and she shivered as she watched him grip his cock and stroke himself. "Get naked and ride me."

Her temperature soared as she yanked her top over her head. Abel never took his eyes off her as he continued to pump his shaft with his hand. Just as she reached for the front closure of her bra, a distant sound caught her ears. Abel's house was set too far back from the main road for it to be just someone passing by. She came back down to earth with a solid thump.

Racing to the window, she saw a cloud of dust moving closer by the second. "Omigod, someone's coming." Frantically, she grabbed her top and yanked it back over her head.

"Who cares?" he cajoled. "They'll go away. Come here." Then he closed his eyes and groaned. "Shit! I bet it's Jackson."

Erin started for the door, but Abel reached out and grabbed her, toppling her back onto the bed. Throwing one of his large thighs over her legs, he pinned her to the mattress. The sound of the vehicle was getting closer and closer, and she struggled to escape Abel's grasp.

The devil just laughed and planted a quick hard kiss on her lips. "Good morning, Erin."

She shot him a harried glance. "I should have known better than to try and sneak over here this morning."

"Why did you?" He tucked a strand of hair that had escaped her braid behind her ear.

"I missed you." She knew her eyes were filled with love as she stared up at him. His green eyes softened for a moment before blazing with passion. He was bending towards her when a truck door slammed.

Erin's head came up off the bed so fast, she smacked Abel in the nose. Laughing, he rolled off her, rubbing his nose as he did. "It's not funny," she hissed in a low whisper. "I can't be caught here this morning of all mornings."

Abel seemed to catch her distress and heaved himself off the bed just as Jackson's voice called up from below. "Are you up yet?"

"Yeah," he yelled back. "I'll be down after I get a shower. Start a pot of coffee."

Erin shrank back against the wall, praying her brother wouldn't come upstairs. "Are you gonna leave me like this?" Abel's cock bobbed as he sauntered towards her.

"Just think of it as foreplay." Erin was desperate for escape. Scurrying to the window, she shoved it up higher, and then swung one of her legs over the sill. She already had one foot planted on the roof when Abel grabbed her wrist in his hand.

"Be careful," he admonished her. "You need to be healthy for later tonight." He slipped his hand between her legs and cupped her sex. "Nice and wet." His fingers rubbed her slit and she widened her legs. "Don't wear any underwear when you get ready later."

She made a sound of protest, but he silenced it with a kiss. "I want you naked underneath that dress. Hot, wet, and waiting for me."

Erin nodded urgently, at this point willing to agree to anything so that he would let her go. She hurried onto the roof, but he was right behind her. Holding her by the wrists, he lowered her to the porch roof. Erin swung herself over the side and dropped the short distance to the ground. Abel watched her while she raced back across the fields.

He'd just climbed back in through the window when Jackson's voice drifted in from the hallway. "Is she gone yet?"

Abel's eyes narrowed as his friend leaned casually against the doorway. The smug look on Jackson's face suddenly penetrated his foggy brain. "You bastard. How the hell did you know she was here?" Clenching his hands, he propped his fists on his hips and glared at Jackson.

"I didn't. Until now." Jackson just laughed and glanced knowingly at Abel's prominent erection. "I figured Erin wouldn't be able to stay away." Pushing and straightening himself away from the doorframe, he sauntered towards Abel and clapped a hand on his shoulder. "Let's just say we're even now for the times you snuck around behind my back. A little abstinence and frustration is good for you. It'll make you appreciate her more later."

Abel grinned wryly and chuckled. "Go make me breakfast while I shower." Stalking out of the room, he headed towards the bathroom.

"Yes, dear." Jackson's mocking laugher followed him down the hallway, and he couldn't stop himself from smiling.

The wind rustled through the trees as Abel stared down at the beautiful woman standing next to him in the garden. The slight breeze ruffled the wisps of hair that had escaped her fancy braid. His fingers itched to smooth the flyaway hair out of her face.

Listening to her promise to love and cherish him for the rest of their lives made his chest tighten with emotion. This was a woman who kept her promises, a woman a man would be proud to have by his side for a lifetime, a woman to grow old with.

She looked beautiful in a strapless white dress that fell to just above her ankles. The material clung to her curves, accentuating her femaleness. Abel knew she damned well wasn't wearing a bra with that dress. But what really had him sweating was wondering if she was wearing any panties beneath it. Her legs were covered with white stockings, and Abel shook himself slightly as the thought of Erin wearing nothing but a garter belt and stockings occupied his mind.

"Abel." He looked down at Erin as she tugged on his arm. His brain registered the fact that there was total silence around them, and everyone was staring at him.

The minister cleared his voice. "The ring," he prompted.

Jackson stood beside him, barely holding back his laughter as he handed Abel the ring. Abel just shrugged, unwilling to apologize for his actions. He took the thick gold band from Jackson and slipped it onto Erin's finger. Then held out his hand as she did the same for him. Taking her smaller, work-worn hand firmly in his, Abel gazed down into her laughing blue eyes, and repeated the vows that would bind them together. Forever.

Her eyes were misty by the time he was finished. Her gaze was solemn as she repeated her own vows to him. He held her hand tight as the minister blessed them. As quick as that, it was all over, and they were turning to face the small crowd that had gathered in the garden of the Connors homestead. The moment the minister told him he could kiss the bride, Abel heaved a sigh of relief. It was over now, and she was his.

Cupping her smiling face in his hands, he bent down and kissed her softly on the lips. She gasped and her lips parted slightly. Abel couldn't resist the temptation and his tongue swept into her mouth, claiming it for himself. She tasted so damned enticing, an addictive combination of sweetness and woman.

Abel could hear laughter in the background as someone thumped him on the shoulder. He reared back with a scowl on his face.

Jackson stood there shaking his head as he plucked Erin out of Abel's arms and gave her a big hug. "Be happy."

Erin's smile was almost blinding as she returned her brother's hug. "I will," she promised.

Then it was Nathan's turn as he picked Erin up and swung her around in a circle. Abel watched them, loving the way they interacted together as a family. Jackson stood beside him as they watched Nathan and Erin together. "Welcome to the family." He stuck out his hand as he spoke.

Abel took his best friend's hand and held it tight. "I'll make her happy," he promised.

Jackson nodded, but then the moment passed and was gone as the other guests swarmed them. Everyone congratulated them all at once. Abel snagged Erin from her brother's arms and kept her close by his side as they shook hands and accepted warm wishes from their guests.

Abel felt a bit awkward when his newfound brother Cain stepped up before him and offered him his large hand. The two men eyed each other as they shook hands. "Thanks for coming." They were finding their way slowly but surely, but it would take time.

"You're welcome," Cain's deep voice rumbled. Then he gave a snort of laughter. "Our wives wouldn't have it any other way." Both men turned and watched Erin and Katie as they chatted and hugged. The women had struck up an instant friendship that only seemed to be getting stronger over time.

"I'm still glad you came."

Cain stared at him for a moment before a rare grin crossed his face. "Me too."

Excusing himself, Cain led his wife away to allow other people to speak to the new bride and groom. Carly was laughing and kissing both him and Erin, and she was followed by a parade of Erin's friends from town. It was a small wedding by most standards, but it was more than big enough for Abel. The thirty or so guests filled the yard as they all milled about chatting and socializing.

It was a beautiful evening for a wedding, and everyone helped themselves to a buffet supper. People sat in clusters around the picnic tables that had been set up around the yard. Food was consumed, toasts were made, and everyone laughed and enjoyed themselves.

Finally, it was time for the first dance. Abel led Erin to the middle of the makeshift dance floor and pulled her into his arms as the local band they'd hired began to play a slow love song. Erin snuggled against his chest and he could feel his cock swelling at her nearness. He'd wanted her desperately since he'd laid eyes on her before the ceremony.

"You look like an angel," he whispered in her ear. He licked behind her ear, and she shivered.

She gazed up at him, her blue eyes luminous and her red hair glowing in the patio lanterns. "Thank you." Shifting closer to him, she pressed her stomach against his growing erection.

Abel laughed and held her close as he swung her around the floor to the whoops and laughter of their friends. "You're playing with fire," he cautioned her.

She just shot him a knowing smile. "Maybe I want to get burned."

Abel swooped Erin up in his arms and turned to the crowd. "Enjoy yourselves. We'll see you in a few days."

Amidst much catcalling and shouted encouragement, Abel carried his new wife to his truck. Carly rushed forward to hand Erin her bouquet as they passed her. Erin buried her nose in the fragrant roses, enjoying their scent and beauty one final time. She looked up at him, gave him a wink, and then tossed the bouquet back over his shoulder. Carly was startled, but caught it in both hands. Erin laughed and waved at her friend as he tucked her into the truck. Giving the group one last wave, he gunned the engine and started the short trip back to their new home.

Nathan walked up behind Carly as she buried her nose in the roses of his sister's wedding bouquet. He wrapped his arms around her and pulled her back against his chest. "I can't wait much longer." His days were filled with frustration, as he and Carly could barely seem to get two minutes together lately.

"I know." She leaned back against his chest and sighed. "I've just been so busy with two of my staff down with the flu."

"And I've been working double shifts. Some of the guys at work are down with the same damned thing." Nathan tugged Carly back into the shadows and kissed the back of her neck.

"Hmm," she agreed as she tilted her neck to one side to give him better access.

"I don't think I can take three more weeks of waiting," Nathan grated out between clenched teeth. His cock was so hard against the front of his pants he thought he might explode. He tortured himself further by rubbing it over her rounded backside.

Moaning, she pushed her ass back against him. His hands started to slide up towards her breasts. "Carly." A woman's voice broke the sensual spell between them. Nathan groaned and buried his face in her hair.

Nathan kept Carly in front of him as her mother walked towards them. Nathan liked both her parents, but right now he wished them to the devil. They'd come home a week ago to spend the month with Carly and help her get ready for the wedding. Since then they hadn't managed to get two minutes alone, even for a quickie.

Carly shot him a pleading look, begging him to understand. He bent down and nipped her earlobe. "Soon," he promised. "I won't wait much longer."

He nodded to her mom before stalking off in the other direction. He needed to be alone for a while. With his cock rock-hard, making a huge bulge in the front of his dress pants, he wasn't fit for polite company.

Chapter Twenty-One

Erin was breathless with anticipation as Abel opened the door to the truck, reached in, and lifted her out of the vehicle. It seemed as if it had been years, rather than days, since they'd made love. Wrapping her arms around his neck, she relaxed as he walked towards the house with her cradled in his strong arms. He lowered her enough so she could unlock the back door and push it open. Carrying her over the threshold, he shoved the door closed with his booted heel. The sound echoed through the quiet house. They were finally alone.

"Welcome home." Erin shivered as his voice and words washed over her. He said nothing else, but continued through the kitchen and up the stairs, not pausing until he reached the door to the new master bedroom.

They'd finally cleared everything out of his parents' old room, and Abel had spent the last week painting and fixing it up just for them. A feeling of rightness settled over Erin as he lowered her legs to the bedroom floor. Standing there, wrapped in his protective embrace, she felt as if she'd finally found her place in the world.

Abel finally pulled away from her, shrugged out of his jacket, and tugged off his tie, throwing them over the chair in the corner. Turning to her, he placed his hands on his hips and stared at her. "Did you?" His voice was low and sexy as he watched her.

"Did I what?" She could feel the moisture pooling between her legs as his heated gaze washed over her. Her nipples were hard and each time she took a breath the sensitive tips were pushed against the material. She bit her lip to keep from moaning aloud.

"Did you wear panties or not, Missus Garrett?" He stalked towards her, a male animal on the prowl.

"What do you think, Mr. Garrett?" She smiled coyly, lifting the hem of her dress slightly, offering him only a glimpse of her white stockings.

Abel sat on the side of the bed and hauled off his boots and socks, tossing them aside. Standing, he unbuttoned his shirt, yanked it off and dropped it to the floor. Erin couldn't take her eyes off him as he continued to undress in front of her. His muscles rippled as he moved and her fingers itched to touch him. Her dress was suddenly way too tight, making it hard for her to catch her breath.

Abel shucked his pants and underwear and sat back on the bed. "Come here." Holding out his hand, he waited for her to come to him.

Erin stepped out of her low-heeled pumps and padded over to him. Spreading his legs wide, he pulled her close to him, burying his face in her stomach. His hands came up to shape the contours of her behind, his fingers tracing the creases at the tops of her thighs.

She bit back a moan as his hands slid down the backs of her legs and then slipped underneath her dress. Her whole body trembled as she waited for him to discover her wet sex waiting for him. His fingers teased her as he took his time, grazing her inner thighs before sifting through her pubic hair. "Thigh-high stockings, not a garter belt," he murmured softly.

Widening her legs, Erin silently encouraged him to touch her. This time she moaned when his large palm cupped her sex, his fingers tracing their wet folds. He growled as his fingers slipped inside her eager body.

"So hot and wet," he muttered as he slid his fingers from her slit and trailed them down her quivering thighs. His eyes blazed as he sat back and stared at her. "Pull up your dress and show me your pussy."

Flames of desire seared Erin's skin as she inched her dress up to her waist, exposing her naked lower body to him. He ran his fingers over the tops of her thigh-high stockings and her hips moved, thrusting towards him. "Spread your legs."

Erin widened her stance and cried out as he thrust his fingers deep into her aching sex. Her muscles clenched hard around them, wanting him deeper. "Do you want me, baby?" Abel's words aroused her even more.

"Oh, yes." Her reply was little more than a throaty whisper.

"Then strip for me, Erin." Abel let her go and settled himself comfortably against the headboard.

He looked enormous lying there in the shadows of the bed. The moonlight was shining through the window, illuminating the extent of his desire. His cock was totally erect, large and thick, as it jutted out from his groin. Erin didn't even realize she'd been staring at it until he gave a low chuckle and began to stroke himself.

"It's going to go to waste if you don't hurry."

Erin smiled wickedly and licked her lips in anticipation as she reached behind her back to unzip her dress. "We can't let that happen."

The sound of the zipper was loud and strangely erotic as she slowly lowered it all the way to her naked behind. The dress dropped to the floor, pooling around her feet, and then she was naked except for her stockings. She reached for the top of her stocking, intending to roll it down her leg, but Abel's hoarse voice echoed through the room. "Leave them."

Erin stepped away from the dress and knelt up on the end of the bed, crawling between Abel's legs. Placing her palms on his rock-hard thighs, she ran her hands over his legs, loving the way his muscles flexed beneath them. He sucked in a deep breath as her fingers hovered over his cock. It bobbed towards her hands, and she wrapped them around it and squeezed it tight.

Moving one of her hands lower, she massaged his sac as her other hand slid over his hardness. She rubbed her palm over the top of his erection, rubbing the milky liquid over the bulbous head. Her pussy was throbbing now, wanting his cock buried to the hilt. But she had other plans first.

Straddling one of his thighs, she lowered her head towards his straining cock. Her tongue flicked the tip, before lapping at the head and sucking it. As she took more of his length deeper into her mouth, she rubbed the mound of her pussy on his leg, trying to ease the ache within her. His thigh was wet with her desire, but she didn't care. Her whole body was on fire with need.

Gripping her head in his hands, Abel thrust his hips towards her mouth. Erin could feel his cock at the back of her throat as she swallowed as much of him as she could. Her tongue continued to stroke his hard flesh as he thrust himself in and out of her eager mouth. Erin hummed with pleasure, as she tasted the salty drops of liquid that seeped from the head of his cock. She could feel his balls drawing tighter to his body as she continued to fondle them.

Abel suddenly pulled his cock from her mouth, reared up, and flipped her over in bed all in one motion. She found herself flat on her back, staring up at her husband. His large hands cupped her breasts, even as his fingers pinched her engorged nipples. Erin cried out as she arched towards him.

He buried his face in her chest, licking, sucking, and lapping at her breasts until she thought she would go mad. Her hands clutched at his head, one minute pulling him closer to her, and the next, tugging him away. Digging her heels into the bed, she levered herself off the mattress, rubbing her clit against his cock. Wanting, needing some relief from the powerful arousal that consumed her.

He groaned and heaved himself over her, taking her breath away in a passionate kiss. His mouth consumed hers as his cock pressed against her mound. Erin was shaking now, needing him desperately.

"Take me, Abel!" she cried out as she tore her lips from his.

Abel's hands and mouth were everywhere, exploring her neck, breasts, and stomach. Then his hands were spreading her legs wide as he captured her clit between his lips and sucked hard. Erin almost shot off the bed.

"Omigod," she repeated over and over as she thrashed from side to side in the bed. Her hands fisted in the covers as she arched back, thrusting her hips towards him.

Abel growled and the sound reverberated through her pussy causing it to clench almost painfully. She brought her hands up to his shoulders, digging her fingernails into his flesh, urging him to take her.

"Tell me what you want," he demanded.

The words tumbled readily from her swollen lips. "Fuck me. Now, Abel. Now."

Abel moved up over her then, lifting her legs over his shoulders, as he thrust his cock deep. His face was a hard mask of desire as he drove hard into her pussy, his entire concentration focused on making them both come. Erin dug her heels into his back, desperately trying to take him even deeper. Abel dug his fingers into her waist and began to pound into her body, filling her totally.

"Yes," she cried repeatedly as he continued to ram his cock into her over and over. Her breath caught in her throat as the shivers started from the very center of her core. Screaming, she came. Hard and fast. Her entire body shook as she convulsed around him.

Abel continued to thrust hard and deep. Then his big body shook, and he gave a shout. She could feel his cock jerk as he came, and her inner muscles contracted around him once again. He gave one final grunt and then collapsed on top of her.

Erin sank back into the pillows and closed her eyes, savoring the little aftershocks that coursed through her body. Abel's head was buried against her shoulder, his shoulders heaving as he struggled to catch his breath. She didn't know how long they lay there like that, but she was more contented than she'd ever been in her entire life.

Finally, Abel raised his head and stared down at her, all his love shining from his sexy green eyes. "I love you, Mrs. Garrett." Leaning down, he kissed her softly before withdrawing from her body. Rolling onto his back, he tucked her under his arms so that her head was resting on his shoulder.

"I love you, too." Snuggling close, she placed her hand over his heart just so she could feel it beating.

About the author:

N. J. Walters had a mid-life crisis at a fairly young age, gave notice after ten years at her job on a Friday, received a tentative acceptance for her first novel, Annabelle Lee, on the following Sunday.

Happily married for over seventeen years to the love of her life, with his encouragement and support she gave up the job of selling books for the more pleasurable job of writing them. A voracious reader of romances of all kinds, she now spends her days writing, reading and reviewing books. It's a tough life, but someone's got to do it.

N.J. welcomes mail from readers. You can write to her c/o Ellora's Cave Publishing at 1056 Home Avenue, Akron OH 44310-3502.

Why an electronic book?

We live in the Information Age—an exciting time in the history of human civilization in which technology rules supreme and continues to progress in leaps and bounds every minute of every hour of every day. For a multitude of reasons, more and more avid literary fans are opting to purchase e-books instead of paperbacks. The question to those not yet initiated to the world of electronic reading is simply: *why?*

1. *Price.* An electronic title at Ellora's Cave Publishing and Cerridwen Press runs anywhere from 40-75% less than the cover price of the <u>exact same title</u> in paperback format. Why? Cold mathematics. It is less expensive to publish an e-book than it is to publish a paperback, so the savings are passed along to the consumer.

2. *Space.* Running out of room to house your paperback books? That is one worry you will never have with electronic novels. For a low one-time cost, you can purchase a handheld computer designed specifically for e-reading purposes. Many e-readers are larger than the average handheld, giving you plenty of screen room. Better yet, hundreds of titles can be stored within your new library—a single microchip. (Please note that Ellora's Cave and Cerridwen Press does not endorse any specific brands. You can check our website at www.ellorascave.com or

www.cerridwenpress.com for customer recommendations we make available to new consumers.)

3. *Mobility.* Because your new library now consists of only a microchip, your entire cache of books can be taken with you wherever you go.

4. *Personal preferences are accounted for.* Are the words you are currently reading too small? Too large? Too...**ANNOYING**? Paperback books cannot be modified according to personal preferences, but e-books can.

5. *Instant gratification.* Is it the middle of the night and all the bookstores are closed? Are you tired of waiting days—sometimes weeks—for online and offline bookstores to ship the novels you bought? Ellora's Cave Publishing sells instantaneous downloads 24 hours a day, 7 days a week, 365 days a year. Our e-book delivery system is 100% automated, meaning your order is filled as soon as you pay for it.

Those are a few of the top reasons why electronic novels are displacing paperbacks for many an avid reader. As always, Ellora's Cave and Cerridwen Press welcomes your questions and comments. We invite you to email us at service@ellorascave.com, service@cerridwenpress.com or write to us directly at: 1056 Home Ave. Akron OH 44310-3502.

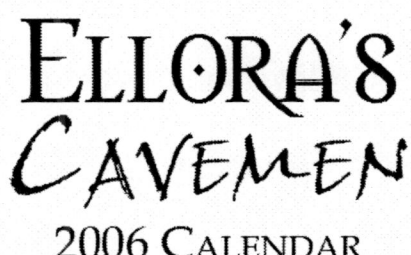

Need a more EXCITING
Way to Plan your Day?

Ellora's
Cavemen
2006 Calendar

Coming This Fall

THE
ELLORA'S CAVE
LIBRARY

Stay up to date with Ellora's Cave Titles
in Print with our Quarterly Catalog.

Lady Jaided

The premier magazine for today's sensual woman

Lady Jaided magazine is devoted to exploring the sexuality and sensuality of women. While there are many similarities between the sexual experiences of men and women, there are just as many if not more differences. Our focus is on the female experience and on giving voice and credence to it. Lady Jaided will include everything from trends, politics, science and history to gossip, humor and celebrity interviews, but our focus will remain on female sexuality and sensuality.

A Sneak Peek at Upcoming Stories

Clan of the Cave Woman
Women's sexuality throughout history.

The Sarandon Syndrome
What's behind the attraction between older women and younger men.

The Last Taboo
Why some women – even feminists – have bondage fantasies

Girls' Eyes for Queer Guys
An in-depth look at the attraction between straight women and gay men

Available Spring 2005

Lady *Jaided* Regular Features

Jaid's Tirade
Jaid Black's erotic romance novels sell throughout the world, and her publishing company Ellora's Cave is one of the largest and most successful e-book publishers in the world. What is less well known about Jaid Black, a.k.a. Tina Engler is her long record as a political activist. Whether she's discussing sex or politics (or both), expect to see her get up on her soapbox and do what she does best: offend the greedy, the holier-than-thous, and the apathetic! Don't miss out on her monthly column.

Devilish Dot's G-Spot
Married to the same man for 20 years, Dorothy Araiza still basks in a sex life to be envied. What Dot loves just as much as achieving the Big O is helping other women realize their full sexual potential. Dot gives talks and advice on everything from which sex toys to buy (or not to buy) to which positions give you the best climax.

On the Road with Lady K
Publisher, author, world traveler and Lady of Barrow, Kathryn Falk shares insider information on the most romantic places in the world.

Kandidly Kay
This Lois Lane cum Dave Barry is a domestic goddess by day and a hard-hitting sexual deviancy reporter by night. Adored for her stunning wit and knack for delivering one-liners, this Rodney Dangerfield of reporting will leave no stone unturned in her search for the bizarre truth.

A Model World
CJ Hollenbach returns to his roots. The blond heartthrob from Ohio has twice been seen in Playgirl magazine and countless other publications. He has appeared on several national TV shows including The Jerry Springer Show (God help him!) and has been interviewed for Entertainment Tonight, CNN and The Today Show. He has been involved in the romance industry for the past 12 years, appearing on dozens of romance novel covers and calendars. CJ's specialty is personal interviews, in which people have a tendency to tell him everything.

Hot Mama Cooks
Sex is her food, and food is her sex. Hot Mama gives aphrodisiac a whole new meaning. Join her every month for her latest sensual adventure -- with bonus recipe!

Empress on the Mount
Brash, outrageous, and undeniably irreverent, this advice columnist from down under will either leave you in stitches or recovering from hang-jaw as you gawk at her answers to reader questions on relationships and life.

Erotic Fiction from Ellora's Cave
The debut issue will feature part one of "Ferocious," a three-part erotic serial written especially for Lady Jaided by the popular Sherri L. King.

COMING TO A BOOKSTORE NEAR YOU!

ELLORA'S CAVE
2005
BEST SELLING AUTHORS TOUR

Discover for yourself why readers can't get enough of the multiple award-winning publisher Ellora's Cave. Whether you prefer e-books or paperbacks, be sure to visit EC on the web at www.ellorascave.com for an erotic reading experience that will leave you breathless.

www.ellorascave.com

Printed in the United Kingdom
by Lightning Source UK Ltd.
107129UKS00001B/11